THE RISING STORM

VOLUME ONE OF THE LEPANTO CYCLE

CHRISTOPHER D. MURPHY

Library of Congress Control Number
2016920764

ISBN: 0-9984410-0-7
ISBN-13: 978-0-9984410-0-9

Murphy, Christopher D.
The Rising Storm
www.lepantocycle.com

Cover design by
BespokeBookCovers.com

Dedicated to
The Virgin of Guadalupe

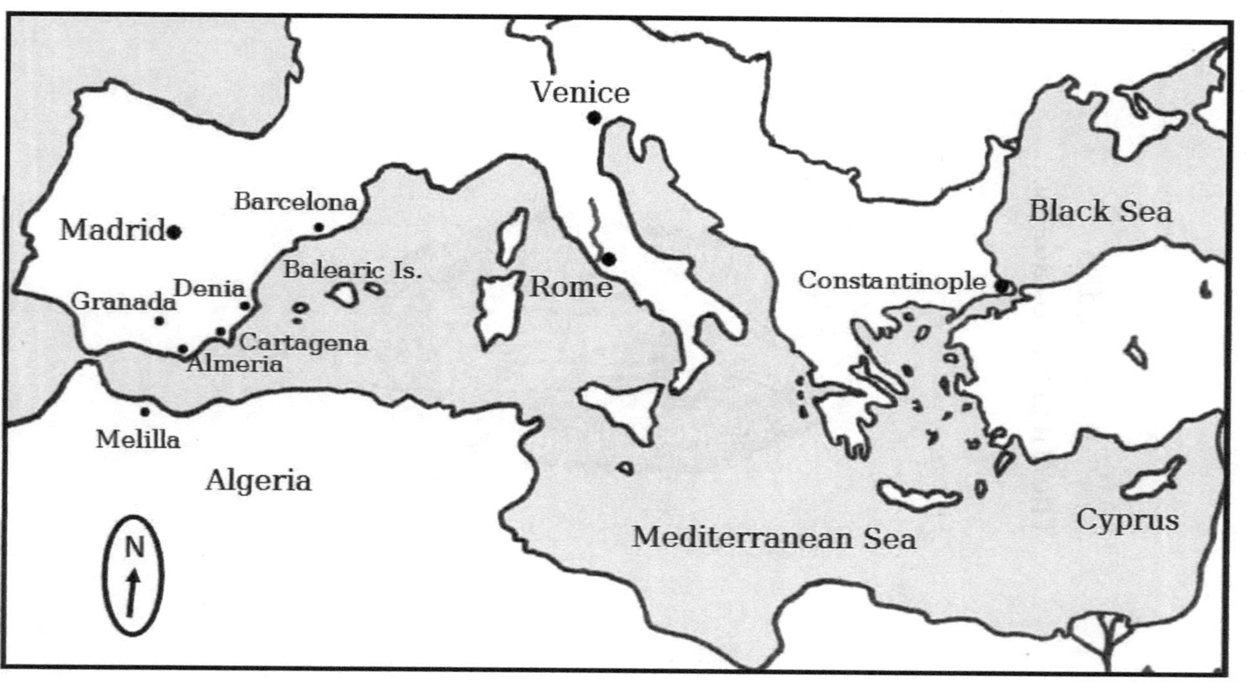

Venice
Madrid
Barcelona
Balearic Is.
Granada
Denia
Rome
Constantinople
Black Sea
Cartagena
Almeria
Melilla
Algeria
Mediterranean Sea
Cyprus
N

Spring 1567

The helmsman was the first to see the ships, five galleys flying the crescent of the Ottoman Empire rounding the promontory north of Cyprus' fortified harbor of Famagusta. "Sir François!" he called.

A tall, lean man with the eight-pointed cross of the Knights of Saint John emblazoned on his breastplate, turned from where he was inspecting the condition of the prisoners chained to the galley benches. "Yes, Johan?"

"Sir, you might want to see this," said the helmsman. François nodded to the boatswain and walked along the catwalk toward the stern of the ship.

"What is it, Johan?" he asked quietly when

he reached the helm.

"There." Johan nodded his head toward the Ottoman galleys. "They are Turks, for sure, and they are heading right toward us."

"That is unusual," said the knight. He looked toward the galleys, wondering what the Turkish fleet was trying to accomplish. Turkish trading vessels regularly conducted business at Cypriot ports, but never the military galleys of the Ottoman Empire. What were they doing here?

As he watched, the Turkish galleys began to shift formation. Four of them formed a line of battle, while the fifth remained behind. *They are trying to protect that ship,* thought François. *And they are willing to offer battle to do so.*

"Sir Claus," he called to a knight on the foredeck. "Signal the rest of the fleet. We form up for battle, but have the *Vallette* attempt to circle the fleet and pursue that one ship that is holding back."

"Yes, sir," answered Claus.

François watched as the seven galleys of the Knights of Saint John lined up. *We have the wind to our favor, and the Turk wants to attack,* he thought. *Let's accommodate him.*

"We attack," he called to Sir Claus. "Get the men ready."

Claus ran to the mast and clanged the bell. The soldiers poured out from below decks, adjusting armor and weapons as they ran to line the gunwales. There was no shouting, only the thunder of boots and the clanking of weapons and armor. By the time the distance between the two fleets had been halved, the Knights of Saint John were ready. François watched the Ottoman ships draw near, the bows and gunwales lined with Turkish bowmen.

He breathed in, smelling the acrid smoke from the burning matches in the hands of the musketeers. The ships drew closer still, and there was still no sign of the Ottoman fleet showing any inclination of backing off.

"Sir Claus," he called again. "You will fire a gun in their direction, but not at them."

"Yes, sir," answered Claus. "And if they do not change course?"

"Then fire *at* them."

"Yes, sir!" Claus ran forward to the cannon in the bow of the ship. He spoke briefly to one of the gunners and stood back.

The galley shook with the recoil of the gun. A moment later, a fountain of water blossomed between two of the Turkish ships. Nothing happened. Then a cloud of smoke enveloped the Ottoman fleet as their cannon answered.

"Wait!" Sir François shouted as gouts of water exploded around the ships of his fleet. He watched the cloud of smoke drift back behind the Ottoman galleys. "Careful," he called to the gunners. "Place your shots well."

Sir Claus again spoke to the gunners, and

the bow of the *Saint Elmo* was blanketed with smoke as her guns fired. The rest of the fleet joined in, and writhing, acrid smoke drifted toward the Turkish ships.

When the smoke cleared, François saw gaps in the lines of Turkish bowmen. "Steer between the galleys," he told Johan, "and then crash one of them amidships."

"Yes, sir!" answered Johan. The *Saint Elmo* turned slightly and made for the gap between the two Ottoman ships toward the west. As the *Saint Elmo* turned into the gap, the Ottoman soldiers rained arrows among the musketeers. They rattled off armor and thudded into unprotected arms and faces. "Fire!" called Claus.

The soldiers lining the decks of the Ottoman ships fell as musket balls ripped through flowing robes and light armor. The *Saint Elmo* veered hard to the port and crashed into a Turkish galley. Grappling hooks were thrown into her rigging, and musketeers leapt over the gunwales of both ships. They charged into the ranks of the surviving Ottoman soldiers, swinging the butts of their muskets into their faces and chests.

On board the Ottoman galley, Claus led his soldiers against the howling Turks defending the stern of the ship. The Turkish soldiers fell back and formed a line of defense. Turning back to the musketeers forming behind him, Claus ordered the rearmost men to reload. He then ordered those in front to engage the Turks. He stepped into the fray and, blocking a sword blow, skewered the nearest Turk. He pushed the soldier off his sword, spun and slashed the neck of another. He looked behind and saw that the solders in the back had reloaded.

"Fall back!" he roared. "And drop! Now!" Around him, solders disengaged from the Turks and dropped to the deck. Immediately, the roar of musket fire filled the air as the musketeers fired over Claus and his men. The soldiers sprang up in the cloud of musket smoke and charged the Turks anew.

Leaping over the fallen Turks, Claus led his men into the decimated Ottoman soldiers. *The muskets made the difference*, he thought gleefully. He charged through the remaining soldiers and bored down on the Ottoman captain.

To the west of the *Saint Elmo* the other the Ottoman ships were swarming with soldiers in hand-to-hand combat. Sir François saw that in every case the Knights of Saint John had been able to board the enemy ships and were pushing the Ottoman resistance across the decks. He looked north and saw that the one Turkish ship that had been hanging back had turned, and using both sails and oars, was fleeing the battle. The *Vallette*, being a heavier ship, was not able to keep up.

He heard cheering, and turning back toward the ship that Claus had boarded, he saw that the fighting had stopped and the Ottoman soldiers were being taken prisoner. He watched as Claus and another soldier climbed over the gunwales of the ships, escorting the Ottoman captain.

"We have taken their ship, sir," said Claus, approaching François. "Their captain has surrendered. I brought him on board to see if we can find out what they were doing here, and why they challenged us to battle."

"Very good," said François.

It was clear that the battle was over. One of the Turkish galleys had been captured, and three were burning. The *Vallette*, not able to keep up with the fleeing ship, had turned back and was rejoining the fleet.

François turned back and looked at the cruel face of the young Turk in front of him. "Who are you?" he asked in Arabic.

The Turk sneered, but did not answer.

"Come, sir," said François, "I must at least know your name and the reason you wanted to fight."

"He had this on him, sir," said Claus. "He seemed upset that we stopped him from throwing it overboard." He gestured toward a soldier who handed François a tightly wrapped bundle of papers.

François opened them. He frowned and

sucked in his breath sharply as he glanced through them. He handed them to Claus.

"It is God's blessing that you were able to capture this ship, sir," said Claus. "This information would not be good to have in the hands of the Sultan. Congratulations on your victory."

Sir François watched as a small smile played across the face of his prisoner. "Victory, Sir Claus?" he asked. "Yes, but not ours." He turned to watch the lone Ottoman ship sailing away in the distance. "This is their victory, not ours."

Chapter 1

June 1567

The Sahara spawned it; over that great expanse of hot sand, the air began to move, swirling the sand into eddies behind the hills, reshaping the desert floor. Northward the air was pushed, gathering strength with each passing mile, picking up sand and dust, rearranging the desert landscape, filtering through the desiccated bones of a lost caravan and depositing sand into an oasis, choking it until the next storm. The sand blasted through the streets of Morocco, swirling around men and women who had their faces covered against the grit in the air. Reaching the Mediterranean Sea, the hot air slowly became humid. Across the sea the sirocco blew, carrying the dust toward the eastern shore of Italy, where, its fury spent, it settled into a cool breeze, past the ruins Ostia and over farmland, moving toward the mountains, until the air began to rise, pushed upward by the Apennines.

Farmers tending their fields loosened their shirts, sodden with sweat from the humidity which had been rising for the last two days. They looked towards the east. At the first sign of a coming storm, they would gather the wheat sheaves and put them under cover; until that time, they continued to work and sweat. The day passed without relief from the heat, and toward midafternoon, a towering wall of black clouds formed over the mountains.

The farmers began to hurry now, trying to get the crops in before the storm, loading their harvests onto carts, shouting and calling for their sons. Horses, donkeys, oxen, and even humans were prodded into motion, moving the harvested grain off the fields. One farmer, along with his three older sons, straining and gasping, struggled to move their overloaded cart by themselves. As they did, they looked to the west, down the old Roman road that connected Ostia with the city of Rome and saw a figure on horseback, cantering east.

The rider rode the horse like a gentleman, but that is where the similarities ended. His boots were those of a soldier, worn but sturdy, while his clothes were those of a sailor. His long, unkempt hair was pulled back into a ragged knot at the base of his neck. His tanned face was made even darker by the beginnings of a beard. Looking at the anvil shaped clouds forming toward the east, the rider kicked his horse into a gallop. He had to reach Rome before the storm broke.

~~~

Black clouds hung low over the city of Rome, filling the late afternoon sky. The sun still gleamed under the western edge of the storm clouds, and Saint Peter's Basilica glowed red in its rays. The great drum rising above its roof for the new dome glowed like a giant cauldron being licked by flames. Marlo Gobeli ran his hand around the open collar of his shirt. *At least I won't be hot for much longer*, he thought, glancing at the dark clouds overhead. The hot, humid weather was going to break soon, at least temporarily. Riding in a torrential downpour with rain blowing in his face was something he usually tried to avoid. Now, though, he looked forward to it.

In spite of the coming storm, he could still hear the calls of the workmen in Saint Peter's, and the cries of vendors in the nearby market rose over the clacking of his horse's hooves on the worn cobblestones of the city. As he turned away from the Vatican, a faint rumble of thunder rolled across the sky, and the voices took on a frantic note as the shopkeepers worked to get their wares under cover.

Near the church of Santa Maria della Strada,
~~~

he swung stiffly out of the saddle. Riding was not something he had done for almost a year, and the gallop from Ostia had made him sore. He took the reins and led his horse across the street and into the stable of the mother house of the Jesuit order.

"Good afternoon," a young man, dressed in black robes looked up from where he was brushing down a brown and white mare. "This is not a public stable, I'm afraid."

"That's alright, Brother," said Marlo. He draped the reins through a ring on the wall and stretched. The ride had given him a knot in his leg. "I am here to see Father Veraccio. I just need a place for my horse to stay out of the rain."

"In that case, come in. If you are going to be a while, take the saddle off and leave it there." The groom pointed to a low wall, upon which a saddle already rested. Marlo unbuckled his and draped it on top of the partition. Opening the flap of the saddle bag, he took out a bundle of papers.

"Thank you, Brother," he said. "I have no idea how long I will be. If you could feed him, I would be grateful." He held up a coin. "This should cover the grain."

"And a bit more, I think," said the groom. "Thank you."

"Use the rest to help someone who needs it." Marlo stepped out into the sticky gloom and, limping slightly, hurried across the street and into the headquarters of the Jesuit order.

On entering through the heavy oak door, he stood in the small white atrium, dimly lit by the gray light that seeped in through a small window. A short, white-haired Jesuit who sat at a small wooden desk on the other side of the room looked up as Marlo closed the door.

"Good evening." The Jesuit stood and walked around the desk. "Is there something you need?"

"Yes, Brother. I need to see Father Veraccio. Is he available?"

"He is saying his rosary. Did he ask you to see him?"

"In a manner of speaking." Marlo hefted the packet in his hand. "I am Marlo Gobeli. I am working for him."

"Come with me." The Jesuit opened the door by his desk. "Wait in here, and I will tell him. Would you like something to eat?"

Marlo gratefully accepted, not having had a chance to eat in the morning, and followed the elderly Jesuit into a small study, equipped with a plain desk, several chairs, and the walls lined with books. A plain wooden crucifix hung on the wall opposite the window. A decanter of red wine was placed on the desk, two glasses, and a platter of cheese and bread. After the lay brother left, Marlo helped himself to the wine and began to eat.

As he finished, the study door opened, and Father Luigi Veraccio strode purposefully into the room, his black cassock and biretta in perfect order. The tall, thin Jesuit sat behind his desk before acknowledging Marlo with a curt nod of his head.

"Well, Marlo," he said abruptly, "how is your leg?"

"My leg is fine. By the time I had reached Cyprus, it had healed, though still a little weak. It hardly bothers me anymore," answered Marlo as he sat down.

"I suspect you will be wanting to rejoin the Guard?" Father Veraccio's tone was flat, almost perfunctory.

"Only if you have nothing of interest for me."

Father Veraccio raised his eyebrows and leaned back in his chair. "You would prefer something else? Well, what do you have for me?"

"Well, let's see," Marlo began. He wanted to make sure that he gave enough detail without taking up too much the Jesuit's time. He suspected that Father Veraccio had little patience for idle talk. "After my injury had healed enough, I took ship to Venice. From there I was able to arrange passage to Cyprus with a detachment of Venetian soldiers who were replacing the garrison there. I befriended some of the soldiers, and was able to visit after they had been garrisoned. After sharing several gallons of wine with them, I got a good picture of the security of Cyprus."

"And is it?"

"Secure? No," said Marlo. "Venice has two garrisons on Cyprus. The capital, Nicosia, and another, Famagusta. The problem is not that the physical strength of these fortifications is lacking; there are hardly any supplies. The Doge keeps enough men to make any casual attempt to take Cyprus seem foolish. However, there are not enough men or supplies to successfully fend off a real attack. And since no extra supplies had been sent with the soldiers I accompanied, I get the impression that more may not be sent."

"So, the Venetians are unconcerned, the garrisons undersupplied. And the Emperor Selim is preparing an army. I fear that he wants to bring Cyprus under Ottoman rule." Father Veraccio sighed. "I don't see how to make them send what Cyprus needs, either. Could the inhabitants help? On Malta, the people were of great assistance."

"Cyprus isn't Malta. The Maltese are Catholic. The Cypriots are Orthodox. They see the Venetians as invaders and occupiers. Unfortunately, I think they would welcome an invasion. And I think that could happen soon."

"How could you possibly know that?" Father Veraccio asked. He frowned. "I don't want unfounded supposition, Marlo. I can't make my report without some evidence. What makes you think that invasion is imminent? I don't think you went to Constantinople and spied on Selim, did you?"

"No, Father," Marlo shook his head. He stood, pulled out the packet of papers from his pouch, and held them ready to hand to the priest. "After looking around on Cyprus, I boarded a galley belonging to the Knights of Saint John. They help patrol the waters around Cyprus. As we were leaving Cyprus we encountered a small flotilla of Turkish galleys leaving from another port. The wind was against them. In spite of the fact that the wind was in our favor, they attacked. We destroyed three and took one, commanded by one of the nephews of Selim himself. On his person was this packet of papers." He handed them to Father Veraccio and watched as the priest opened them. "When we attacked, one ship fled and escaped. I would guess its captain had a copy of these as well."

Marlo sat back down as Father Veraccio began to read the contents of the packet.

"You have seen these?" Father Veraccio asked gravely. Marlo nodded, and the priest resumed his review of the papers. After turning over the last page, he went to the open window and looked out over the cloister. He was silent for some time, watching the black clouds lower over the city. The room grew darker, and Marlo could hear the distant rumble of thunder.

Father Veraccio stepped back from the window as the wind began to blow. He closed the casements and sat back down.

"If all you did in Cyprus was get this information, you would have done well." The priest picked up the papers again. "But you also confirmed that Cyprus is not prepared for invasion. And these reports indicate that Selim is preparing for just that. Well done."

"Thank you, Father," said Marlo, pleased that Father Veraccio thought he had done well. "If I might ask, though, do you think that Selim will attack Cyprus? I know what is in those papers, but could this just be a feint to distract Venice from something else?"

"That is a possibility," answered the priest. "However, Cyprus is a Christian stronghold in the midst of their waters, and their spirit for holy war never rests. It has never rested. I don't believe it ever will. For nearly a thousand years they have warred against Christendom, and Suleiman even almost made it to Rome. He drove the Knights of Saint John out of Rhodes, and later came close to destroying them at Malta. If he had won there, he would have been free to move on Rome. No, Selim will try to finish what his father started. And if he does, Christendom will exist no longer. And those who refuse to accept Allah..." Father Veraccio paused, and glanced at the crucifix.

"Are you familiar of the recruitment process for the Janissaries?" he asked softly.

Marlo nodded. The Janissaries were the strongest fighting arm of the Ottoman army. Stirred into a frenzy by Imams, these well-trained soldiers became fearless in their dedication. They had no fear of dying in battle. Under Suleiman, they had become almost invincible. They had been defeated at Malta, but such defeats were rare. And they were not even Moslem by birth.

When they Turks conquered a territory, they would permit the surviving Christians to keep their religion, but only if they paid higher taxes and suffered the kidnaping of their children. The girls were enslaved as concubines, while the boys were trained in warfare and incorporated into the Moslem faith. This was the price of being Christian in Ottoman territory – to see your own sons fighting to bring the rest of Christendom under similar enslavement.

Marlo shifted uncomfortably in his seat. He had no love for the Moslem world. His uncle had been a merchant and was now chained in an Ottoman ship, if he was still alive. His own family had fled to Switzerland from the coastal region of Molise in southern Italy several generations ago to escape the pillaging and raiding that had been occurring along the coasts of Italy.

"So, you think Selim will strike soon?" he

asked.

"Venice is building up her fleet, but so is Selim, and at a faster rate. And Venice may have no one to help. Christendom is divided; the Holy Roman Empire has been weakened by the Protestants; Charles of France has no inclination to be involved, and Philip of Spain has shown himself to be hesitant to come to our aid, as was seen at Malta." The priest sighed slowly. "Venice is strong, but her navy is no match for Selim's. Therefore, we must do what we can to prepare our defense. The rest is in God's hands."

"Our defense, Father?"

Father Veraccio rose from his seat and walked back to the window. The storm clouds were lower and darker. Thunder rumbled in the distance, but the storm had not yet inundated the Eternal City. "No, the Turk will attack. They will attack soon, and Cyprus is only the beginning. The storm about to break may wash away all of Europe. Unless God wills otherwise.

"I am afraid that I can't let you rest more than a couple of days," he said to Marlo who had stood when the priest had. "I have another task, if you are willing to help."

"What do you need?"

"I need you to go to Spain. I have heard rumors about an unsettled situation in Granada that may be related to all of this, and King Philip has made it clear that the Jesuits are not welcome. We do have houses established there, but are viewed with suspicion. Besides, our priests and brothers would not be able to go where you can. It might be dangerous, but I need to know what is going on there."

Marlo hesitated. His last task had been a mild adventure, something interesting to do instead of standing guard in Rome. He had been involved in a small battle, but that had been unexpected. This time, Father Veraccio was asking him to place himself in danger. But if he could help drive back the infidels? He thought of his uncle, and nodded.

"What are you expecting me to find out?"

"I am not sure. I will give you more information once I have put it all together. I was not expecting the need to investigate this, but what you just brought me makes it necessary. You can stay here until I have a chance to speak to Father Borgia."

"Thank you, Father." Marlo moved to open the door.

"Marlo," Father Veraccio called. Marlo turned. "Good work," the priest said with the first smile Marlo had ever seen from him.

~~~

The cool morning breeze made Marlo shiver as he walked through the streets of Rome. The rain of the last two days had brought cooler air
~~~

and had washed the streets of the city. The early morning sunlight glowed off of wet cobblestones and buildings. He turned toward the Vatican, making for the Offices of the Inquisition.

The entrance was watched by two Swiss Guards. Marlo eyed them carefully as he came closer. He squinted as he tried to make out their features. He crossed the street and moved opposite them. A smile spread across his face as he recognized the one on the right, Franz Bohren.

Franz stood, holding his halberd in his right hand, feet spread slightly. Marlo grinned and moved opposite to him. Spreading his feet, he stood at attention and held out his right fist, striking the same pose as Franz. Unlike Franz, though, Marlo did not keep his face expressionless; he grinned mischievously.

Marlo stood there for a minute before Franz raised his eyebrows in recognition. Relaxing, Marlo said, "I'll see you at Angeletto's when you get off duty." Franz gave a slight nod, and Marlo limped away, whistling.

He knew Franz reasonably well; after all, he had served with him. At the age of sixteen, he had joined the Swiss Guards and was sent to Rome. Of all the courts in Europe, the posting at Rome was the most prestigious. He had taken his assignment seriously, not just because he had been part of the personal guard of the head of Christendom, but also because he was Swiss. The Swiss never failed their duty.

Fourteen months ago, Marlo was exercising the Guards horses. He was jumping them and putting them through maneuvers. His horse had timed a jump poorly, hit the top bar with its fore hooves, and rolled upon landing. The horse was unharmed. Marlo was not. The horse had landed on its side with Marlo's left leg trapped beneath it. His leg was broken in three places. Unless it healed completely, he was out of the Guard for good.

The apothecary who had set the leg must have been drunk, for it had healed crooked. Not enough to prevent him from riding a horse or walking, but enough to disqualify him from the Guard—and even then, only because of the disagreement he had with his commander. And that was what had really hurt. It still did, even though he was still serving the Holy Father.

There were only two other people in Angeletto's when Marlo arrived. He took a seat in the corner where he could watch the door, ordered a meal, and leaned back in his chair to wait.

He wasn't sure why he had asked Franz to meet him here. It was not like he wanted to enlist his help to be readmitted into the Guard. He rather enjoyed his new occupation. Standing still all day paled in comparison to espionage.

Franz arrived about two hours later. "Marlo!" he shouted hurrying across the crowded room. "Where have you been? You gave me quite the shock this morning! I thought you were gone for good. What have you been doing?"

Marlo grinned. Franz's excitement lifted him out the self-pity he had been wallowing in. He stood and was thumped in the chest by Franz. "Well, you certainly have not changed," said Franz laughing. "You are still the same rascal that you ever were. Are you rejoining the unit?"

"Not yet, if ever." Marlo sat back down and put the wine bottle in front of Franz. "Have something to drink. No, I think I'm done with the Guard," he said, as Franz sat and filled his glass.

"What are you doing here, then?"

"Getting my next assignment."

"Assignment?" Franz looked rather puzzled. "Next? Be clearer! What have you been doing?"

"Working for the Jesuits as a courier. I have been traveling around the Mediterranean."

"You're running errands for the Black Pope?"

"Father Borgia wears black, yes," Marlo leaned back in his chair and stretched out his legs under the table. "But he is not the pope. And yes, you might say that I am working for him. After my accident, I was asked to run some errands, as you said, for Father Borgia regarding some of Venice's interests." The circumstances surrounding how he had become employed by the Jesuits was a bit more complicated than that, but Franz did not need to know the details, and Marlo was not sure that he was ready to say more. He was glad that Franz did not seem to know what had occurred between himself and his commander. "I will be off tomorrow morning."

"So what is Father Borgia like?"

"I haven't spoken to him, but from what I hear, he seems a determined man. Elderly, strong, and, according to the lay brothers at the Jesuit house, holy."

"Holy?" laughed Franz. "And a Borgia? What is happening to Rome that 'holy' can be applied to a Borgia?"

"I don't know," Marlo shrugged. "But he works for the Holy Father, and I take it that Pius is taking advantage of the fact that the Jesuits are spread out over Europe and Asia. Their network probably gives the Holy Father a political advantage in European affairs."

"You're not trying to recruit me, are you?" asked Franz. "I wouldn't know anything about world affairs."

"No, you wouldn't," Marlo chuckled. "You are the type that is quite content to stand guard here in Rome. I thought I would see you before I leave. I am going to Spain. Here one day and gone the next."

"Why Spain?"

"I do not know." Marlo frowned. He was wondering that same thing. Father Veraccio had not told him, just that the Father General was worried about something. "I leave tomorrow; I will know soon. I just wanted to see how you were doing."

"Leaving tomorrow? That is very sudden."

"Well, I have to catch a ship that Father Veraccio says is setting sail soon. But that is for tomorrow." Marlo reached for the bottle of wine and gestured to the glass in Franz's hands. "Today, I have nothing to do; so drink up, and tell me how you have done since I left."

Chapter 2

June 1567

"Here is what we know." Father Veraccio stood at the window with his hands clasped behind his back. "The Algerians are increasing their pirate activity, and Spain seems to be the target."

Marlo shifted in his seat. In spite of his assertion that his leg was fine, he had been sitting for a while waiting for his meeting, and the muscles in his left thigh had cramped again.

"Your leg bothering you, again?" asked the priest.

"Some." Marlo shrugged. "It will be fine once I get a chance to walk it off."

"Come," Father Veraccio nodded to the door. "I will fill you in on your assignment while we walk."

Marlo stood, grateful, and followed the priest out of the office.

"We will go into the street." Father Veraccio held the main door open for Marlo. "Our conversation will not be noticed in the crowd. How often does your leg bother you?" Father Veraccio looked at Marlo as they turned left and walked in the direction of the Via Sacra past the crumbling façade of the Maria della Strada.

"Inactivity is a problem," Marlo grimaced as he limped alongside the priest. "But not enough to be incapacitating."

"Good, because you may need to travel a lot. I expect you to spend most of your time on horseback the next few months." Father Veraccio was silent for a moment. "So, what do you know about Spain?"

"Not much. Philip II rules the largest empire in the world – Spain, the Netherlands, the New World. And there is some animosity between Philip and England."

"How is your Spanish?"

"Passible."

"Good," the priest nodded. "Well, I suppose I need to give you some background. Spain was practically overrun by the Moors eight hundred years ago. And the Moors turned the Iberian Peninsula into the jewel of the Islamic world: Andalusia. The Spanish kingdoms eventually reconquered their lands, taking over Granada about seventy-five years ago. Queen

Isabella forced the Moriscos of Granada to convert to Christianity at the insistence of an Archbishop Ximines, a prelate of great zeal and little prudence. Because of that, Spain could have some internal problems in the near future."

"The Moriscos might revolt?"

"Not likely. The problem would not exist, except that Spain has colonized the New World. The only ones who went to Mexico were the Christian soldiers. The Moriscos would have nothing to do with the Spanish army, so they remained in Granada. Many Spanish also followed the army to Mexico, leaving Spain rather short of farmers."

"So, where is Spain getting its grain?"

"From Sicily. The grain needs to be shipped and the Algerians have been taking advantage of that. The Pasha of Algiers is a puppet of Selim, and their piracy against Spanish shipping has increased just as Selim is building up his navy. What I need to know is how dependent Spain is on Sicilian grain."

"Rather dependent, I would think," interjected Marlo dryly. "Isn't Philip doing something about this?"

"Again, we do not know. If Spain is faced with the prospect of a famine, then I suspect that Philip will be assembling a fleet. I just hope that a real threat exists."

"Why is that?" asked Marlo, surprised.

"Because, if Philip builds a fleet, then that fleet can help with the Turks. The information you brought from Cyprus shows that Selim has plans to take Cyprus, and the Holy Father is afraid that Cyprus is only the opening move of an Ottoman attack on Venice. He needs Philip to help defend Venice, which he cannot do if he has no fleet, or if that fleet is too involved with protecting his shipping. I need you to find out how close Spain would be to famine if Philip used his fleet to defend Venice for a year. If the Holy Father knows the situation in Spain, then he will be able to negotiate more effectively with Philip."

Father Veraccio paused. "There is a ship, the *Santa Cecilia*, at Ostia now. It is a Spanish merchant vessel. She can provide you passage to Almeria. I think you should travel as a young gentleman, bored with European politics, and seeking something a little more interesting. Maybe having an eye on joining the Spanish in the New World."

Marlo nodded. "How shall I communicate with you?"

"Send regular reports. Unless you tell me where you are going to be, I will send any instructions to Granada and Cartagena. While in Granada, I recommend you visit the Marquis of Mondejar. He is a good man, according to Bishop Castagna, the nuncio to King Philip's court. You have some latitude in this assignment, just keep me informed. And use caution with the locals. The Moriscos have little love for Christians, and our priests in Granada report that some of them have taken to banditry. It is not safe for one to be alone in the villages and hills around Granada."

"I'll be careful." Marlo shrugged.

"Are you sure you want to do this?" Father Veraccio asked. "You are free to step aside."

Marlo considered as they walked along the Via Sacra. He looked at the ruins of the old Roman Forum, its remaining columns pointing upward and telling the story of invading armies that had successfully reached Rome. The Visigoths and Vandals had destroyed the civilization that had built this city.

He had come to love this city during his service here, and not just because it was the center of Christendom. The rebirth of art and architecture of the last century had given the Eternal City a new vitality. And now, the same army that had destroyed the Byzantine Empire was now planning to destroy this city. There would be no rebirth if that happened.

"I'll do it, Father," said Marlo.

"Thank you, Marlo," said the priest. "Let's go back to my office. I have funds for you, and if they run out, I will give you a note of credit that you can use at any of our houses in Spain. Even though we are not trusted there, we do have several priests in the region."

"One question, Father. How much time do I have?"

"Not much. A few months, maybe a little more. The Holy Father intends to open negotiations soon, and he needs this information. I am afraid that you will need to be on board the *Santa Cecilia* by tomorrow morning."

~~~

It was two days after Marlo's departure from Ostia that the storm struck. The *Santa Cecilia* bobbed and danced on the violent waters. Pedro, the captain, had stowed the oars and ordered the storm sail set. He stood by the helm, expertly keeping his balance, rocking with the constantly changing angle of the deck. Below, alone in a cabin reserved for affluent passengers, Marlo was trying, without much success, to keep to his bunk. He realized, that in a storm like this, he would only be in the way on deck. When a sudden contrary wave threw the ship sideways, Marlo landed on the floor of the cabin. Instead of climbing back into his bunk, he sat against the roughhewn bulkhead and groaned. His stomach would not keep still and he feared he was going to be sick.

"This is terrible," he muttered. "I hope I never have to do this again."

This was the first time that he had been sick at sea. He had thought that he was immune to seasickness, but this storm was too much. He
~~~

needed something to look at besides the closed walls of the cabin. He crawled to the cabin door, sometimes losing ground as the ship was tossed about on the sea. Reaching the door, he pulled himself upright. Griping the frame and the latch, he stood with his head out of the cabin, muscles tense, breathing deeply, and braced for the next crashing plunge into the sea.

Outside there was very little light. The dark clouds blended into the dark sea, and the wind threw a mixture of rain and salt spray into his face. The ship climbed a wave. When it reached the top, the sail cracked sharply as it was suddenly filled with wind and the *Santa Cecilia* leaped forward, only to plunge sickeningly down the far side.

In the forward part of the main deck, two sailors were lashed to the gunwales. They were holding the lines that kept the sail in trim, ready to let them off their cleats if a contrary wind threatened the ship. The ship rose, pointing steeply upward as it climbed a swell, righted itself, and then plunged down, the bow crashing into the base of the next. A torrent of water poured over the front half of the ship, overwhelmed the two sailors, washed down into the recessed rower's deck, and rushed toward Marlo, cascading over the empty benches of the rowers. Just as he was about the step back into the cabin and shut the door, the ship lifted above the water and the flood drained through scuppers.

Seeing the full fury of the storm, Marlo forgot about his unsettled stomach. The very sound of the wind and crashing water deafened him, yet that was nothing compared to the resounding crash that followed upon a sudden bolt of lightning. *I hope we make it*, he thought.

He tried to close the cabin door, but a sudden gust of wind tore it out of his hand and sent him sprawling onto the slick deck with nothing to hold on to. The ship climbed another wave, and he started to slide. Twisting, he tried to catch himself and rolled against the bulkhead a few feet from the entrance to his cabin. The ship leveled off at the top of the wave, and Marlo scrambled on hands and knees into the small cabin and closed the door. As the ship plunged down into the sea with another sudden crash, he was sent sprawling onto the floor. Crawling over to the bunk, he wedged himself underneath to wait out the storm.

~~~

In the morning the sea was calm, and Marlo made his way out of the cabin, across the deck to the water barrel, and washed his face. There was a light breeze and only a few clouds in the sky. Land was nowhere in sight. Wondering where the ship was, he went to the helm in search of Pedro.

"Good morning, Señor," called Pedro cheer-
~~~

fully. "The small blow doesn't seem to have dampened your spirits too much."

"Small?" asked Marlo grumpily. "Small? I was tossed about the cabin all evening long. I have bruises from being thrown out of the bunk and landing against the floor and the walls." He gestured dramatically. "You call that small?"

"Small? Yes," answered Pedro. "'Big,' the ship would have been damaged, and 'great,' the ship would not exist. We got through it without damage. It was a small blow."

"Where are we now?"

"We are completely off course. We needed to sail northwest to reach Almeria. The storm moved us almost due south into waters that are frequently patrolled by Algerians. We are sailing north to try to get back into Spanish waters. As soon as the prisoners are recovered enough, I will have the oars manned. That should be quite soon."

"Have you seen any other ships?" asked Marlo.

"Not really," said Pedro. "The lookout thought he saw a sail to the west. He wasn't sure. He could have seen a cloud on the horizon. He didn't see any color that would indicate the presence of a banner or flag. And as you can see, we have taken ours down. Maybe our sail will look like a cloud to any curious ship." Pedro shrugged expressively. "I only hope that any Algerian ships that were in these waters were blown to the south as we were."

Marlo nodded and looked out to sea as Salvador, the ship's boatswain, approached Pedro. "We are ready to use the oars, Captain," he announced.

"Very good, Salvador," replied Pedro. "Carry on."

The boatswain blew his whistle, and the oars began their rhythmical sweep. The *Santa Cecilia* shuddered and began to move faster.

The prisoners rowed throughout the morning, and the ship glided through the clean waters, with no sign in the sky of the storm of the day before. At midday Marlo ate and went up by the helm to stay upwind of the smell coming from the sweating galley slaves. He sat against the rail and closed his eyes. He was tired from the lack of sleep the previous night. He jolted awake as the lookout shouted.

"Captain, captain," he called, "you need to come and see this, at once!"

"What is it?" Pedro asked.

"A ship, working its way from the southeast. I'm not sure, but it looks to me like it is Algerian." Pedro nodded and moved toward the stern. Marlo followed him.

When they reached the rail, Pedro pointed the ship out to Marlo. It was close to the horizon, almost too far to be seen clearly. "See, it is heading in our direction."

"It doesn't seem to be heading for us," said Marlo.

"No it isn't," replied the captain. "It is on a course that will allow it to intercept us ahead somewhere. And the wind is directly behind it. Do you see the flashes on the sides of that ship?"

"Yes, they are also using their oars. They want to catch up with us. But if they are indeed friendly, they can catch up with us in port, don't you think?"

"They can at that," answered Pedro. He turned toward Salvador. "Salvador, we will increase our speed. At once!"

Salvador shouted, and the rowers stood as they pulled back against the sea, sat as they raised the dripping oars and moved them forward, and dipped them again into the sea. The *Santa Cecilia* creaked and shuddered as she began to pick up speed.

Even though the slaves were pulling harder, the ship was slowly gaining on the *Santa Cecilia*, and it seemed to Marlo that unless the *Santa Cecilia* changed course, they would be attacked. "Don't we need to go in that direction?" he asked Pedro, pointing to the northeast.

"If we head in any direction," answered Pedro, "that ship will have the advantage of the wind. The only thing we can do is try to outrun them."

Marlo stayed out of the way of the sailors as

they prepared to be boarded. Pedro kept an eye on the trim of the sail, while sailors opened the hatches to the holds. Weapons were brought onto deck. The other ship was closer now. Its prow rose on the swells, throwing up spray as it fell. He hoped that the *Santa Cecilia's* rowers would be able to last long enough.

"It is going to be close," said Pedro, as he joined Marlo and watched the progress of the other ship. "If we can go just fast enough, they will lose speed when they slip behind us. It is going to be close," he repeated.

Marlo gestured to the open hatches. "Are you going to throw your cargo overboard?"

"Not yet. But I have everything ready in case I have to. These pirates have been making trade difficult for Spain. If we eject our cargo, the pirates have succeeded, even if we escape. We won't discard the grain unless we have no other option. The owner of this ship is expecting us in Almeria. I would save the cargo, if I can." He moved toward the compass and checked the sails again. He came back to the rail.

"Definitely Algerian," he said after a moment. "You can make out people now. They are Algerians. They have been getting more aggressive. We usually stay close to shore so we can duck to a port if we are sighted. The storm pushed us too far south." He pointed at Marlo's sword. "Do you know how to use that?"

"Yes."

"Good. Stay here in the stern. If we are boarded, I think it will be here." He left Marlo and climbed down the ladder to the lower deck. Marlo took off his cloak and stowed it near the tiller, and turned to watch the pursuing ship.

The Algerian ship was close enough that details could be seen. The deck was lined with men, their heads wrapped in turbans and their short curved swords in hand. Their captain was dressed in white, with a red fringed vest. A jewel set in his turban flashed in the sun. His long beard was black against his chest. Marlo watched as their oars rose from the water, the sunlight reflecting off the wet blades. The oars dropped into the water, moved back, and rose again.

Pedro came back. He studied the Algerian. "I don't think they are going to cut us off. Now let's hope they don't catch us." Marlo nodded and watched as the pirates drew closer. "Keep them rowing for all they are worth!" Pedro shouted at the boatswain.

Now the pirates were alongside the *Santa Cecilia*, about three boat lengths away. Marlo could hear the jeers and calls of the Algerians. Behind him, the prisoners at the oars were panting and groaning as they pulled their oars through the water. Marlo drew his sword. He was determined to kill the first pirate to board the *Santa Cecilia*.

The other ship drew closer and then began

to tack. The new course would bring them on a path that would bring it behind the *Santa Cecilia.* The pirate sailors let off the lines and began to hoist the spars over the top of the masts. The forward spar was successfully lifted and was being set into its new position. The spar on the aft mast was raised, passed over the top of the mast, and fell to the deck in a tangle of sailcloth and lines. Part of the sail blew over the edge and tangled with the oars.

"God be praised!" shouted Pedro. "Keep them rowing," he shouted to Salvador.

Marlo watched the ship and grinned. They were pulling away! Shouting, he leaped onto the rail and grabbed a stanchion line. He waved his sword around and laughed.

"What happened to them?" he called to Pedro.

"A line broke," answered Pedro. "The storm must have weakened it."

The Algerian ship had ceased rowing, and men were crawling about the deck, cleaning up the damage. The *Santa Cecilia* crossed in front of them beyond the range of their guns.

Marlo laughed again. He leaped back onto the deck and returned his sword to his side. Cupping his hands around his mouth, he began to shout at the retreating Algerians. "You misbegotten spawn of swine! You twisted followers of Satan! You're too slow!" Marlo laughed again.

"Señor Gobeli," Pedro called out to Marlo. The captain was laughing. "You are wasting your breath!"

"They have no respect for a victor who doesn't gloat," Marlo replied. "And I will gloat over them every chance I get."

Turning back toward the receding pirate vessel, he cupped his hands again. "Hey you, the one with the turban and jewels! Your toothless wives are better sailors than you!"

Chapter 3

June 1567

"See, Maria, there is our ship." The gray-haired, dignified-looking man pointed out into the harbor where the *Santa Cecilia* was working its way to its designated place. "It has made good time," he finished.

Maria disengaged her hand from her father's arm and brushed back her dark, wind-tossed hair and wrinkled her nose. "I think I can smell it from here," she said. This was her first time traveling with her father to Almeria as he checked on his shipping concerns. He usually left her home in Granada, but had decided to bring her this time. He had taken her to visit one of his galleys, and she had been revolted at the stench arising from the unwashed prisoners who manned the oars. She had no intention of ever boarding another.

Turning her dark eyes up to her father, she smiled. "I am looking forward to getting home."

Out in the harbor, the *Santa Cecilia* let down her anchor and swung to a stop. Two ragged shoremen rowed out to her, and Maria watched as three figures climbed over the side of the ship and got into the boat. Her father took her arm and walked down to the quay to wait for the boat to arrive.

The boat had beat them to the quay. By the time Maria and her father got there, only the captain of the *Santa Cecilia* was there, paying the harbor pilot. The other two men had already left.

"How did she weather the storm, Pedro?" asked Maria's father.

"No damage, Señor Montoya," said the captain walking toward them. "We did have a close call with an Algerian, though."

"Algerians?" asked Maria. Her father motioned for the captain to join them as they walked away from the quay. Pedro bowed to Maria.

"Pirates, Señorita. Moslem pirates from North Africa. They have been rather arrogant, of late. His Majesty will have to take care of them soon. Much Spanish shipping has been lost to them."

"Papa, you aren't taking risks with your business, are you?" asked Maria.

Montoya shrugged. "The ships stay close to shore. The Algerians go after those who can't dart back to port when enemy sails are sighted." He put his arm around his daughter of sixteen. "Besides," he added with a smile, "Pedro is a cautious sailor and will make sure the *Santa Cecilia* is never in any danger." He turned back to the captain. "I see you had some passengers."

"Yes, Señor, I did. One of them is a young man that I think will be a charming companion for the Señorita here."

"Companion!" Maria stopped walking and put her hands on her hips. She glared mockingly at Pedro. "Companion? I certainly hope you are not trying to suggest something."

"Now, what could I possibly be suggesting?" asked Pedro.

"You are not trying to set me up with a husband? Because if you are, I'll make up my own mind, thank you!"

Pedro's face broke into a bright smile. "Now why didn't I think of this young man as a husband? Perfect, the idea is perfect!" He laughed and placed a calloused hand on Montoya's shoulder. "Señor, I have found the ideal man for your daughter. Your worries are over!"

"Pedro, you have lifted a great weight from my mind," answered Montoya, laughing heartily at his daughter's expense. He placed his arm around his daughter's shoulders. "My dear, I am happy for you! You will let me meet this young man of yours sometime soon?"

Maria felt her face grow hot. The continued laughter of her father and Pedro added to her embarrassment. She shook off her father's arm and brushed past Pedro. Tossing her head, she gracefully stalked away, the laughter of Pedro and her father echoing in her ears.

Turning a corner, she walked quickly to escape them. When she reached the church at the end of the road, she looked over her shoulder and saw that her father and Pedro were only halfway down the street. Without slowing down, she moved past the church, turned down another street and arrived at The Gull, the inn where she and her father had been staying. She rushed through the open door and collided into the back of a man who was standing just inside. He staggered forward several steps to regain his balance.

"Fool," gasped Maria, "you don't own this place. Standing in front of the door without any thought of who might be trying to come in behind you. A courteous man would have stood to the side."

"And a well-bred lady would have looked where she was going and apologized," replied the young man, quietly. "I shall set the example, however, and apologize." The man swept aside his cloak and bowed, deeply. "I am extremely sorry that I didn't have a servant outside to warn those entering that I was just inside the door, standing in their way." The man's tone was serious, but one corner of his mouth twitched in an ironic smile. He straightened the fall of his gray traveling cloak, placed his left hand on the hilt of his sword and bowed again. "I am greatly pleased to make your acquaintance. May I escort you to a table, lest you collide with someone else?"

"You may not," said Maria, her rising anger at the young man's sarcasm made her voice hard. "Now, if you are done being rude, I would appreciate it greatly if you would just step aside."

"I still would like an apology," the young man crossed his arms. He looked at Maria without moving.

"You will not get one!" snapped Maria. "Now just let me pass."

The young man looked over his shoulder toward the stairs. "If you are careful," he said turning back to her with a grin, "I think you can make it to those stairs without knocking anyone over." He stepped aside and gestured for her to pass. "I will be dining here this evening, so you can easily find me if you feel like running into someone again. Just give me a little warning, though."

Her eyes smarting, Maria stalked pass the man and deliberately climbed the stairs, the worn wood creaking under angry footfalls.

Reaching the top of the stairs, she strode down the dim hall and opened the door to her room. She closed the door behind her, sat on her chair, and wiped her eyes. She let down her wind-blown hair and began brushing it violently. The gray-clad young man was impertinent. Where did he learn his manners? He had made her look like a fool, and then, instead of being contrite, had addressed her with sarcasm.

Running her hands through her hair, her thoughts were diverted. She had her mother's hair, and she missed her. She put down her brush and leaned back in her chair. Her mother. She had not thought much about her mother since she had started traveling with her father a month ago. She missed her mother. She had been full of life and joy. Years ago, her father had been traveling near Venice and had met a Gypsy family. Her mother's family. Sela had left her family and followed her father back to Spain. She and Montoya had married. They had two children, but Maria's younger brother had died of a fever when he was still an infant.

Maria got up and moved toward the window, looking out over the city and the harbor glinting in the evening sun. Her graceful walk had also been a gift from Sela. Sela had loved to dance. She had even danced when she was preparing food. Even when Sela used to walk in the streets, it looked like she was dancing. Maria grew up with the same love and grace. Her friends even called her "la Bailadora", the Dancer. Three years ago Sela had caught pneumonia and died.

Maria crossed herself, whispering a prayer for her mother. She wiped her eyes and sighed. One of the reasons her father had brought her along, she thought, was to lift her out of the melancholy that she still felt. Or maybe he had her along to lift him out of the melancholy he felt.

She had regained her composure when her father knocked on her door. "It is supper time," Montoya said, the mockery gone from his voice. "Let's go down." She smiled and stepped out into the hall and waited as Montoya closed the door. "We will eat with Pedro," said Montoya taking her arm and leading her down the hall.

"As long as you don't spend the entire meal planning my life." Maria tossed her head playfully and accompanied Montoya down the stairs.

The dining room was brightly lit by the late afternoon sun which filtered through the open porticoes on the west side of the room, and Maria was led by her father around the room toward a table with two men. One was Pedro. The other had his back to them. They stood when Maria approached, and the man with Pedro turned toward her. Her hand flew toward her mouth in shock. There, standing before her, was the young man who had been so rude to her earlier.

~~~

Marlo watched as the dark-haired, gypsy-looking girl registered shock and dismay. He had not expected to see her, though he should have realized that the girl who had ran into him earlier was the daughter of Señor Montoya. He had just excused himself to get her.

"Good evening, Señorita!" said Pedro. "I would like you to meet Señor Marlo Gobeli who traveled with me here. He says that he is going to Granada. Maybe he will travel with you?" Not waiting for a reply, Pedro turned toward Marlo and clasped him on the arm and made a self-satisfied smirk, "This beautiful young lady is Señorita Maria Montoya, the daughter of the owner of *Santa Cecilia*. It will do your humility much good to spend time with her."

"You don't need to introduce us," Marlo grinned. "We already met. Rather forcefully, in fact."

"Eh? How's that?"

"Well, there I was," Marlo placed his thumbs behind his belt buckle and rocked back on his heels. "I had just entered the common room here and was looking around for someone who could serve me with some wine, when all of a sudden, I was sent sprawling, and found myself
~~~

being admonished by this young lady. I made my apologies and offered to help her. But she refused. She even refused to apologize for running into me." He rolled his eyes upward, "I can't imagine why!"

"And you will not get one," said Maria hotly. "You don't deserve it." She turned on Pedro. "If this is the 'pleasant young companion' you told me about, you can keep him company. You two should be perfect for each other. Father," said Maria as she turned back to leave the table. "I will have my meal in my room."

Marlo watched Maria as she walked purposefully toward the stairs. *I really should apologize*, he thought. Later. After she had time to settle down. Right now he did not think that he could get a chance to speak without her cutting him off.

"I'm sorry," said Montoya after she had left. "Her mother was headstrong, and ever since Sela passed away, I haven't had the heart to try to curb her stubbornness."

"At her age," said Pedro with a shrug, "that can be hard. Sometimes the youth need to learn on their own."

"But she is a good girl, otherwise," said Montoya.

"Tell me, Señor Montoya," said Marlo, sitting down and adjusting his sword so it would not be in the way. "Does your daughter accompany you all the time?"

"No, this is the first time." Montoya took the wine flask, poured some for himself and offered to pour for Marlo. "I expect her to marry into a trading or merchant family, so I want her to have some idea of the nature of the business. By bringing her with me, I am hoping she will get a sense of what is involved in trade."

"As long as you don't bring her on ship, Señor," said Pedro. "We don't want to lose her."

Marlo saw the opening he needed. Since meeting Montoya, he had wanted to inquire about the nature of his trade and see to what extent the Algerians were damaging his business. He was not averse to informing Montoya that Rome needed to know what was happening to Spanish food trade, but he felt that Montoya would be less guarded in his conversation if he was not aware that Marlo would be reporting his words to Rome.

"Loose her?" he asked frowning. "As long as she only sailed during the trading months, there would be very little chance of the ship being lost from a storm."

"Storms are the least of our concern," said Montoya. "We are losing shipping to the Algerians. Quite regularly, in fact."

"The Algerian that chased us earlier was not an isolated event," put in Pedro. "We are keeping closer to shore to try to avoid them. We travel slower. Either way, trade is hurt. We either loose the cargo, or the cargo comes in late."

"How has your trade fared?" asked Marlo.

"Better than others, and worse than I could like," said Montoya. He put down his wine glass and leaned back in his chair. "My ships all hug the shore. I lost two last summer, and none this year. But shipping takes more time, so I can't move my merchandise as fast, thus profits are down. We'll survive."

"What would happen if not enough grain is brought in?"

"That would mean that almost all of our Mediterranean trade has stopped," said Pedro. "And that could happen. The Algerians are getting bolder."

"I think there would be a real food shortage," added Montoya. "How much, I don't know."

"That is sobering," said Marlo. He refilled his wine glass and helped himself to some meat and bread. He passed the platter to Montoya.

"Thank you," said Montoya. "An what about you? What brings you here to Almeria?"

"Boredom, wanting to see something different," said Marlo evasively. "I used to be in the Guard. I could have gone back to Switzerland, but I wondered if there would be an opportunity for me here, maybe in the New World."

"I thought you had something of the soldier about you," said Montoya. "The Marquis of Mondejar is a good captain. Stop in to see him when you are in Granada. He might want to employ someone like you."

"I just might do that."

~~~

After the meal, Marlo strolled along the harbor front. The information he had received from Montoya merely confirmed the suspicions of Father Veraccio, but it did not give any more details. He kept along the harbor, watching the ships that swung at anchor. He saw one in the process of offloading its cargo and walked toward the quay and waited for someone to notice him.

"Good evening," he called to the dockhand who had looked in his direction. "What ship is that?"

"She's the *Stella*, Señor. Just in from Sicily."

"Do you know if she encountered any Algerians?"

"How would I know?" said the dockhand. "I wasn't aboard her. Ask them." he pointed a dirty thumb over his shoulder toward a group of sailors who were overseeing the landing of the cargo.

"Hey, Esteban," called the dockhand before Marlo had a chance to speak. "This fellow wants to know if you saw any of those pirates."

"Why should you want to know?" asked Esteban.

"I came in earlier on the *Santa Cecilia*, there,"
~~~

said Marlo pointing to where the ship swung at anchor. "We had a close call with one, and I was just curious if anybody else had encountered them."

"Not us," said Esteban. "But they're out there. I've seen them before, and there have been ships that have not come to port."

"Well, thanks," said Marlo. He nodded to Esteban and continued his way down the quay. The Montoya's were leaving tomorrow, and he debated asking to accompany them. They were only from one class of people, and he could not get an accurate picture of Spain's food supply from them. He needed to speak to some of the farmers themselves, maybe to some of the garrison commanders.

But then again, traveling with the Montoyas could help him give him a place to stay while in Granada as well as provide a source of information on Spain's troubles. He would just have to put up with Maria. He paused and looked thoughtfully out over the bay. Father Veraccio wanted information quickly, information that he probably would not get from the Montoyas. On second thought, he decided to travel alone and get to Granada as soon as possible.

Chapter 4

June 1567

Marlo rode out of Almeria as soon as it was light. He had secured a horse the evening before, and was up and ready before dawn. He rode through the quiet streets of the city and onto the well-traveled road that led through the Aljuperas Mountains and on into Granada, its dirt surface ground into powder by centuries of heavy travel, and as the day progressed, Marlo encountered many wagons and travelers heading toward Almeria.

Towards the evening of the second day from Almeria, Marlo saw that some men in the small towns along the road were wearing the long tunics and large turbans of the Moors. *These must be Moriscos,* he thought. They tended to ignore him, almost to the point of being insulting. As he had traveled, he had exchanged pleasantries with those he encountered on the road, but the Moriscos either did not respond, or viewed him with ill-concealed hostility, as if they were insulted that he would dare to speak to them. The animosity bothered him, and he grew wary as the day progressed.

Shortly after sunset, he rode into the town of Juviles and tied his horse outside an inn. He nodded to a dark complexioned man who was lounging nearby and walked in through the arch of the door and into a common room lit with lamps.

Marlo looked about the room. He saw no-body at the tables. He started to walk toward a table to sit.

"You!" A hand grabbed Marlo's shoulder. He was spun roughly around and the dark face of the man he saw outside frowned into his. "Why are you here, dog?"

"Because I am hungry and need a place to stay." Marlo brushed the hand off his shoulder. "You need to ask me a question, ask it properly." Marlo rubbed his shoulder and smiled in answer to the glare he was given. "You could chase guests away – guests that would pay for some peace. Bad for the business."

The Morisco's face contorted as he shouted something in Arabic. He pulled a long dagger out of its sheath, held it like a sword at waist height and lunged. Marlo stepped to the side and back, circling so his back was not to the room. He eased around until he was able to reach behind him and touch the plaster wall.

His assailant lunged again, and Marlo spun out of his path. There was a faint ring as the dagger glanced off the wall. It fell out of the Morisco's hand and clattered to the floor, followed by the man himself, who smacked his head on the wall and collapsed. Breathing heavily, Marlo backed away from him, easing towards the entry.

"You were lucky." A tall man, dressed in worn clothes and wearing an apron walked across the room toward Marlo. "Ali, here, is distrustful of strangers. Especially those who are armed. Afraid that you were one of the king's men. Come, sit down. I will bring you some food."

"What about him?" Marlo pointed to the huddled form of Ali, who was beginning to stir.

"Pay him no mind," said the innkeeper. "He won't bother you again. Will you, Ali?"

Ali looked up at Marlo and grunted. He slowly stood, and with his hand on the wall, carefully walked out.

"He will leave you alone now," said the innkeeper apologetically. He held out a chair for Marlo and helped him sit. "So, why are you here?"

Because this is an inn, and I need to eat and sleep, said Marlo to himself. His reception here was not what he had been expecting. The innkeeper looked at him calmly, but Marlo could see in his hard eyes that a wrong answer would not be taken lightly. *What is going on here?* he thought.

Father Veraccio had warned of danger, but Marlo had not expected to be attacked in an inn. This attack and the innkeeper's offhand dismissal of Ali made him suspicious. Had not Father Veraccio said something about the Moriscos being forced to convert or leave? The animosity of the subjugated Moriscos must be stronger than the Italian Jesuit suspected. He took a deep breath and let it out slowly, trying to calm his nerves. He had to get this right.

"Going to Granada," said Marlo. He glanced toward the entry as a couple of men in plain woolen clothes, sweat stained and dirty walked in and sat at the table closest to the door. He leaned forward to the innkeeper. "I figure Granada to be a better place than where I was a month ago. Healthier. I'm greatly attached to my head."

"I believe we all are," said the innkeeper. "Let me get you something to eat." He left through a narrow passage opposite of where Marlo sat. Before he left, though, Marlo saw him look at the two laborers and nod. Marlo turned to look at the laborers, and found them staring at him.

"Good evening," said Marlo. "Are you passing through?"

"Live here," said one, his creased, sun-darkened face showing no expression.

"Then you might be able to help me."

"Won't help." Again, there was no expression one the man's face.

Marlo shifted his chair so he could keep the men and the entry in view. There clearly was something amiss here. He was curious. Father Veraccio would probably like to know about his reception here, but that was not the point. Marlo needed to know what was going on in the region if was to avoid being killed.

"Can I get you something?" Marlo asked the two. "Some wine? Something to eat?"

"Buy nothing."

Marlo sighed and stood as the innkeeper came back into the room. "What is going on around here?" he demanded. "I ride in, and I am attacked as soon as I enter, never mind the insults I encountered on the road. Then these two by the door won't speak. Well, one hasn't, and the other might as well have said nothing."

"Sit," said the innkeeper pulling out a chair and sitting himself. "Those two are just keeping an eye on you."

"Why?"

"Let me ask you again, what are you doing here? You speak Spanish, but like a foreigner, you look like a soldier the way you walk, the way you're used to your sword. Are you in the army?"

"No army, not anymore," Marlo scowled. The innkeeper's questions did nothing to settle his anxiety. "When an officer insults you, and you defend your honor by killing him, you are out of the army."

"Where?"

"Switzerland."

"And why Granada?"

"Seemed a good place as any." Marlo shrugged. "When one needs to get moving, he often does not think of where he is going. The ship I took was bound for Almeria, so here I am."

"Are you being pursued?"

"I hope not. Just in case, I figure the mountains here would be a great place to loose myself for a while. I hope to find somebody in Granada who could guide me through the hills and not say a word about seeing me."

"I wouldn't think you need to go to the city for that," the innkeeper shook his head. "Men around here know these hills. They might even be able to get you to blend in."

"Blend in?"

"I know you are light on your feet; you were able to move very quickly in spite of your limp when Ali went at you. How well can you use that sword?"

"Good enough. Why?"

"There might be a use for you. In exchange for hiding you, I think you could teach a few men how to fight. You would be too valuable."

"If Ali was any indication of local ability, I can at least ensure that your men can hold a dagger and not injure themselves. Why, though? Not that it really is any of my business," Marlo added hastily.

"No, it's not," agreed the innkeeper quietly. He stood. "It could become your business, though, depending on your reliability."

"Suits me," said Marlo leaning back and stretching his legs under the table. "I can live with that, as long as I get to live." He gave a half smile. "For that matter, I would do just about anything to live."

"That's good to know. I will have Ali wake you in the morning. He will be your guide, and probably your first pupil."

Shortly after daybreak, Ali woke Marlo and led him to an empty stable. He shut the door, blocking all but the rays of morning light shining in through the small window set high in the walls. Ali then turned and pulled out his dagger. He advanced on Marlo. "Teach me."

"I thought we were going into the hills," protested Marlo.

"We go when I say. But you start teaching now. And if you teach good, then we make sure anyone looking for you does not find you. So, teach."

"Put that knife away, then. We will use short

pieces of wood, at first. Until you learn how to use a dagger against an opponent." Marlo rummaged through the old straw that had piled up along the walls and found two sticks that would serve. He tossed one to Ali. "First, hold the dagger like so, and not like a sword. The dagger needs to be an extension of your forearm, and it points toward your opponent, except when you slash, like this."

After a couple of hours, Ali called for a halt. He had learned quickly, and using the sticks, he and Marlo dueled. He wiped his face, dirty from the dust they had kicked up. "Good," he said. "You know how to use a blade. Tomorrow, you will teach again."

For the next week, Marlo would get up at daybreak and meet Ali at the deserted stable. Ali always brought a different man with him every morning, and demanded that Marlo teach them how to use a dagger. Sometimes, Marlo would be led to the field behind the barn in order to show some men how to handle a sword. He would say nothing about when Marlo could expect to be taken into the hills, but from some of the comments he heard from the inn-keeper and those who would come in at night, he got the impression that there was a camp of men to the southeast. It was during his eighth evening in Juviles that he overheard the inn-keeper tell Ali to lead the men Marlo had taught to the camp. Slipping to his room, Marlo sat by his window and waited for night. He needed to find out what was going on. There was something more here in Granada than just hatred of Christians.

Juviles was silent, and the moon had just set, when Marlo slipped out of the inn. He stood in the deeper shadow of the doorway and looked around. He saw nobody. Slipping along the building, he moved south, ducked between two houses, and, keeping to a crouch, left the town.

Traveling slowly, he worked his way into the hills, following the trail that lead to the south. He could just distinguish the trail in the starlight, and could see nothing of the terrain, until a dark mass loomed to his right. It was a steep hill, almost a cliff.

The silhouette of the cliff against the night was only about six to eight feet tall, and climbable. Marlo adjusted his sword so it would not interfere with his climbing and worked his way up and into the cracked and jumbled rocks. He reached the top and lay down in a depression, covered himself with his cloak, and waited for morning. He hoped he had come in the right direction. There was no going back to Juviles, even if he did not find Ali and the men he was leading.

Later, after laying there all night and then sitting in the morning sun for about three hours, Marlo heard the sound of feet on the trail below him. He raised his head above the boulder. A column of twenty-three armed men was passing below him on the mountain path that led into the valley. The man in front wore a turban and was not carrying any weapons that Marlo could see. The rest of the men carried an odd assortment of weaponry: swords, scimitars, muskets. Nobody looked up to where Marlo was hiding.

He slid down behind the boulder and crawled back. Keeping himself bent over and out of sight of the column, Marlo ran behind the ridge that paralleled the trail. Stopping abruptly, he crouched in a depression in the ground, behind some low scrub brush that stood twenty feet off the trail. He took his dirty gray cloak and spread it over himself, hoping that he would not be seen.

He forced himself to breathe normally as the column rounded the outcrop and came into view. His heart raced. He was taking a risk positioning himself this close to the trail, but he needed information.

The man leading the column did not seem to be worried about being seen. He was not scanning the land ahead or to the sides of the trail. His gaze was focused on the ground before his feet, and as he drew closer Marlo saw that it was Ali.

The men following carried supplies and plodded wearily along, and as they passed Marlo, he noticed that they were all of disparate ages, some of them were still boys, and some of them were the men he had taught.

He remained still until the column had vanished. Standing up, he moved furtively alongside the trail and up the hill until he could see the men in the distance. Moving cautiously from shrub to shrub, he followed the column's progress, keeping out of sight.

As the sun was setting, Marlo sat for a moment on a boulder, his throat parched. He had traveled harder than the men he was following. Several times during the day, he had gone off the trail and climbed the hills and moved forward in an attempt to spot the column's destination. He had not brought enough water.

Taking a deep breath, he stood up and plodded along the trail, keeping an eye on the disturbed rocks and soil. He staggered up a steep hill, crested the top and saw the men below him. He crouched, hoping he had not been spotted.

The men clambered down the slope before him and passed into a valley, shaded from the setting sun and filled with trees and shrubs. Marlo waited until the column entered the wooded area before he began his descent.

The mountain slopes glowed orange and red above the twilight of the valley, and Marlo shivered a little in the cool air of the valley floor. He could smell moisture and began to look around for the stream that he knew had to be there.

Moving furtively from tree to tree, he caught up with the column in time to see Ali hold up his hand and call for the men to halt. Marlo slipped behind a tree to watch.

A figure stepped out of the gloom of the forest and approached Ali. He said something, which sounded Arabic to Marlo's ears. Ali answered him and turned to the men following him. "We have arrived. Follow me."

The path was a dark ribbon that wound through the trees, and Marlo continued to follow the column, now augmented by the black robed sentry. The men trudged silently for about ten more minutes before the forest opened up onto a small level plain on the valley floor. Crude huts and tents reflected the red flickering light from several campfires. The men picked up their pace, heartened at the prospect of rest and food.

Stopping at the nearest campfire, Ali turned to the men and they sat. Taking one with him, he moved wordlessly through the huts towards a tent on the far side of the stream that ran through the encampment. The two splashed through the cool water and approached an armed man sitting at the entrance of the tent. Ali and his companion waited as the guard stood and entered the tent for a moment. Then he returned and held the tent open for Ali to enter.

Marlo kept just outside of the clearing and circled until he was able to reach the stream, out of sight of the camp. He knelt on the bank, cupped his hands, and drank greedily. Refilling his water skin, he stood, waded the stream and, at a crouch that sent fire though his weak leg, moved toward the lone tent on this side of the stream.

When he began to hear the murmur of voices, he dropped onto his hands and knees and crawled, carefully avoiding loose stones and sticks that would betray his presence. He was about ten yards from the back of the tent before he stopped and lay down.

"...and I think we can get more from the farms," he heard Ali say.

"Do you? And who will take care of their farms for them while they are here?" The speaker had a deep, smooth voice.

"We could use the men," objected Ali.

"No, we could use secrecy. How is your new weapons trainer?"

"Good. He is running from something, and I think he should come here."

"Tell, me Ali. Why would you bring a Christian here? When we rise, we need surprise."

"He only wants to live. He has no loyalties. And he is good with a blade." Marlo could almost hear the shrug in Ali's voice. "Besides, we could make sure he doesn't leave here.

"Fine, bring him. And I have word that Selim considers helping us restore the Crescent to Granada. He has even promised soldiers. That might help those who are unsure of our chances for success. Go join your men. I will speak to them tomorrow."

Marlo remained motionless as Ali left the tent and crossed back over the stream. He eased back away and drifted into the dark beneath the trees. He had to get to Granada without getting caught, and now he would have to walk the entire way since it would be too risky to return to Juviles for his horse. For now, though, he just needed to get out of the valley under cover of darkness. He needed to get word to Father Veraccio as soon as he got to Granada. The Jesuit would want to know about this.

Chapter 5

June 1567

The inn's serving girl knocked on Maria's door before sunrise to wake her up. She lit a couple of candles and brought fresh water for Maria to wash with. Promising to be back with breakfast, the girl left.

Maria climbed out of bed and washed. She dressed and began arranging her hair for travel. The girl came back with food: bread and watered ale, and some cold meat from last night's meal. Maria ate, put on her deep red traveling cloak, made sure her belongings were gathered, and that her trunk was completely packed. Going to the door, she opened it, crossed the hall to her father's room, and knocked on his door.

"Come in," he answered.

Maria opened the door and found her father

finishing his breakfast.

"Good morning, Papa," she said, kissing his cheek. "I hope you didn't stay up too late visiting with Pedro?"

"Late, but not too late," he replied, wiping his mouth and standing up. "Are you ready? We should be heading home."

"Everything is packed. Are we traveling alone, or will Señor Gobeli be traveling with us?"

"He has probably left already. Last night he told me that he decided not to travel with us since he had something pressing to look after." Montoya shrugged with a small smile and shook his head. "Now, that is an unusual young man. He asked about my business, and the business of my associates, but he is not a merchant at all. Knowledgeable about world affairs and polite, but gave very little information about himself."

"I didn't like him, and I am relieved he is not traveling with us. I hope we never see him again."

"I'm sorry, but I'm afraid you will have to see him. He asked if he could visit when he is in Granada."

"And of course you said yes," Maria sighed. "Papa, you like everybody you meet."

"At least until I have a reason not to." Montoya took Maria's arm to lead her out of the room and down the hall. "Are you ready to go?"

"I am ready to go. I just want to stop at the church on our way."

"What for?"

"I want to light a candle for our safe trip. And another one for mother."

Montoya put his arm around her shoulders. "I'll go with you. We will light those candles together." Taking her arm, he led her down the hall and down the stairs. At the bottom, they met the old landlord. "Our trunks are ready. Can you have the wagon hitched and the trunks stowed?"

"At once, Señor. It has been good to have you here, again. Señorita." The landlord turned to Maria and took her hand. "It has made my heart young again to see you. I hope you will come back with your father again and dance for us, no?" He kissed her hand.

"We shall see." Maria laughed. "I do thank you for your hospitality. I enjoyed my visit."

"I shall get about those trunks, Señor. May the angels guide your way." Bowing, the landlord went upstairs.

Outside, the sky was beginning to lighten in the east. There was a slight breeze coming from the south, bringing with it the fresh smell of the sea. On shore, the roosters were beginning to offer their welcomes to the new day, competing with the cries of the sailors preparing their ships. Maria and her father walked arm-in-arm to the Cathedral of the Incarnation and went in. Genuflecting, they went to the image of the Mother of God, lit four candles, and knelt in prayer for a few minutes.

Leaving the cathedral, Maria and her father walked slowly back to their inn. Maria thought that Almeria was beautiful in the dawn. The delicate stonework of the Moors glowed in the morning light, making the streets and buildings seem as if they were made of graceful, golden stone. To the northwest rose the *Alcazaba*, or rather, what remained of the fortress. Even the ruined walls possessed a delicacy of line and form that reminded Maria of Granada. She had been told that the *Alcazaba* had been ruined by an earthquake, and since the Reconquista was over, there had been no reason to rebuild it. She imagined that the completed structure had been as beautiful as it had been strong.

Before returning to the inn, Maria and her father walked along the harbor, breathing deeply the clean salt air. The morning sun reflected off the harbor, and Maria stood for a moment watching the gulls circling above the water.

"Señor Montoya!" came a voice behind them. They tuned and saw a well-dressed middle-aged man was walking quickly toward them. His face showed the same relief that was carried on his voice.

"Good day to you, Padilla," answered Montoya. "I don't think that you have met my daughter, Maria?"

"I have not," said Padilla taking her hand and bowing. "I am delighted to finally meet you after all the times your father has spoken about you."

"Thank you." Maria smiled. "Are you one of Papa's partners?"

"No, but I am a trader and sometimes do business with your father." Padilla turned his attention to Montoya. "Señor, I was hoping to find you. There is something I think you need to hear."

"What is it?"

"Not here. Let me take both of you to where I am staying. I'm sure you would like to eat."

"Very well," said Montoya. "Come, Maria. It looks like we are going to get a good meal before we return to Granada."

"I was afraid you were going to take your daughter on ship," said Padilla looking at Maria. "Señorita, I am relieved to see that is not the case."

"Señor, thank you for your gracious greeting, yet I think I am as confused as my father. Why are you so relieved to see us?"

"Let's eat first, Señorita. I will explain afterwards. If you would allow?" Padilla held out his arm for Maria.

"Thank you," said Maria. She took his arm

and he escorted them away from the church.

Padilla led them to an inn surrounded by open porticoes. He explained that this had been a Moorish bath, but following King Philip's prohibition against public baths, it had been converted into an inn. Padilla led them to a table overlooking the sea. The view of the harbor in the setting sun was broken by the delicately carved pillars and arches of the portico. Maria thought it a harmonious blend of nature and art.

Over a meal of fish, bread, and fruit, Padilla and her father discussed trade and the economic situation of greater Mediterranean Europe. Whenever the conversation led to pirates or any of Montoya's business associates, Padilla would change the subject, saying that such things could wait until they were done eating.

Padilla seemed most interested in Montoya's account of the close encounter the *Santa Cecilia* had with the Algerians. He asked after Montoya's business plans, and steered away from all questions concerned with his own news.

When the meal ended, Montoya leaned back in his chair and frowned at Padilla. "I think it's time that you explain what it is you have been so mysterious about," he said. "You have been evading the issue ever since we sat down."

"I was asked by a few of your friends in Cartagena to come here and make inquiries into how your business was doing. And to caution you: almost every ship that has left Cartagena has been attacked or taken by the Algerians. To be frank, I am quite surprised that your ship made it into port. You were very lucky. Many have not been."

"I think there is something more," said Montoya. "Come, you had better tell us. There has to be something else. Otherwise you would not have waited till after we ate."

"Yes," said Padilla slowly. "It concerns Señor Carlos."

"The silk merchant?" asked Maria.

"Yes." Padilla seemed reluctant to continue.

"What about him?" asked Montoya.

"Señor, you set a bad example by telling him how you wanted to involve your daughter in your business. Two months ago, Señor Carlos visited me in Cartagena. He had with him his daughter and son. He was planning to go to Sicily, just like you are thinking of doing."

"So that's were Isabella went," interrupted Maria. "She left home a while ago and I had no idea where she'd gone. I was worried that something had happened. Well, I am glad she went. Papa has told me that Sicily is beautiful."

"They did not make it to Sicily," said Padilla. He sighed before continuing. "They were on two ships. Señor Carlos and Isabella on one and Juan on the other. The *Asuncion*, Juan's ship, came back to port a month ago. When we heard what had happened, I was sent to tell you."

"Well, what happened?" demanded Montoya tightly. "For God's sake, stop stalling and tell us!"

"The *Juanita* was taken by the Algerians. The *Asuncion* was further away and made good its escape, but not before seeing what happened. Señor Carlos and his daughter were captured."

Maria moaned through her hand. She knew Isabella well. They had spent much time together since her father and Señor Carlos were business associates. When her mother died, Maria had spent much of her time at the Carlos family home while her father was either away or busy with his business. She moaned again and tears welled in her eyes. *This cannot be true,* she thought. *Not Isabella. Not her!*

"Worse," continued Padilla almost ruthlessly in his determination to be done with this disagreeable task. "I arrived here five days ago. Two days ago some Spaniards ransomed from the Algerian galleys came into port. They claim that Señor Carlos and Isabella were seen being put aboard a Turkish ship, and that its destination was Constantinople. I'm afraid that as pretty as Isabella is..." Padilla did not finish. He did not have to.

~~~

Maria and her father did not leave Almeria until midday. Montoya was distressed at the news, and had spent some time discussing the
~~~

event with Padilla. While waiting for her father, Maria had gone to the cathedral and sat before the altar, unable to pray. She knew she should be praying for her friend. But she would hold back whenever she started, afraid that God would not answer her; that she would be angry at Him if He did not.

The first day out of Almeria, she was miserable, anxious for what might be happening to Isabella. By the following morning, her anxiety had abated a little, and she was able to take some joy in the pleasant weather. She sat in an open carriage with her father and gloried in the smell of the trees and flowers. She did not miss the smell of the sea, and if she never smelled it again she would consider herself blessed. She only looked forward to the end of the journey and the security of being home. Isabella's story made her feel vulnerable.

When they were only a day away from the city, the road became more heavily traveled. Maria found herself the object of open stares from the men, and even though it was hot, she veiled her face.

Even Montoya himself soon became uncomfortable with the attention of the men on the road.

"We are almost home, Maria," he said. "You will be safe from all this attention there."

Maria was not convinced. The men who were staring at her as she passed were swarthy, and they were not looking at her with appreciation. Rather their gazes were filled with a thinly disguised animosity, disdain, and maybe even hate.

They spent the night in an inn some seven miles outside of Granada, and resumed their travels early in the morning. Montoya was anxious to be home, and Maria had to admit that she was as well. Clean clothes, a bath, and a chance to rest properly had strong appeals after days on the road.

They reached the city without mishap, and in the teaming throngs of the city's residents, Maria felt somewhat secure from the frightening stares she had encountered on the road. Their carriage made its slow way through the maze of elegant streets, buildings, and squares. The light, Moorish architecture of her home city was a welcome sight indeed.

The carriage halted outside of the Montoya's house, and Señor Montoya climbed out to help Maria alight. The driver rang a bell and a servant hurried out of the house.

"Señor Montoya!" he called. "Welcome home. And you too, Señorita. I am happy to see you safe. We were worried that you might not return."

"I can well imagine, Carlos," said Montoya affably, "after the report of what happened to Francisco and his daughter."

"That is horrible," said Carlos shaking his head, "what happened to them. Praise God, it did not happen to you." With the help of the driver, Carlos lifted Maria's trunk, and they made their way toward the house.

"How are things here?" asked Montoya to change the subject.

"Well," said Carlos as he entered the house and set the trunk down, "business has been better. But it has been worse. We are almost out of wool. For some reason there has been a high demand for cloth. The grain supply is nearly exhausted. Our spices, though, are not moving well at all."

"Well, it does seem that things are sufficiently in hand," said Montoya. "Tomorrow I will go over everything with you and see precisely how the business stands. For now, I intend to use the remainder of the day to rest. It has been a long and difficult trip."

"Of course, Señor," said Carlos. "Let me get your things into your rooms and I will have baths made ready and food prepared. Welcome home, again."

Chapter 6

June 1567

Two evenings after spying on the Moriscos, Marlo, hot and dusty from two days' travel on foot and a night spent outdoors, arrived at the outskirts of Granada. The *Alhambra* loomed over the surrounding city to the east, and Marlo trudged wearily toward it. He climbed the street that led to a gate guarded by a sentry.

"Is the Captain-General available?" asked Marlo, his dry voice rasping.

"Not usually to strangers. What do you need to see him for?" asked the guard.

"Is there another officer somewhere I can talk to?"

"I can summon one." The guard rang a bell and Marlo sank down on the bench. He did not have to wait long before an unarmed soldier approached the sentry.

"What is it, Carlos?" he asked

"Captain, this man wants to see an officer," said the sentry, pointing toward Marlo. "He asked for the Captain-General." The captain nodded and walked toward Marlo who slowly stood.

"What can I do for you, Señor?" asked the Captain, surveying Marlo's dusty clothes and unshaven face.

"Captain," Marlo bowed slightly, "Can we go someplace else?" asked Marlo. "I have been on my feet for the last few days, not to mention sleeping outside. I would appreciate something to drink."

The captain studied Marlo for a moment. "Well, I can at least do that. Follow me." He led Marlo through the gate and into a courtyard. Turning to the right, he opened a door and gestured for Marlo to enter. "Come in. I'm Captain Guiterrez. Sit down and tell me what you need to inform the Captain-General about." Guiterrez went to a small table on the opposite side of the room, picked up a pitcher and filled a cup with water.

"Thank you," said Marlo, taking the cup and sitting down. He emptied it.

"More?" asked Guiterrez.

"Yes. I have been walking from the hills south of Juviles. This is hot weather for hiking."

"What were you doing there?" asked

Guiterrez as he refilled Marlo's cup.

"Spying," Marlo chuckled at Guiterrez's raised eyebrow. "On my own initiative. I have some friends here in Granada that I was going to visit. Señor Montoya, the merchant?"

"I don't know him."

"No matter, I should be able to find where he lives. I met him in Almeria, and he invited me to see him when I pass through here."

"Where are you going?"

"I'm not sure," Marlo shrugged. "I used to be in the Swiss Guard and was discharged due to an injury. Now I am looking for something to do. Mexico and the New World sound interesting."

"If you are a trained soldier, we could use you here." Captain Guiterrez lifted his hands expressively. "We are understaffed. The Marquis needs more men."

"If it's trouble with the Moriscos, I have some information about that." Marlo paused and drained his water again. "I ran into some malcontents in Juviles."

Guiterrez nodded and motioned for Marlo to continue.

"The short version is that I grew concerned there. I was assaulted, so I got curious. I pretended to be running to protect my life, and was willing to trade work for my security. The innkeeper had me training some men in weapons use for about a week."

"Learning how to use weapons might be disconcerting, but what makes you think it is an indication of a serious problem?"

"No, but an organized, armed camp in the mountains is. The men I trained left town a few days ago, and I followed them through the hills and found their camp. I was even able to get close enough to overhear that they were preparing to rise, and that Emperor Selim was interested in helping them. I figured that the Captain-General should know about this."

"Do you realize that since you have vanished, they have been alerted and have moved camp?" Guiterrez sighed. "You should not have gotten involved in something that clearly was not your affair. Now they will probably never be at Juviles again, and the innkeeper will only claim ignorance and protest his loyalty." Guiterrez shrugged. "The Marquis has suspected something of this nature, so your news is not surprising; it confirms our suspicions. The Marquis will probably send a detachment out tomorrow and they will find that the camp has been abandoned. The Captain-general will more than likely use your report to try to convince the king to bolster the garrisons around here. But right now, His Majesty just does not think we have a developing issue here."

"I was afraid I would not be believed," said Marlo with relief.

"We have been seeing unrest grow for the

last few years. Ever since His Majesty closed the public baths, the Moriscos have been grumbling and even openly rejecting the king's prohibition against Islamic practice."

"And the king doesn't believe the Captain-General?"

"I don't know. I would like to hope that your report will be what is needed."

Marlo stood and stretched. "Well, I have done my Christian duty and reported what I saw. I think that I will go hunt up the Montoyas."

"Are you sure that we can't convince you to sign on here?" Guiterrez walked over to the door and opened if for Marlo. "As I said, we can use extra men."

"I don't think so. I have had my fill of sentry duty in Rome. The New World sounds better."

"Come back if you change your mind. And thanks for the information. And next time," Guiterrez put his hand on Marlo's shoulder, "don't do something so foolish again. They would have killed you if you had been found spying on that camp."

"I'll remember that," said Marlo, smiling crookedly. He nodded at Guiterrez and limped toward the gate.

~~~

Señor Montoya's house was easy to find. All Marlo had to do was ask a merchant in the
~~~

marketplace just outside of the *Alhambra* and he was directed to a street about a mile away.

Standing outside Señor Montoya's house, he smiled. He looked forward to a meal and a real bed. He knocked. The door opened shortly, and a plain dressed, gray-haired man stepped out. "Can I help you, Señor?" he asked.

"Is Señor Montoya here?" asked Marlo. "I met him in Almeria and he asked me to stop by."

"*Si*, and you are?"

"Marlo Gobeli."

"Come inside and wait. I will go and tell him." Marlo stepped inside and waited for the servant to close the door. He followed the servant into a small room. "Wait here, Señor." The servant bowed and left.

Marlo sat on a plain wooden chair. His clothes were too dusty for the cushions on the chairs near the marble fireplace. He straightened the fall of his doublet, grimacing at the dust it left on his hands. He must have looked like a tramp to the servant.

Quiet voices came through the door, and Marlo stood as Señor Montoya entered. "Marlo!" The merchant smiled. He took Marlo's hand and clapped him on the shoulder, raising a small cloud of dust. Montoya tried to wave the dust away from his face and coughed.

"Sorry about that," said Marlo. "My horse was left at Juviles, and I had quite the detour through the hills in coming here. No place to clean up along the way."

"Never mind that. You're welcome here. I will have Carlos draw a bath. Carlos!"

"Señor?" Carlos put his head in the doorway.

"Carlos, can you get a bath and a room ready for Marlo?" He looked at Marlo. "Have you eaten?"

"No." Marlo shook his head.

"And get some food, as well as some clothes that he can wear while his are being cleaned."

"*Si.*" Carlos bowed and left the room.

"I should have asked before I spoke to Carlos, but do you have lodging?"

"It seems that I do now," Marlo grinned. "I don't know anybody here, and since you asked me to stop by…"

Montoya waved his hand. "Of course, of course. You are more than welcome." Montoya walked toward the chairs by the fireplace. "Come, sit down."

"I'll get that chair dirty," protested Marlo.

"And I will have it cleaned. Sit down. Now tell me," he continued as Marlo sat, "what were you doing that you lost your horse and had to hike through the hills? The road from Juviles is easy to follow."

"I had an unusual reception in the inn there. I was attacked upon entering." Marlo stretched his feet out and leaned back with a sigh. "I have been called a rascal, but the only fights I have had are ones I have picked myself. To be attacked by a brute just because I wanted a meal was something new."

"You don't appear to be injured?"

"No. He did not know how to fight. He was just an angry fool. The innkeeper, on the other hand, was a scheming devil; so I thought it would be better to play along. It's a good thing I did. There is something brewing in this region."

"What would that be?" asked Montoya frowning.

"What do you think about the Moriscos around here?" Marlo asked in return.

"They're good people. They've grumbled a little bit ever since His Majesty ordered the baths closed." Montoya shrugged. "So would I if I was in the habit of frequenting them. Why?"

"I followed a group of them into the hills. I know," Marlo raised a hand to quell Montoya's objection. "I am a bit on the curious side. My inquisitiveness has gotten me in trouble before. But, as I said, I was attacked without provocation, and I wanted to know why. And I found out."

Montoya raised an eyebrow.

"Señor." Marlo sat up and leaned forward, resting his forearms on his knees. "These Moriscos are anything but peaceful. I followed them into an armed camp. Since it was night when they arrived, I was able to sneak around. From what I overheard, they are planning an insurrection."

"They can't be." Montoya shook his head in disbelief. "I deal with them every day. You must have just found a camp of bandits."

"They were talking revolution. And the possibility of help coming from Emperor Selim," said Marlo quietly. "And Captain Guiterrez at the *Alhambra* is concerned about what the Moriscos might do. He even tried to recruit me."

Montoya was silent for a while, frowning into the empty fireplace. "Even if this group is planning violence, that doesn't mean that they all are. No." He shook his head. "The ones I deal with and meet on the streets are good people. I really don't think that there is much to worry about."

"With them, there is always something to worry about. Moors, Arabs, Turks – they are all the same. Señor, my uncle was captured and is probably pulling an oar for them, if he was not killed outright. They attack the coastal towns; capture, kill, and burn wherever they go. Just look at what they did when they invaded Constantinople. Your 'good' Moriscos are simply jackals waiting for a chance to tear your throats."

"Not these people. Even if they are, the king is too strong for them. They have no hope of success, and they know it."

Marlo nodded. He doubted that Montoya was right, but there was nothing to be gained by arguing the matter. "How is Maria?" he asked in an effort to change the subject.

"Enjoying being back," Montoya smiled fondly. "Traveling didn't make much of an impression on her, though she did have some hard words to say about you."

"She would," Marlo chuckled. "We both had some hard words for each other in Almeria."

"Señores?" Marlo turned and saw Carlos at the door. "The room is prepared," the servant continued. "And the bath is almost ready."

"Thank you, Carlos," said Montoya. He stood. "Well, Marlo, you must be tired. Go with Carlos. We will talk more in the morning."

"Thank you, Señor." Marlo stood and joined Carlos. "One thing." He stopped and turned back toward Montoya. "It would probably be best to keep a closer eye on things here. You may be right about the Moriscos, but it doesn't hurt to look around."

"I'll do that." Montoya nodded. "Have a good night."

"I will, thank you."

Marlo followed Carlos down the corridor and up a wide staircase. The carvings on the stone walls were only just glimpsed in the flickering candle light. Stopping at the first room at the top of the stairs, Carlos opened the door and gestured for Marlo to enter.

"This is your room Señor. When you are ready, cross the hall. You will be able to wash there."

An hour later, Marlo lay luxuriating on the first comfortable bed he had slept on since he had left Rome. He thought about starting his report for Father Veraccio, but decided to wait. He had not slept well the last few nights, and he was tired.

~~~

The sun was high in the sky when he awoke. He flipped his blanket back and swung his feet out of bed. Squinting in the bright sunlight streaming through the arched window, he rubbed his face and looked about the room.

It was large enough for his bed and a small writing desk. The plaster walls were unadorned, except for a niche over the bed with a small wooden Madonna. His clothes, cleaned while he slept, were draped over the chair by the desk. He stood, stretched, and began to dress.

There was no one in the hall when he left his room. Going down the stairs, he looked into the room where he had met Montoya last night and found it empty. Walking toward the back of the house, he opened a door and looked into a large patio garden, lined with a colonnade on three sides. In the far corner, he saw Maria tending a rose bush.
~~~

Marlo grinned and made his way quietly along the colonnade. When he was opposite her, he folded his arms, and leaned against a column and waited.

Maria clipped off an old blossom and tossed it into the basket next to her. She raised her head. Marlo could hear her sharp gasp from across the garden. He was amused at the range of emotions that flitted across her face, passing from shock and dismay, to disgust and anger. He pushed away from the column and started walking toward her, still smiling.

"Good morning, Señorita."

"Good morning." Maria's voice was precisely polite. "I did not realize you were here. Does Papa know you've come?"

"Yes, I saw him last night, and was hoping to see you"

Maria wiped the back of her wrist across her forehead, pushing back her loose dark hair. "Señor, I do not particularly want to see you."

"Why?"

"Beyond the fact that you are rude? Señor, I do not know you. My father really does not know you either. Why are you here?"

"I am just passing through and I was invited, if you remember." Marlo paused and clasped his hands behind his back. "And I also need to apologize for insulting you back in Almeria."

"Papa might have invited you," answered Maria sternly, "but he likes everyone he meets.

I don't know you enough to trust you."

"Señorita, I am not a vagabond to be turned off the doorstep," Marlo said in exasperation. "What have I done that makes you suspicious?"

"You've only followed us here after a single brief meeting," Maria snapped. "Papa has been taken advantage of before."

"Señorita, I am not trying to take advantage of your father."

"Then find someplace else to stay."

"I can't easily do that without offending Señor Montoya," Marlo raised his hands helplessly. "But since you do not trust me, I will leave you alone. Good morning." Marlo bowed slightly and walked slowly back into the house.

Maria's suspicions disquieted him, and he was worried that she would voice them to Montoya. Staying here was a matter of convenience, but he had come to like Montoya in Almeria. The merchant's seriousness combined with his genuine affability had won Marlo's respect, and now that there seemed to be trouble brewing in the area, he had become concerned that the Montoyas would be destroyed by the barbaric warfare the Moriscos were sure to unleash. He wanted to convince them of the danger, and, he admitted to himself, win Maria's respect. He only knew one way to do that, and that was to do what he did best: he needed to investigate the sentiment on the streets of Granada to find out the extent to which the thirst for blood had infected the Morisco population, not just the grain situation that Father Veraccio had tasked him to study. He would begin right away.

Chapter 7

June 1567

Maria watched Marlo limp slowly away. He reminded her of a speculator who had introduced himself to her father a couple of years ago. Señor Diaz had been well mannered and charming, but ended up selling Montoya on a venture to Asia to trade for spices and had vanished with Montoya's money. She was afraid that Marlo was also trying to take advantage of her father's generosity.

Maria resumed her work pruning and deadheading the roses. She would have to try to warn her father. That would be difficult. Once Montoya was convinced that he liked somebody, it became difficult to change his mind.

Once the roses were pruned, she took the basket of clippings inside to the kitchen and left them with the cook to dispose of them. She went to her room and straightened out her hair, then went to her father's study and knocked on the door.

Montoya was sitting at his desk, marking off entries in his ledger. He looked up and nodded before resuming his calculations. He finished the column, put down his quill, and sat back.

"Good morning, Maria," he smiled.

"Good morning, Papa." Maria walked over to his desk and sat down on a nearby chair. "When did Señor Gobeli arrive?"

"So you have seen him? He came late last night."

"He didn't ask you for any money, did he?" Maria frowned with concern.

"No, no," Montoya shook his head. "I don't think that is why he is here."

"Then, what is he here for?"

"After running into some bandits on his way here, he somehow has a silly notion that there is going to be a rebellion in Granada." Montoya shook his head again and smiled. "He says he came to warn us. But he is only passing through and will be gone once he either finds something to do here in the city or decides to look elsewhere."

"A vagabond then," Maria stated.

"I wouldn't say that. Do you know he used to be in the Swiss Guard? Now that his leg is injured, he is disqualified from service. He told me he either wants to join the army here or continue on to the New World. The Guard is a respectable company. Señor Gobeli is just trying to find something that suits him now. I find him to be a decent young man."

Maria sighed inwardly. Just as she feared, her father already thought highly of Marlo. She would have to keep an eye on Marlo's comings and goings. She could only hope that business in the city would keep him away.

~~~

And for the most part, it seemed that Marlo was very busy. He had a lot to do in Granada. For three days, he left early and returned late. Maria only saw him once, during the afternoon of the second day of his stay when she saw him coming out of her father's office, and then he merely nodded to her. By the end of the third day, she was becoming angry that he not would give them the common courtesy of visiting with them. A guest in the house, and he would not take the time out of his schedule to visit with his hosts. She was glad when Friday came and she was invited to her cousin Jacinta's house for the evening.

Before she left, she went to her father's study to let him know she was leaving. Montoya was sitting by the window, staring out onto the street, frowning.

"Papa, what's wrong?"

Montoya shook his head. "My dear, I am just
~~~

thinking about business and this situation with the Moriscos. I have been talking to some of my associates, telling them about Pedro's escape from the pirates. They inform me that goods are not making it into the city. And some of them are worried. It seems that more and more Morisco young men are heading into the hills. Some of the merchants are beginning to think about relocating."

"Do you think we should, as well?"

"I do not know, yet. I am afraid to move too prematurely. Marlo is convinced that something is going to happen, but I don't know. What if this discontent is just a passing thing?" Montoya shrugged. "I don't know," he said again. He looked up at Maria and smiled. "I take it you are on your way to Jacinta's"

"Yes, Papa," Maria nodded, grateful at the change of subject. "Why don't you come, too?"

"No." Montoya patted her hand. "There are some things I need to go over with Carlos. But, I am sure you will still enjoy yourself without me."

Maria left her house and walked to Jacinta's. Her flowing dress billowed and swirled around her in the breeze. There were only few people in the streets and so the person coming towards her was noticeable. He was a man with the dark skin of a Morisco, and he was even wearing traditional Morisco costume. Aside from festivals in which the *Zambra Mora* was performed, and the occasional man in the villages on the road to Almeria, Maria had rarely seen anyone in in the city clothed as a Moor. Such apparel had been forbidden for as long as she could remember.

The Morisco noticed her and kept his eyes fixed on her as he drew closer. Maria began to feel uncomfortable and moved to the side of the street to try to avoid him. She kept her face averted, but noticed, nonetheless, that he angled toward her. When he was no more than five paces away, he called out to her, "Señorita, a moment!" Maria paused and looked at him. He looked at her and smiled. "What a treasure!" he breathed. He met her eyes and bowed. "You are truly the Pearl of Andalusia, and I am honored to have seen you. Does your family live here?"

Maria was uncomfortable with the unsolicited praise, but she felt that she had to answer. "Yes, my father is a merchant."

"Where does he do his business, my beautiful one?"

"His offices are just down this street."

"Then I shall look for him." The Morisco bowed again. "I hope to see you again, for you are as the sun in the morning after a storm, and your beauty is beyond that of the heavens." He smiled and turned away. Maria, uneasy with the flattering words of the Morisco, hurried away.

Glancing behind her as she left, she saw that the man had turned back and was staring after her, a strange smile on his face.

She increased her pace until she reached Jacinta's house, looking behind frequently. She saw no sign of the Morisco. She sagged with relief against the wall. Her anxiety passed, and she entered the courtyard of the house.

One of Jacinta's younger brothers was in the courtyard. "Maria's here!" he called. He ran up to her and bowed. "This will be the first evening that I will enjoy myself since you left for Almeria," he said.

"Come, now," said Maria archly, "I know you have enjoyed not having to make music for us girls."

"But I have missed making music for you," he protested.

"Hernan, you are getting better," Maria laughed. "Who has been teaching you how to flatter?"

"I need no inspiration around you," he said with a smile. He looked around and leaned forward with a conspiratorial air. "Just between you and me, there is this fellow who has been paying court to Jacinta. I thought I would try a few of his lines on you to welcome you back."

Maria's peal of laughter rang through the courtyard. Smiling she leaned forward and kissed him on the cheek. "You are becoming a good young man, Hernan. And I am glad to be back."

"Is Hernan trying to pay court to you, too?" Jacinta asked as she approached. "I must warn you, he has been trying to court every pretty young lady he meets, married or not." Hernan looked sheepishly at Maria and flushed. Maria laughed again and allowed herself to be escorted in by her friend.

"I have the whole group coming," said Jacinta. "Now that you are back we will dance every week." She led Maria into a room where several young ladies were fixing their hair and preparing their dance costumes. "Look who is here," she called.

Maria found herself the center of attention as the ladies began asking questions about her trip to Almeria. Remembering that Isabella would never be part of this group again, she evaded most of the questions and made her way to the inner courtyard where the dancing was to be done. The girls began to follow.

In the courtyard, Jacinta's brothers were preparing their instruments, and when they saw the young ladies they began playing. With the sound of the music, Maria forgot the strange Morisco and her annoyance with Marlo. She immersed herself in the pleasure of the *Sevillana*, her feet clicking on the stones and arms moving gracefully.

Those watching began clapping to the music, in time with the movement of the dancers' feet. When the dancers brought out their fans, the watchers cheered, and as Maria began using her fan, waving it and her arms with the music, one of the young men cried out, "Look, *La Bailadora* has returned!"

The afternoon progressed, and Maria danced almost without stopping. The few times when she stepped aside, her face flushed with happiness, she was immediately showered with congratulations on her safe return and expressions of joy that she was among them.

During one period of rest, she managed to spend some time away from the exuberant youths and visit with Jacinta's grandmother. The elderly matron teased her about the attention of the young men, and asked her if she was going to choose any of them. The time was quickly passing for her to marry, after all.

Maria shook her head. "Not one of these."

"Well, I will find someone for you," said Señora Lopez. "At my age, the only recreations I get are my grandchildren and match-making." She adjusted her shawl. "I noticed that you seem to be avoiding speaking about your travels." She looked sharply at Maria. "Something unpleasant happened?"

"Several somethings," said Maria. "I still don't feel like thinking about them."

"My dear." The matron laid her hand on Maria's. "At times, unpleasantness loses it sharpness when it is shared. But only to those who can recognized it for what it is." Maria looked at the old lady's face and before she realized it, she was telling her about the loss of Isabella and her father's concern about the Moriscos. Señora Lopez looked at her with concern and understanding.

When Maria was done, Jacinta's grandmother clasped her hand. "By the grace of God and His saints your father didn't try to take you to Sicily. Even though I have not left this house, I was with you. I never liked the idea of your father taking you on this trip—I have heard about Morisco bandits." She shook Maria's hand slightly. "I prayed for your safety every morning and night. It seems that my prayers were answered." The old lady smiled at Maria. "Thank you for telling me. Now go, enjoy yourself."

Maria rejoined the ring of dancers. Her recent talk with Señora Lopez had eased tension, and she joined the dance with a lighter heart.

Shortly after the Angelus rang from the church of San Salvador, the evening meal was served. Maria and the other guests were led into the house for dinner. Jacinta's family sat Maria at one end of the table in the place of honor, and there was some competition as to who would get to sit next to her. She solved the issue by asking Señora Lopez to join her, and the elderly grandmother skillfully steered the conversation away from the topic of Isabella, dwelling instead on things that had happened while the Montoyas were gone. Jacinta was seated on the other side of Maria and spent her time eagerly praising the virtues of Francisco, the young man who had been visiting her recently. The intervention allowed Maria to enjoy the evening without the intrusion of any unpleasant memories.

As she was preparing to leave, Hernan offered her a flower. "Maria, I am glad you are back. I promise I will never tire of playing music for you."

Maria smiled and took the flower. "You know, I think there is a little bit of the rascal in you." She slipped the flower into her hair and leaning toward him, whispered, "Don't worry. You'll outgrow that someday. But not too soon, I hope. I think it's cute." Maria smiled and touched his cheek. "You still have five years before you reach my age, and then I will be an old maid. Still," she said mischievously, "maybe I will wait after all." Chuckling at Hernan's discomfiture, she left the house.

Smiling, Maria hurried home, her dress swirling about her legs. She ran up the steps and opened the door and twirled through the entrance, her skirts flaring out about her. Closing the door, she skipped her way to her father's study. She went in and stopped short: Montoya was clasping the hand of the same

Morisco who had spoken to her earlier.

"Come here, Maria," he said. "I want you to meet this new customer. He is a wool dyer and has purchased most of our remaining wools." Maria approached slowly and curtsied slightly.

"Good day to you," she said quietly.

"And to you, Señorita," the man said.

"Maria, my daughter," said Montoya, his voice echoing the relief that shone on his face, "we are in good fortune. This man, besides buying wool from us, gives us news from the hills. The so called 'malcontents' have only moved to the hills so we won't be bothered by them." Montoya's face was filled with relief.

"Yes, Señorita," said the man. "Your father has told me of your worries, and I assure you that they are unfounded. Yes, we have returned to the ways of our fathers, but we mean you no harm. In the hills, we can use our language, our fashions, and practice our way of life."

"That is good to hear," said Maria doubtfully. She realized that she should be relieved, but the meeting with this Morisco on the street disturbed her.

"Please be assured, Señorita, that no unpleasantness is being planned," continued the man. "The rumors about impending revolt are not based on reality. Some of us are upset with Spanish policy, but what can we do? We leave the cities and go to the hills to practice our way of life, and yes, for some of us, even our religion. But we have no intention of trying to take back Granada. And besides," he smiled, "any attempt to do so would only destroy the beauty which Allah has given you." Turning to Montoya, he bowed. "My congratulations to you Señor. Allah has favored you with a beautiful daughter."

"Yes, I am blessed," answered Montoya taking Maria's hand. "See, my dear, we have nothing to worry about. These men are peaceful, and only desire peace. They may not be following the letter of the king's law, but they will respect the king's peace and only come to the city to do business."

"And as for that," said the man, "I am desirous of purchasing more wool. I will return in a month, and if you can set aside some for me, as much as I purchased today, I would be most grateful."

"I am expecting a shipment soon," said Montoya. "I will have the bales set aside for you."

"We will meet again then." Turning to Maria, he added, "You are the Pearl of Andalusia. Allah grant that your beauty is appreciated by others as it is appreciated by me." He bowed again to Montoya and said, "*Salaam.*" He glanced at Maria and turned to leave the room.

"Wait," said Maria. "What is your name?"

The man gave a slight smile, his eyes hard. "My name," he said, "is Farax."

Chapter 8
July 1567

For three days Marlo prowled the streets of Granada. He stopped at every market he could find and spoke to as many bakers and vendors as he could. Almost all the grain being sold was from Sicily, and many merchants were selling Sicilian wheat to buyers in Castile. Father Veraccio had been right: there were not enough farmers in Spain to grow what was needed, and the grain prices were rising as the Algerians restricted Spanish trade.

On the fourth day, a Saturday, Marlo returned to the Montoya's at midday. He saw no one as he entered, so he went upstairs to his room. Taking his boots off his tired feet, and loosening the doublet at his neck, he stretched and sighed. He had to write his report to Father Veraccio. And he was going to inform the Jesuit about the Moriscos as well. He hated writing

An hour later, he leaned back in his chair and let his right hand dangle from the armrest, shaking it and flexing his cramped fingers. He could hold a sword and fence for an hour, but something as light as a quill made him sore. But at least the report was done.

He took the six sheets of paper, folded them, dripped wax, and pressed the pommel of his sword onto the red wax. Flipping the packet over, he addressed it to Father Veraccio. He stomped his feet back into his boots and picked up the letter.

Downstairs, he found Carlos in Montoya's study. "There you are, Carlos," he said. "I will be gone for just a little bit. I plan to eat here tonight."

"Good, Señor," The lines of Carlos's face creased further as he smiled. "I will let Señor Montoya know to expect you."

"Thanks," said Marlo. He tapped the letter thoughtfully against his open hand. "And I think I will be leaving tomorrow. Would you know how I could get to Almeria and avoid Juviles?"

"Take the road that goes out of the south. I'll draw you a map."

"That would be appreciated. Thanks." Marlo nodded to Carlos, strode down the corridor, and, opening the door, went back into the heat of Granada's streets.

The nearby church of San Salvador was staffed by two Jesuit priests. Usually the Jesuits would try to open schools wherever they were stationed, but the distrust King Philip had for a religious order that was answerable only to the pope prompted them to keep a low profile. But Marlo trusted they would get his letter safely to Father Veraccio.

~~~

"So, Marlo, what have you been doing with your time here?" asked Montoya. He filled Marlo's wine glass and sat back. "You seem to have been quite busy."

"Mostly looking around," evaded Marlo. "This is my first time in Granada."

"But even visitors would take time to eat," said Maria sharply.

"But I did eat, Señorita. And I am eating now." Marlo smirked. He looked at Montoya. "In answer to your question, I have been a victim of my curiosity."

"The last time almost got you killed."

"But this time, I was more circumspect. I was investigating the Morisco situation."

"You didn't have to waste your time. I have that figured out," Montoya smiled. "I think that they are just wanting to be left alone. Remember, I live here and do business with them. I just spoke to one of them the other day who came to buy wool. There is nothing planned.
~~~

The Moors were defeated a while ago, and they have no hope against Spain's army. Everything suggests that the bandits you saw do not represent the general Morisco sentiment."

"The Moors are not defeated," said Marlo. "I have seen, even here on the streets of Granada, a strong undercurrent of animosity and defiance. They are still Moslem at heart." Marlo paused and sighed. "To tell the truth, I am here at the request of Rome. The Holy Father wants to find out the true scope of the Islamic threat Europe faces. There is trouble brewing, Señor. It would be good for you to stay out of Granada."

"You are working for the Holy Father?" Maria's eyes were wide with surprise; then she frowned. "You are not just making that up, are you?"

"No, Señorita. I have been tasked to find out how severely the Algerians are interrupting trade to Spain. That is what I have been investigating both here and in Almeria. During the course of my investigations, I discovered that the Moriscos are on the verge of revolt. One of the reasons I stayed here was to warn you father."

"Oh," said Maria softly.

"I think you are overreacting," said Montoya. "Besides, my business is centered out of Granada. I don't think I can afford not to be here for an indefinite period of time."

"Then at least make arrangements for your daughter to stay elsewhere for the time being."

"Señor Gobeli," put in Maria. "I am right here. I would appreciate you not making plans for my life without consulting me."

"Of course, Señorita. My apologies. And you can be sure that I won't do it again. I am leaving tomorrow morning."

"Where are you going?" asked Montoya.

"Cartagena, I think."

"At the request of Rome, as well?"

"You could say that," Marlo smiled. "I have seen all I can here."

"You are welcome if you come back," said Montoya. "Maria and I would be pleased to have you as a guest, again."

~~~

The first thing Marlo noticed when he arrived in Cartagena was the fleet. He had sailed from Almeria two days ago and had seen no military galley on the waters. Upon arrival, it seemed that they all were in Cartagena's harbor. As his ship sailed into the harbor and set anchor, Marlo noticed that the fleet was being repaired and rigged. He wondered what was going on.

Marlo was silent as he was rowed to the docks. He made note of the warships that they passed, trying to gauge their state of readiness. Something was being planned. Most of the
~~~

ships seemed in good repair, and those that were not were being worked on. On some of the ships, carpenters were replacing old spars and re-caulking the seams. One ship was in the process of mounting a cannon, and another was being loaded with powder and shot. All the ships were manned by watch crews.

"Do you know what these ships are here for?" he asked the harbor pilot in the boat with him.

"No, Señor, but more keep coming."

Marlo nodded. King Philip was obviously preparing for something. Once he had landed, Marlo shouldered his pack and trudged up the streets to the Cathedral. He knew that his last letter would not have reached Rome yet, but Father Veraccio could still have sent him instructions. Tomorrow, he would begin the same process of inquiry he had done in Granada.

There was a letter and a priest waiting for him at the monastery attached to the Cathedral. Father Andrea, a thin Dominican, had arrived with a letter for Marlo with instructions for him to proceed to Madrid with Father Andrea if possible. Otherwise he was to proceed to Madrid as soon as possible and meet Father Andrea there.

"Why a Dominican, Father?" asked Marlo after he had read Father Veraccio's short note.

"I am going to Madrid, and His Majesty does not like Jesuits." The priest shrugged. "Besides,

I am going for the pope."

"And I am to go with you." Marlo indicated Father Veraccio's letter.

"So it seems. When could you be ready?"

"Tomorrow, I think. I would need to get horses and find out about the road to Madrid."

"I'm grateful you happened to come. I have been here a week not knowing if you would arrive. I was not looking forward to traveling to Madrid alone."

"What are you doing there, Father?"

"I bring a message to the Nuncio, Bishop Castagna. The Holy Father is requesting negotiations for the formation of an alliance with Venice."

"So, it begins," sighed Marlo. "I had better see about those horses and lodging for the night."

When he arrived at the stables, there was no one in sight, so he sat on the rail and waited. In a matter of minutes, a man came out of the neighboring public house with a small loaf of bread and a pot of ale. Seeing Marlo, he walked toward him.

"Are you looking for a horse?" he called.

"Yes, I am. But there doesn't seem to be anyone about."

"That would be me. I went to get a bite of food. What do you need the horse for, young man?"

"That would be two horses," said Marlo, getting off the rail. "One of them has to have a very easy gait and gentle manners. My companion hasn't ridden much recently. And I need to buy them."

"Well, I don't rightly know," the man mused. "The demand for horses for local traffic is very high with the extra soldiers at the Castle and all. I don't know if I could afford to get rid of any."

Marlo laughed and clapped the man on his shoulder. "High demand, indeed. The garrison at the Castle is set for ship duty, not cavalry." He was only guessing, but the number of ships in the harbor made this seem reasonable. "And the Señorita at the inn over there said that helping me would be a special favor."

"Well, for the beautiful Señorita I might be able to part with a horse or two." He took a large bite of his bread and chewed thoughtfully. "Let me see," he said around his mouthful of food, "I have a couple that I got the other day. I was hoping to keep them. They're good horses, mind you. And they cost me a lot." He gulped down a large swallow of ale.

"Can I see them, please?" asked Marlo.

He followed the man into the stables. The building was poorly lit and the stalls were not as clean as those of the Swiss Guard. In fact, they were filthy. The stone walls were blackened with mold and filth, and Marlo had no idea of what material the floor was. The smell of old horse urine and manure was overwhelming, making his eyes water. The horses that Marlo could see were just as bad. Most of them were unkempt and listless. In spite of what the man had said, Marlo did not think that there was much use for these animals. Regularly used horses would have some signs of being groomed and saddled. Most of these did not show any signs of being handled recently.

"Here they are," said the ostler. He set his pot of ale and half eaten bread on a shelf and opened the stall gate. "These are the two new ones I was telling you about. Go in. Take a look. Like I said, these are good animals."

Marlo went in. *If these are his good horses, his bad ones must be corpses*, he thought in disgust. They were gaunt: ribs and shoulder bones protruding prominently. One had a bad knee. He went up to them and looked in their mouths. Both of them were very old; their teeth were worn.

"How much are you asking for these nags," he asked the ostler.

"Nags?" exclaimed the ostler. "You insult me! I thought you would appreciate what I'm offering. I really can't afford to part with any of these, but since the pretty Señorita asks..." He shook his head in disgust. "Nags!"

"Whether you can afford to sell these or not doesn't change the fact that these are nags.

And old ones. What's your price?"

The ostler leaned against the wall and ran his hand through his thinning gray hair. "Four escudos. Each." Marlo rocked back on his heels and clasped his hands behind his back. He just stared at the ostler who, after a few moments, shrugged. "Well, since it is a favor for the Señorita, I will take only four escudos for both."

"I would only give you a half an escudo for both," said Marlo, looking at the ceiling, "and that's because that would be about how much I could sell them at a tannery. They can't be ridden all the way to Madrid. I doubt they will even make it out of this city without collapsing."

"I could take three escudos for both," said the ostler mournfully, "without the bridles and saddles, of course. You make things very hard for me."

"I told you what they were worth. There is no way I could even consider a price six times their value." Marlo started to walk out of the stall.

"Wait," said the ostler. "Since you were sent by the Señorita, you can have them both for an escudo. With saddles," he added as Marlo continued to walk away.

"Still too expensive," said Marlo glancing back at the ostler as the man closed the stall gate. As he looked over his shoulder, he saw a horse stick its head over its stall gate. That was not the head of an old, underfed horse. "Are you sure you don't have anything else? What about further down the stable?"

"Well, I don't rightly know," said the ostler. He took a long swallow of his ale and wiped his mouth with his sleeve. "I might have something down here." He went to a stall which had a unkempt chestnut mare.

"A bit ragged, this one," said Marlo as he went in. But aside from not being groomed, this horse was acceptable. He would have to try her though. Considering the state of the stables and the horses, he could very easily imagine the ostler selling him a horse that was not broken. Without saying anything, he walked over to the mare's stall. Without waiting, he opened the gate himself and went in. Inside was another mare but black with white markings on the face and two of its feet, and this one seemed to have a little more spirit than the chestnut. "I'll give you an escudo for each of these mares," he said.

"I can't do that," the ostler gasped. "These hoses bring me most of my income. They are frequently hired out."

"Come on," said Marlo, and he pointed to the side of the chestnut. "This horse is unkempt, and I should see saddle and girth marks. There are none. And not on that one either. Neither of these have been ridden or groomed in a long time."

"Alright. Since you are a friend of the Señorita, I will sell them. But I can only go as low as
three escudos each."

"Two escudos, each. These might just be
worth that. It's hard to tell in this filth. And
they haven't been properly cared for. Don't expect me to go any higher. We both know that is
what these horses are worth in their present
state."

"You are a hard man, Señor. But, for the Señorita, I will take two escudos each."

"Saddles and gear included," said Marlo
quickly.

"Do you want my shirt and the food out of
my mouth, too?" the ostler whined. "Señor, I
can't just give you my livelihood. Have some
pity on an old man!"

"If you took better care of these horses, you
might do better. And don't try to sell nags as
good horses. Four escudos for these two horses.
And because you asked for pity, I will give you
one for the saddles and gear, but no bargain
until I see if both these horses can be ridden."

"Agreed," the ostler sighed. "And only because of the Señorita."

"Enough of the Señorita, if you please. I have
not cheated you out of anything. You are selling these horses and gear for a fair price. Better, in fact, since they haven't been groomed
and are filthy. Now get me a saddle and bridle. I
need to see if a person can ride these animals."

Early the following morning, Marlo stood outside the stables attached to the cathedral and held the reins of the horses waiting for Father Andrea. The Dominican priest had just completed his mass and was collecting his few traveling items. The morning air was cool, but the breeze coming off the sea was warm and moist, smelling of salt and fish. The chestnut mare shifted, stomping her hooves. Marlo ran his hand along her neck and spoke softly to her.

"Well, here I am," said Father Andrea, approaching Marlo. "Sorry to have kept you waiting."

"No more than a couple of minutes, Father," answered Marlo. He took the priest's bag and tied it behind the saddle of the black and white horse. He made sure the saddle was tight and held the reins as the priest mounted. Father Andrea took the reins from Marlo and waited for him to mount. Marlo swung into his saddle and they rode out of the stable yard and into the streets of the city.

The city was starting to wake up. Some people were on the streets, heading to various churches for morning mass, the bakeries were putting out their first batches of bread, and travelers and wagons were, like Marlo and Father Andrea, beginning to make their way out of the city. Overhead, the gulls were circling and filling the air with their raucous calls. The two travelers moved north through the empty markets of Cartagena, soon to be full of goods and people. Now there were only churchgoers and travelers in the open squares.

In a couple of hours, Father Andrea and Marlo were out of Cartagena and moving at a leisurely pace through the countryside. While Marlo was used to riding, Father Andrea had not ridden for a number of years as he usually walked when traveling. Marlo did not push his companion. He planned to take two days to travel the thirty miles to Murcia, giving the priest time to become comfortable in the saddle.

After the manner of the Dominicans, Father Andrea prayed the rosary as they rode, and Marlo joined him. Several times during the day, they would stop at a roadside shrine so Father Andrea could pray his required office. The day was hot and the arid landscape reflected the sun's heat into their faces, so Marlo took advantage of these times of rest to water the horses.

It was early evening when they reached a small roadside inn, and Father Andrea climbed stiffly out of the saddle. "It has been too long since I was in the saddle," he sighed as he rubbed his lower back.

"I thought the Domincans were a mendicant

order," said Marlo as he took the priest's saddlebags.

"Yes, but we usually walk as we travel. And we rarely go that far from the monastery."

"So, this is your first time in Spain?'

"Yes, I grew up the son of a farmer near Genoa. At thirteen, I came to Rome and entered the Order. That was thirty-one years ago. I have been there ever since, except for missions in cathedrals and villages within the Papal States. I have not done that for a few years, though. When the Holy Father was elected, he kept me in Rome as a liaison between various ambassadors and prelates. Usually I just listen to people complain about how strict and demanding they feel that Pius is."

"Demanding?" Marlo laughed. "They should try the Jesuits! They never let me rest."

Father Andrea looked at Marlo and chuckled. "Youth is never satisfied. When you have nothing to do, you complain that you don't have adventure, and when you are active in some life-threatening occupation, you complain that you are not able to rest."

"That's because we never get to do what we want," said Marlo, "which is probably best in the end." He swung the saddlebags over his shoulder. "Shall we go in?"

"So you are finding out information for Father Borgia?" asked the Domincan as they walked toward the inn.

"Yes, and now he also wants me to be your guide."

"And report about my mission, I assume?"

"He seems to think that I can find out things that are meant to be kept secret. You know, I could have been killed a few weeks ago doing just that? I only hope the intrigues of the royal court are less dangerous than traveling through Granada."

Marlo opened the inn's door and let the priest enter. Since there were usually a large number of pilgrims traveling to Cartagena each year, there was a church next to the inn, and Marlo waited as Father Andrea made arrangements to say mass in the morning.

After mass, they mounted and rode into the Sierra de Carrascoy, a small mountain range just south of Murcia. The heat of the day gave way to thick, black clouds. Marlo urged that they ride faster. They had almost made it out of the mountains when the storm broke.

Chapter 9

July 1567

Father Andrea and Marlo were soaked when they rode into Murcia. Ever since the rain had started, they had ridden without rest. Father Andrea was sore and exhausted and agreed to stop at the first inn they saw rather than looking for a religious house for the night. There was only one room available, and Marlo got the shivering priest out of his habit and into bed. After getting a mug of hot broth from the kitchen and bringing it up to him, he went to take care of the horses.

The sun rose in a clear sky the following morning Father Andrea said mass, and they left Murcia and rode north. The road was well traveled, and they had much company. At times they fell in with farmers who begged the Dominican to offer prayers for good weather.

Their conversations were filled with speculation on the coming harvest and the rising prices of grain. Tinkers entertained them with stories and songs, and soldiers provided boisterous cheer. The days passed quickly with the company.

To encourage Father Andrea to rest, Marlo insisted that they stop at the numerous roadside shrines that they encountered. Not only did this give an opportunity for rest, but it provided time for the priest to say his required prayers. Marlo also took the time to pray for the success of their venture and for the safety of Señor Montoya and Maria. They should be safe living so close to the *Alhambra*, but a Morisco riot could sweep their street long before the soldiers could get there.

By their second evening, they had left the hills, and the land opened up around them. The only shade was found in barns and old roadside shrines, and the land stretched flat and unvaried, except for farmhouses and fields of grain. Though the days were hot, Father Andrea grew stronger with each passing day. They began to travel further and faster. By the eighth day, they were traveling close to twenty miles a day.

They were traveling to Albacete, a small city that had grown wealthy off of the region's farms. There, Marlo hoped to find out if the Algerian activity had affected the inland regions of Spain. The harvesting that he saw along the road indicated that this area would not be feeling the impact of the loss of Sicilian trade. Father Veraccio might be interested in what he discovered.

On the ninth day of travel, Marlo welcomed the opportunity of joining a caravan of local farmers and their families bringing grain into Albacete. At their invitation, Marlo and Father Andrea joined them for the remainder of the journey to the city.

The caravan consisted of twelve wagons of grain and four families. The youngest children rode perched on the sacks of grain or with their mothers. The older ones walked alongside, occasionally playing tag as they went along. Marlo and Father Andrea were able to travel further since the priest was able to ride on a wagon when he got tired.

The first night with the company they stopped at a small shrine. Next to the shrine was a well and the ground showed signs of frequent use. The men tended to the mules, while the women lit the cook fires and began to prepare the evening meal. A group of five young girls ran about the camp, laughing.

"Do you always bring your families to the city when you bring in your harvest?" Father Andrea asked one of the men whose name was Manolo.

"Not always, but this time of year there is always a holiday in honor of Saint James. Most years, the first harvest is early enough for us to be present. We will be in Albacete in time for the first day of festivities."

"Did you have a good harvest?" asked Marlo.

"Good enough," answered Manolo. "I think I will get a good price this year."

"Because you are one of the first?"

"Because grain is in short supply," said Manolo. "We grow enough in this region for Albacete itself, but nowhere else. There are buyers from other cities trying to get grain, and they bid the price up. I have not seen many caravans from the ports this year, so imports are down." Manolo shrugged. "That means I get paid more. We have reason to celebrate at the festival." The farmer smiled. "Why don't you join us? You won't be delayed much."

"Do you hear that, Marlo?" said Father Andrea. "Providence has arranged for the possibility for you to combine duty and celebration."

"I shall do my best to bear that cross," said Marlo grinning, "but I'm afraid my constitution is not hardy enough to handle such austerities."

"Santiago!" roared Manolo. "We need to get you into shape, then. Roderigo!" A short man with a heavy black beard looked up. "Music! We need something to cool the ardor of this young buck's tongue." Laughing loudly, Manolo shoved Marlo into the group of children. "We will start you off gently. The *sardana* first."

The travelers formed a circle and held hands, and as the music started, the group began a slow, stately dance that consisted of a pattern of delicate footwork. After Marlo caught his feet against his ankles a few times, he quickly caught on to the pattern. When they were done, Roderigo began a fast melody and Marlo was introduced to the *jota*, an acrobatic dance from Aragon. At the first leap, he landed on his bad leg and fell. He was rewarded with laughter from the other dancers. His leg caused him to fall several times, much to the amusement of the other participants.

Together, they all danced until the food was prepared. When Marlo returned to Father Andrea's side, he was flushed and in good spirits. He carefully lowered himself to the ground to sit next to the Dominican.

"That's how you are supposed to get to the ground," called Manolo, "slowly."

"Why didn't anyone tell me that sooner?" Marlo laughed. "And here I was thinking that the only way to land on the ground was at great speed, and preferably on a rock!"

"Father," asked Manolo, "does nothing make your companion serious?"

"Not much," answered Father Andrea, "but he does concern himself for the well-being of others and...," Here the priest paused thoughtfully. "I was going to say he *might* be serious at the prospect of battle; however, he was laughing as he told the story of having been chased by pirates."

"Pirates!" said one of the boys. "Did you actually fight pirates?"

"No," said Marlo. "I couldn't. You see, I was waiting for you to come and help and you never showed up."

"I want to fight pirates when I grow up," said the boy, his voice now serious. "My grandfather is in Mexico and he writes letters to my father. He said that the English pirates keep attacking the Spanish ships. When I fight the pirates, I will be helping my grandfather. Have you fought in many battles?"

"No. I only fought in one sea battle, and that was over rather quickly."

"Did you kill anyone?"

"Just one. When our ships collided, a Turk leapt across the gunwales. He had his sword raised and I was not wearing a helmet."

"What did you do?" asked the boy, his eyes wide with excitement.

"Well, I couldn't let him kill me, so I just stuck my musket out and shot him. Then I helped take the ship."

For the remainder of the evening, the young boy watched Marlo as he talked to the other travelers, and listened to Marlo converse with them about the situation in Europe, the Church, and especially the pope's struggle against the rise of Islam.

"I think you have become a hero," Father Andrea remarked.

"I hope I don't disappoint him, then," Marlo answered quietly.

"I don't think you will." The priest smiled.

"Father?" Manolo came out of the shadows. "It is time for the children to sleep. Could you give them your blessing?"

Together, Father Andrea and Marlo joined the gathered families and the priest blessed them. Thinking of the threat to Christendom still before him, Marlo joined in the singing of the *Salve Regina.* The full-throated singing of the men overpowered the voices of the women and children, reverberated off the ground, and shook the air around them.

~~~

The next day the caravan arrived in Albacete in the middle of the afternoon. The streets were crowed with people preparing for the beginning of the festival. After vespers, the holy day would begin, and would last until the following night. But the celebrations would last a week. Marlo looked forward to the prospect of taking part in the morrow's celebrations. He had not been involved in a city-wide festival since he had been living in Rome. He enjoyed the pageantry, while avoiding the riotousness always to be found among some of the people.

Father Andrea planned to rest the following
~~~

day and resume travel on Wednesday, and Marlo stayed with the Dominican since the inns would probably be full. They stopped at the Cathedral of San Juan and then made arrangements for themselves and the horses. Once they had washed off the dust of travel, they joined the people for vespers.

Early Wednesday morning, Father Andrea said mass. After he and Marlo had eaten breakfast, they saddled the horses and rode along the streets, still littered with crushed flowers. The city was quiet now. The houses were still festooned with flowers and fabrics. The celebration had continued throughout most of the night, and Marlo suspected that it would still be many hours before the revelers got up. The festival spirit would continue throughout the week, but more subdued. There would be daily parades and processions, but they would be shorter, and the parties would move back into the homes.

"Are you aware that all of this will be lost if Venice is overcome?" asked Father Andrea. "The joy we saw in the last few days would be replaced with absolute misery if I am not able to convince King Philip to unite with Venice. There is no room for this type of festivity in Islam."

"Then you must not fail," answered Marlo.

Father Andrea did not respond for a few moments. Then he sighed. "I am afraid that the

Holy Father will have much anxiety to suffer before he succeeds in stopping this threat. But this is in God's hands. I will do my part."

By midday, they had ridden past most of the farms to the north of the city and passed wagons carrying produce into the city. The day was already hot, and Marlo determined to end the day's travel early to avoid the heat of the afternoon. They were able to get some water from a few farmers on the road, and Marlo bought a pair of wide brimmed hats from a family of Gypsies. "This is not quite clerical," he said giving one to the Dominican, "but this will help keep the sun off your head."

"Thanks." Father Andrea put the hat on with evident relief. "This sun is hotter than I am used to in Italy."

"This will also help." Marlo took the hat off of Father Andrea and moistened the crown and brim. "As long as the hat is damp, you will find it refreshing. If you can keep the hat damp, you will find the heat to be a little less oppressive. We will have to carry more water tomorrow."

Father Andrea chuckled. "You know, if I had been a Moor invading this country eight and a half centuries ago, I would have turned around right here. The heat and dust are unbearable."

"If you had been a Moor, this would have felt like home. You would have grown up on the edges of the Sahara and used to hot, dry conditions and few trees. But I think we shall be stopping soon. I see a couple of buildings up ahead. We should begin tomorrow as soon as it is light enough to see."

The buildings were those of a house and barn. The farmer and his wife were most welcoming. They provided grain and hay for the horses and a bed for the priest. Marlo elected to sleep in the barn rather than put his hosts out of their own bed. Father Andrea, exhausted from the heat, rested along the shaded side of the house. After tending to the animals, Marlo joined the farmer and helped him load his wagon with produce and tend to the livestock.

"Where do you come from?" asked the farmer when the work was done.

"Originally, from Switzerland. Most recently from Rome," answered Marlo. "We are traveling to Madrid with a message for the Nuncio. Rather, Father Andrea is carrying the message, and I am to help him on his way."

The farmer washed his face and hands at a basin outside the door. "Is the message very important?"

"Yes," said Marlo handing the farmer a towel. "It seems that the followers of Mohamed are trying to devour Spain again. And not just Spain, but the rest of Europe as well. The Holy Father wants your king to help."

"We won back this land a long time ago," said the farmer opening the door for Marlo. "You are welcome to our table. And thanks for your help this afternoon." he clapped a rough hand on Marlo's shoulder. "I wouldn't worry too much about us. Saint Fernando will not let the Moors conquer us again, as long as there is a Spaniard left to resist. Let's go in."

Chapter 10

August 1567

Madrid was hot. Marlo and Father Andrea made their way to the Royal Alcazar, the new seat of King Philip's government. The midday sun was oppressive, and it seemed as if the entire city was taking its siesta. They rode as swiftly as possible, anxious to reach their destination and find relief.

Their journey from Almeria had taken a week, and in spite of the difficulties and excitement they had experienced since leaving Cartagena, the second half of their route had been uneventful. Except for the heat.

Their clothes were sweat-stained and covered in dust. The Dominican's white habit was now a mottled tan. They attracted some stares from the few people who were on the streets.

Approaching the iron gates that opened into

a large courtyard that lay in front of the palace, they dismounted and Marlo enquired if Bishop Castagna was in residence. On being informed that he was, the priest presented papers to the guard and requested that the bishop be informed of their arrival. The guard rang a bell and a servant came and led away the horses. Marlo, carrying their bags, followed another servant into the castle.

"Tell me," said Marlo, "will we be able to clean up as soon as possible?"

"Yes, Señor," answered the servant. "I will have baths ready for you as soon as I have shown you your rooms. I assume, Father, that you wish to be quartered with the clergy of the Royal household?"

"For the time being, if that isn't a problem," answered Father Andrea. "Depending on the length of my stay, I may go to a monastery near the castle, if there is one. But for now, my business with His Lordship will keep me here. I hope."

"Very well, Father," said the servant.

He led them to a clean room where Marlo placed his bag. "Do you want me to carry your bag to your cell?" Marlo asked the priest.

"No need. You stay and rest. I will come for you after I clean up and pray. Then we will make our official request to see the bishop." Father Andrea left with the servant. Marlo took off his cloak, sword, and boots. In a few minutes, there was a knock on his door and he was informed that a bath had been made ready for him.

He followed the servant across the corridor and undressed to wash off the two weeks of accumulated dust. He handed his clothes to the servant. "Could you see about having them washed and dried? I will wait for them in my room."

"Of course, Señor. There is a cloak that you can use hanging on the wall behind you. Do you need me to stay and help?"

"No, thank you," said Marlo. "I can bathe myself."

The servant bowed and left.

After washing, Marlo wrapped the cloak around him and went back to his room. He found his boots gone, and a servant with food waiting. After eating, he sat by the window and waited for his clothes.

A knock on his door woke him. "Your clothes and boots, Señor," said the servant who had brought him to his bath. Marlo let him in and dressed. He was pulling on his boots when Father Andrea tapped on the door and entered.

"Ah, Marlo, I see you have gotten cleaned up." The Dominican's habit was white again and he looked cheerful. "I have just received word that Bishop Castagna will see us in a half an hour. If you are ready, I would like you to accompany me. We should present the Holy Father's message together."

"We?" asked Marlo. "I thought that was your job. I came along as a body guard and travel companion."

"Yes, but I thought you could be of assistance. You have learned much about the Turkish threat and can give a firsthand account of what you have seen."

Marlo shrugged. "I rather think that you only need to present the letter from the pope, and that will be enough for the Papal Nuncio."

"For Bishop Castagna, yes. But His Excellency also needs to convince His Majesty, and anything that will help him do that should not be withheld. The Holy Father stressed that time is short before the Ottomans make their move against Venice."

"Very well," said Marlo. "However, since this is your task, I will remain silent until you ask me to speak." He hung his sword near the fireplace and draped his gray cloak over it. "I am ready to go."

"Aren't you going to wear your sword?" asked the priest.

"No," said Marlo. "I am not a knight, so I don't have the right to wear one here in the palace. I could make the case that as your bodyguard I could, but that might not be the most diplomatic approach, especially when we are trying to gain the goodwill of the king." He closed the door, and walked alongside Father

Andrea as they headed down the corridor. "Do you know where to go?"

"Yes, in fact I do. The bishop's apartments are near the area where the clergy are quartered. I was shown them before I came for you."

They passed through ornately carved and decorated corridors. Scaffolds and workmen were seen in several rooms and courtyards. Philip had only recently transferred his court here, and there were still renovations to be done.

The chambers of the Nuncio were, while still part of the same castle, simply furnished: a desk, several chairs, and shelves of books that lined a wall. They were asked to wait by a priest while the bishop was informed of their presence. After a minute, Bishop Castagna entered the room. Marlo and Father Andrea stood.

"Good afternoon, Father and Señor Gobeli," said the bishop. "I trust you were able to refresh yourselves?"

"Yes, My Lord," said Father Andrea kneeling and kissing the bishop's ring. "We have washed and eaten. However, I believe that you would want to see and discuss the message from the Holy Father without delay."

"Come," said the bishop. He led them into his study and dismissed his secretary. He gestured to Father Andrea to sit. Marlo stood off to the side. "My Lord, here is the letter from the Holy Father," said Father Andrea. "He requested that you read it in my presence."

Castagna inspected the seal and then opened it. He sat and as he read, his face grew grave. When he was done, he looked up. "This is serious. Have you seen the contents of this?" He held up the letter.

"Yes," answered the priest, "and I can assure you that the threat is quite real."

"Far be it from me to question the Holy Father," said the bishop. "Yet, how do you know that this is real? I have heard nothing that would indicate that the Ottoman is moving on Venice. That does not mean that what the pope communicates here is not true. I just have not heard, especially since His Majesty does not communicate diplomatic information readily."

"As for the veracity of the report," said Father Andrea, "this young man here, Señor Marlo Gobeli, can attest to the situations in Cyprus as he has just been there and is the primary source of the Holy Father's intelligence in these matters."

"And how is that, Señor Gobeli?" asked the bishop. Marlo could not tell whether the bishop was doubtful or just trying to gather background information.

"Your Excellency," said Marlo stepping forward, "for two years I was a member of the Swiss Guard in Rome, and I like to think that I served well. However, due to an injury, I have not been a member of the Guard for the last year. Instead, I was asked to investigate Cyprus. Father Andrea just gave you copies of the information I gathered there."

"How did you obtain this information?"

"I was sent to assess the garrisons there. After making my inspection, I took ship with the Knights of Saint John. As we were leaving port, we were attacked by Turkish galleys. We took this information off of one of their captains. As you can see, these are complete maps and plans of the military fortifications of Famagusta and Nicosia."

The bishop sat back and contemplated what Marlo had said, then picked up the papers and began to study them. After a few minutes, he stood and walked over to a window and looked out into the evening. "I believe your assessment," he said quietly. "However, the need for immediate action may or may not be there. The Holy Father charges me to make this information known to His Majesty as soon as possible. I must warn you that King Philip keeps his own counsel close and is very cautious. He does not make a move until a situation has been thoroughly studied and he never lets anyone know what that move is until it has begun, and sometimes, not even then.

"Don't get me wrong," he continued turning back to them, "Philip is no coward. Yet he is in the midst of a web of European politics. The French are fearful of a strong Spain, especially since Spain and the Holy Roman Empire are on either side of them. Then there are the Protestants in the Netherlands and England. William Cecil has never forgiven Philip for marrying Mary Tudor, and now that the throne is in Elizabeth's hands, Cecil is doing everything he can, directly and indirectly, to weaken Philip's power.

"I do think the king will act on this information, but I would not expect that his answer will be immediate. You will probably have to wait many months before you find out what his answer will be." He picked up the papers on his desk. "I will communicate with the king as soon as he permits an audience, which should be tomorrow or the next day. I would ask that both of you remain in Madrid so the king can speak to you if he wishes to."

"Of course," said Father Andrea standing. "I will be staying with the palace clergy. Later I might move to a monastery in the city, but for now I will be here until I am sure that I won't need to be available at a moment's notice."

"Very good, Father," said the bishop. "And you, Señor Gobeli, since you are an eyewitness, please stay here in the palace. I believe the king may require your presence."

"Yes, My Lord," said Marlo, kissing the bishop's ring. Castagna led them out of his office and dismissed them.

"That didn't go too badly," commented Marlo as they walked back to his room. "I expect the bishop is disposed to believing communications from the Holy Father."

"That hasn't always been the case," said Father Andrea. "I don't know the history of Bishop Castagna, but just because one is a bishop and a personal representative of the pope, doesn't make him free from ambition. There have been prelates and nuncios who have not had the good of the Church as their primary object."

"Castagna seems a good man," objected Marlo. "I noticed that he wasn't ostentatious, nor did he seem concerned about his position."

"No, I rather think he would have done as the Holy Father requested even if you were not there. I believe that Pius has a worthy ally in his cause in the person of Bishop Castagna."

"Let us hope that he is the ally that the pope needs," said Marlo.

~~~

The next morning, Marlo attended mass and ate breakfast with Father Andrea. Afterwards he found the stables and went in to check on their horses. The animals were being well cared for, and after running his hand over the neck of his horse, he walked along the stalls and exam-
~~~

ined the condition of the others. One of them was a remarkable brown stallion, tall and sleek. He ran his hand along its neck speaking softly.

"You! Leave that horse alone!" Marlo jumped and turned. He saw a groom running toward him. "That horse is not to be handled."

"My apologies," said Marlo stepping out of the stall. "I was here checking on my horses and saw this one. It is a beautiful animal. But if I am not to handle it, I won't."

"It is a good horse, but it is the prince's. He is particular and doesn't care for anyone to touch it except the palace grooms. In fact, he has demanded it, and if you would have been in this stall fifteen minutes from now, he might have had you lashed for handling it."

"Who is this prince?" asked Marlo.

"Don Carlos," answered the groom. Marlo moved away and began brushing his horse, hoping to see this hot-tempered prince. A short time later a pair of young men entered the stables. One of them went to the stallion and took the reins. "The saddle better be cinched up tight enough," he snapped at the groom.

"Yes, Your Highness," said the groom checking the saddle. "I think you will find this to your satisfaction."

Don Carlos pulled on the saddle. It did not move. He swung into the saddle. "Mount up, John," he called to the other person, a well-dressed young man of about twenty.

John took the reins of his horse, thanked the groom courteously and started to lead the horse out of the stable. On seeing Marlo he paused. "Good morning," he said, "That is a good animal you are brushing. I saw it last night. Is it yours?"

"Yes, Señor, it is," answered Marlo.

"Don, not Señor," said John with a laugh. "I am pleased to see that you seem to know the value of that animal. *Vaya con Dios!*"

"*Vaya con Dios,*" answered Marlo as Don John left the stable. Wondering who this young knight was, Marlo left the stables and headed over to the armory. On his way he saw Father Andrea heading toward him.

"I thought I would find you here," said the Dominican smiling. "I have just received word that Bishop Castagna will meet with His Majesty in about half an hour. He would like us to be available in case the king wants to see us."

"In that case, I should make sure I am fit for the king's presence. I will be ready in my room."

"I'll come and get you in about fifteen minutes. We should be waiting outside the reception room in case we are needed."

Thirty minutes later, Marlo and Father Andrea were waiting outside the king's reception hall. Several other people were there as well, waiting for their chance to present their petitions to the king. Father Andrea was sitting, his rosary in hand. Marlo silently added his prayers to his.

"Father Andrea and Señor Marlo Gobeli, His Majesty awaits." Marlo turned and saw the king's secretary at the door. "Please follow me." Father Andrea stood and joined Marlo. They followed the servant into the reception room, approached the king and knelt.

The king was tall and dark haired. His eyes were troubled. "Father Andrea, as emissary from His Holiness, Pope Pius the Fifth, you are most welcome, even though the message from the Holy Father is most grave," said the king. Marlo noted there was none of the imperiousness he had witnessed in the prince. "Señor Marlo Gobeli, I understand that you can give an eyewitness verification for much of what the Holy Father has to say to me. Please, be seated."

"Thank you, and God save you, Your Majesty," responded Father Andrea. He and Marlo seated themselves near Bishop Castagna.

"Father Andrea," said the king when they were seated, "I have been apprised of the mind and wishes of the Holy Father, as well as the information the Turks have obtained regarding Cyprus. Since you are the Holy Father's messenger, could you explain the situation with the Turks as Rome sees it?"

"Of course, Your Majesty," said Father Andrea inclining his head. "The Holy Father is seeking the defense of Europe. The victory of the Knights of Saint John at Malta was only a temporary reprieve, and the timely death of Suleiman halted the Ottoman push into Europe. Selim, however, is ready to continue his father's dream of conquest. The Holy Father fears that an attack on Venice will shortly follow the fall of Cyprus. At the same time, I fear that Selim is involved in keeping Your Majesty otherwise occupied so you will not be able to come to the aid of Venice."

"What steps do you think Selim is taking to accomplish that?" asked Philip.

"The Pasha of Algiers is a puppet king of Selim, and the Algerians are threatening your shipping. If Your Majesty builds a fleet and uses it to remove the Algerian threat, Selim would not have to worry about Venice receiving help."

"Yet my ships will be occupied in trying to defend our shipping from the Algerians. How does the Holy Father expect that I can help with a naval battle?"

"I do not know the answer to that," answered Father Andrea. "All I know is that the Holy Father stressed the importance of forming an alliance for the defense of Venice and of Europe in general. If such an alliance is formed and is able to defeat the naval might of the Ottoman Empire, then Europe will be secure, as the logistics of an overland march of a Turkish army would render such an enterprise difficult.

"The Holy Father requests I stress that if Venice falls to the Turk, then Rome will also fall. Suleiman had bragged about one day flying the crescent over Rome, and Selim desires to do just that. Up until now, it is only the naval might of Venice that has stood in the way. But the balance of power is changing. Both the Ottomans and the Algerians are building up their fleets, which are now about twice the size of Venice's."

Philip was silent for a moment. "Señor Gobeli, there is more to this than just an alliance with Venice. I have been informed by Bishop Castagna that you have firsthand knowledge of some discontent in Granada?"

"Yes, Your Majesty," answered Marlo. "While there a month ago, I came to the belief that there is something boiling in Granada, something that may prevent you from helping Venice: a rebellion amongst the Moriscos. And if the malcontents are successful in their plans, Europe will be caught between two prongs of the Islamic Crescent."

"Your imagery is apt," smiled the king, "however, my men have not reported anything as dire as what you suggest. Why should I believe you?"

"Your Majesty, any protestation of honesty on my part would not add one bit of proof to what I report. I did find an armed camp in the hills near Granada and overheard that Selim's vizier, Sokoli, desires to help the Morisco revolt. I did report this to an officer at the *Alhambra* in Granada. I implore Your Majesty to send spies into the hills around Granada—men who can speak the Moorish tongue and can blend in with the malcontents. And God willing, I hope I am wrong, because that will mean that many innocent Spaniards won't be slaughtered."

"Your Majesty," said Father Andrea, "if Venice falls, then there will be no way to defend Rome. With Rome and Venice under Ottoman rule, Selim will be free to march north into France. If what Señor Gobeli says is true, then a Morisco revolt in Granada will allow the Algerians to land a large force which could sweep through Spain and meet up with Selim in northern Europe. Christendom may be about to be destroyed."

The king was again silent for a moment, his face expressionless. "Your information on Cyprus is interesting." Turning to Father Andrea and Bishop Castagna he continued, "Tell the Holy Father that I must look to Spain first. If what this young man has to report is true, I may not be able to help with this alliance, however good the idea is. Inform the Holy Father, further, that in spite of the differences that exist between us, I am most grateful for the trust and confidence he places in us, and as I do not want to see Christendom and Rome fall, I shall endeavor to determine the wisest course of action."

Bishop Castagna and the others rose and bowed. "We shall so inform the Holy Father," said the bishop.

"Thank you, Your Majesty," said Father Andrea, "we are at your service." Marlo and the priest bowed again and left.

"A perfectly unsatisfactory meeting," Marlo said when they were alone in the courtyard. "To have my report dismissed, however politely, especially when it is good enough for the Holy Father..."

"Patience, my son," said Father Andrea. "I don't think he absolutely dismissed your report. Remember what Bishop Castagna said about him, that he is cautious and keeps his counsel close. I think he just wasn't letting us know what he thought. Even his message to the Holy Father was non-committal."

"How long will we have to wait before we know what he will do?" asked Marlo.

"That," said Father Andrea gravely, "I think, is only known to God and the king."

Chapter 11
September 1567

September had just arrived when Father Andrea heard from the pope. By this time, he had moved out of the palace and into the Dominican monastery of Our Lady of Atocha. The luxury of palace life was not suited to his life of voluntary poverty. He was finishing the office of vespers when the messenger arrived. Father Andrea took the message and went into his cell. Lighting a candle, he broke the seal and read the contents. With a smile of relief, he folded up the letter and left his cell and was soon walking through the streets of Madrid.

When he arrived at the palace he approached a guard. "Have Marlo Gobeli sent here, at once. Tell him that I have the message that he has been waiting for."

"At once, Father." The guard rang a bell and

informed the servant of the priest's request. "Won't you come inside and sit in the courtyard, Father?" asked the guard.

"Thank you. I will just sit on that bench there." Father Andrea sat and composed himself. It was not long before Marlo joined him. "Ah, Marlo," said the Dominican, "come, let us go someplace private."

"Let us go to my chambers, then," said Marlo.

When they reached Marlo' apartments, he opened the door and gestured for Father Andrea to enter. "Would you like something to eat or drink?" he asked.

"No, I will have something when I return to the monastery. This shouldn't take long." After sitting down, he took out the letter from the pope and gave it Marlo. "Read this. It concerns you as well."

Marlo took the letter and went to the window for better light. As he read, his face grew grave. When he was done, he carefully folded up the letter and gave it back to the priest.

"So you have to leave," Marlo said, "and the pope is not satisfied with His Majesty's answer. I wonder if Bishop Castagna should be informed."

"I think so. And what about you? How are you going to spend the winter?"

"I don't know. This last month has been hard. For the last three years I have been occupied—in the Guard or traveling. This is the longest stretch of time that I have had nothing to do. Father Veraccio wants me to keep him informed about what His Majesty is doing about the Ottoman threat. How can I do that?" He thumped the table in exasperation. "I am in no position to be privy to the king's decisions. He could send an army against Rome, and I would know nothing."

"Marlo, we can only do our best. God does not expect anything more. However, I think Bishop Castagna is in a position to help you. I fancy that he could introduce you to some knights and officers, and your charm and ability to disarm any apprehensions about yourself should help you do the rest."

~~~

Four days later, Marlo was riding through the streets of Madrid. His companion was the pleasant Don John. Don Carlos had gone to Valladolid, and Bishop Castagna had arranged, at Marlo's request, an introduction to Don John two days ago.

The bishop had received Father Andrea and Marlo the day after the pope's letter had arrived. He did not seem surprised at the Holy Father's decision to recall the Dominican.

"His Majesty did not give much of an answer to the Holy Father's request. It was just a diplomatic platitude. I will speak to His Majesty
~~~

and see if he is willing to send a representative with you, Father, to discuss directly with the Holy Father on this matter. The king is cordial, even if he is not forthcoming, and he is sure to reciprocate the honor and send someone."

"That would be good, Your Excellency," said the priest. "I was not looking forward to making the journey to Rome alone."

"I will present that wish to the king as well. You will have at least one companion."

"Your Excellency, I was wondering if you could help me with my task," said Marlo.

"In what way, Señor?" asked the bishop.

"Rome is asking me to report on what His Majesty does regarding the Moslem threat. I don't know anyone here, except for a few servants and soldiers, and they are not likely to know what is happening. Some introductions in the right places to the right people would help."

"I can do that," the bishop smiled. "I know just the person."

~~~

The next day, Bishop Castagna invited Marlo to an evening banquet. It was a farewell gathering for Don Carlos who was leaving the palace for the winter. There the bishop introduced Marlo to Don John.

In the morning Marlo said farewell to Father Andrea, who was happy not to be traveling
~~~

alone. King Philip had seen the merit in the request of the bishop and was sending an emissary to the pope. Don Luis de Torres and three companions were accompanying the Dominican to Rome. Don Luis was given powers to discuss the matter of an alliance with the Holy Father.

Don John arrived in the courtyard and waited until the group had left before he approached Marlo. "Señor Gobeli, tomorrow I am going for a hunt. Would you be interested in joining me?"

"I would be delighted," said Marlo. "The enforced idleness of the last month has been hard. The stimulation of a hunt, as well as a chance for entertaining conversation, will be a welcome relief."

Now he was riding alongside of Don John through the narrow streets of Madrid, followed by two attendants with hawks on their wrists. John, speaking loudly to be heard above the ringing hooves on the stone street, turned to Marlo. "I suppose the boredom of court life does not appeal to you?"

"No, my lord," said Marlo with a grimace. "One of the reasons I did not return to the Guard was because I was tired of standing around all the time. I find the Spanish court to be second to Rome for its implacable slowness."

John laughed. "If my Royal Brother could

hear you, he would make you sit through hours of briefings just to show you what slowness is."

"Not likely," Marlo commented dryly.

"No, but after a day of that, you would appreciate weeks of having nothing to do." The prince grinned at Marlo. "Did you know that I tried to run away to war, once?"

"I hadn't heard of it," said Marlo.

"No, you probably wouldn't have."

"I notice you said, 'tried'. I take it you didn't succeed?"

"I succeeded in running away, but not to war. I found myself on a sickbed. When Malta was being attacked a couple of years ago, I had begged my brother to let me go, and he absolutely refused. He wanted me to enter a monastery and serve the Church! So one night, I left and headed south. I reached port, but was not able to board ship as I had fallen to a fever that left me bedridden for a couple of weeks. Philip figured out where I was going, and long before I was well enough to sail, Don Luis Quixada had joined me and forced me to return."

"Malta was a bloodbath, My Lord. It is providential for you that you were not able to make it."

"It would seem so. My attempted escape was providential in another way: it convinced my brother that I was not destined for the life of devotion, but for the army. I have been under the tutelage of Don Luis ever since."

Marlo nodded. He wondered about the possibility of Don John being given military command. The prince was quite young, no older that Marlo himself. "My lord, I wonder if I could ask you a favor?"

"What would that be?"

"Could I join you if you are given a command in the near future? I would be grateful for something to do."

John was silent for a moment. "So, tell me, why did you really leave the Guard? I doubt it was because of your injury."

Marlo shifted in his saddle. The question embarrassed him. "Not for anything I am proud of."

"I wouldn't think so," said the prince, "but you are still trusted enough to serve as a bodyguard for a papal messenger. If you want to join my entourage, though, I think I have the right to know what happened."

Marlo sighed. "I had an argument with my captain."

"Insubordination, then."

"Not really." Marlo shifted in the saddle again. "I had a political difference with my commander. I accused Jost von Meggen of having sympathies for the Hapsburg control of Italy. My family was from Ticino, in southern Switzerland, and had to relocate when Emperor Charles took over that canton."

"So, you have little love for the Hapsburgs?"

asked the prince in an even voice.

Marlo sighed. This was an awkward situation. He was not merely troubled about the accusations he had hurled at von Meggen and the heated argument afterwards, but Don John was the son of the same emperor who had chased his family out of their home.

"My lord, Charles was crowned by the pope," he began carefully. "And territories change hands. But Rome was sacked under the Emperor, and my grandfather fought against the imperial forces. Italy is probably better off under the guidance of the Emperor, but the cost of that guidance has been quite high. And I was in a lot of pain when I had my argument. Not that that's any excuse."

"At least you are honest," said John. "And even though I am the son of an emperor, I was not raised in my father's court. The sack of Rome was an atrocity. Now that I am part of the Spanish court, I am quite frustrated with some of the decisions that are made or rather," he paused, "the decisions that are not taken by the king."

"Not taken, my lord?" asked Marlo.

"My Royal Brother is a good man, but there are times when I think he puts the good of the realm over the good of Christendom. What you have said about the threat is of such serious nature, that any concern the king would have about the position of Spain in European politics needs to be set aside. Christendom and the Cross are more important."

"Might you get in trouble with such open criticism of His Majesty?" asked Marlo with some surprise.

"No," said John ruefully. "Though I perhaps should be more guarded in my speech with a relative stranger. My brother knows that I am hotheaded, and will probably pass off my critique as nothing more than a product of the impatience and inexperience of youth. He does have the responsibility of an empire larger than any other in the known world. I do not. As much as I might be frustrated with his caution, I would probably be the same way if I were king. But I do not have to worry about that." The prince chuckled. "As the 'natural' son of Emperor Charles, I will never inherit."

"Does that bother you?" asked Marlo.

"Not really," said John. "I at least can focus on the army."

By this time, they had left the city and were in a large field alongside a sparse wood. There was a slight breeze in the air and the scent of the coming autumn.

"My Lord," said one of the prince's attendants, "will you take your hawk?"

"Yes." John slipped on his leather gauntlet and took the hawk, made sure its hood was on and its leads gathered securely in his fist. "Marlo, do you know how to hunt with hawks?"

"No, My Lord," answered Marlo. "My family is respectable, but I am not of the nobility. My duties in the Guard never included hawking."

"Then, Señor Gobeli, it is time for you to learn! Give this man a bird," he called to one of his attendants. "Here, Marlo, put on the gauntlet, and gather the leads into your fist," said John with a smile of satisfaction. "Anyone who has been a member of the Guard has received more training in warfare than many a Spanish *grandee*, and you serve as a guard to an emissary of the Holy Father. You have earned the right to hunt as a noble." The young prince clapped Marlo on his shoulder. "Next time, wear your sword." With that, Don John kicked his horse into a canter.

"Yes, My Lord," answered Marlo. He kicked his horse and followed the prince into the fields. After a little bit they reined in and allowed the attendants to move ahead to attempt to flush out the game.

"Now, Marlo, when you see a bird or rabbit, remove the tresses from the feet of your hawk, like so. Pluck off the hood and cast your arm up and forward. Your bird is well trained, and will go after the game. When it has brought the animal down, I will show you how to get the hawk back onto your wrist. For now, while we are waiting, speak to it that it might grow comfortable being with you."

They rode along at a slow walk. Marlo spoke to the bird and kept a watch for any game. "Don't watch the attendants beating the brush," said the prince. "Look slightly ahead of them. But not too far. Rabbits and birds have a tendency to wait until the last possible minute before moving, hoping that they will be passed by. Sometimes, a partridge will fly only when those beating the brush stop suddenly. Look!" he exclaimed. "There one flies! Go ahead, you go first. The tresses. Now the hood. Just so."

Marlo cast the hawk up into the air and watched as it beat its massive wings. It gained altitude quickly and spread its wings, circling. Marlo thrilled in its stately power and grace. All at once, it swooped and dove toward the partridge. Marlo clenched his fist in anticipation as the hawk fell out of the sky. All at once, there was a cloud of feathers as the hawk struck. The stunned bird tumbled to the ground and the hawk dove after it.

Marlo and Don John galloped up toward the downed bird and were joined by one of the attendants. He took the tresses from Marlo and tied them to the hawk's feet. Then he lifted it up to Marlo and transferred it to his fist. Marlo took the tresses and was about to replace the hood when Don John stopped him.

"Wait," he said, "give it a piece of meat first."

Marlo took the scrap of meat from the attendant and laid it on the top of his gauntlet. The hawk bent down and swallowed the food.

"Now put on the hood," said the prince.

The attendant picked up the downed bird, made sure its neck was broken and went back into the brush to try to flush out more game.

At midday they stopped under the shade of the trees to eat. The prince's attendants took the hawks and Marlo sat on the ground in the shade. Don John sat back against the trunk of a tree and sighed.

"Thank you for coming with me today," he said. "With Don Carlos gone, there is no one to spend the day with, and I have enjoyed your company."

"It was my pleasure," said Marlo.

"A pleasure I hope is repeated. Do you know how long you will be here?"

"No, I don't. I am at the mercy of the Holy Father and of your brother. As soon as His Majesty makes known his decision regarding Venice, I will probably be recalled to Rome."

"That is not likely going to happen anytime soon," said John. "And if by chance his plans involve me, I grant your request to join me. Don Luis Quixada, my mentor, is giving me the necessary education in military matters, but I may want someone with youth, energy, and experience to help me."

"We shall see what the Holy Father commands," said Marlo philosophically.

"Yes, and the king may have other plans. This is all wishful thinking." John sighed and then grinned. "But then, maybe this time, my brother will let me go." He stood and brushed off his clothes. "Come, let's hunt."

~~~

It was indeed quite some time before King Philip did anything. Marlo spent the winter in Madrid, passing the time with Don John and Don Luis Quixada, learning from the old Spanish warrior.

Don Luis was a knight who harkened back to the days before gunpowder, when a valorous fighter could turn the tide of battle. He was eminently noble, and strove to impart his ideas of honor to Don John who clearly respected the old warrior and eloquently discussed the virtues of chivalry with Marlo.

In his monthly reports to Father Veraccio, Marlo mentioned Don John. In a reply from Father Veraccio, he was informed that the negotiations with Don Luis de Torres had yielded nothing regarding the formation of an alliance against the Turks, but based on something Don Luis had told the pope, it seemed that Don John would be put in charge of a major military operation in the near future. Accordingly, Father Veraccio informed Marlo, the Holy Father desired that Marlo remain in the company of Don John.
~~~

The winter passed slowly for Marlo. Even though he was able to keep up his training and his studies with Don John, the knowledge of the looming Moslem threat made him impatient even though the Turk would not be moving toward Cyprus until the weather improved in the Mediterranean.

One morning in early May, Marlo was summoned to Don John's apartment. When he arrived, the prince was eager and excited.

"Come in, Marlo. Come in." The prince showed Marlo to a seat by a fire and picked up a letter from a table. "I want you to read this," he said.

Marlo took the letter and read its contents. As he read, his heart began to race, and he stood in excitement. "Captain of the Seas," he whispered. "You have been given a command!"

"Yes," said John, "I know nothing about naval matters. But that is no real problem since I will be accompanied by Don Requesens. He will make sure I don't make any mistakes, as well as be my brother's eyes and watch my every move." The prince grimaced.

"What assignment do you have?" asked Marlo. "Do I dare hope..."

"No, you are not allowed to hope," said John with a chuckle. "Hope means that you are desirous of something that is not a distinct possibility. And there is no longer the possibility of action against the Algerians," John glanced at

Marlo's face with a smile. "There is no possibility, because it is happening!"

"Happening," sighed Marlo. "At last. Thank God!" Marlo clasped John's hand. "My congratulations on your assignment. When do you sail?"

"As soon as I can get to Cartagena and assemble my officers. Don Luis will accompany me to the harbor, but he will not be joining me on ship. He says that he is too old and I should learn from someone with more naval experience. I am also ready to grant the request you made several months ago. I hope that you will be able to accompany me as well?"

"I am able to," said Marlo, "if that is what you wish."

Marlo hurried back to his room. He immediately began writing a letter to Father Veraccio, requesting that any information regarding movements of ships of any Islamic nationality be sent to him a Cartagena. After sealing it, he went to Bishop Castagna's apartments.

When he arrived, Marlo was asked to wait. The bishop was praying his office and so Marlo waited in the chapel until he was finished.

Entering the chapel, he genuflected and knelt in the back. The sound of the Latin chant helped to calm his excitement and he prayed for the success of the coming expedition. When he saw the bishop close his breviary and walk slowly out, Marlo got up and returned to Castagna's apartments. There he found the bishop waiting for him.

"Señor Gobeli, I was informed that you needed to see me on a matter of some importance. Come in." The bishop opened the door to his study and motioned Marlo to enter. Marlo entered and kneeling, kissed the bishop's ring.

"Your Excellency," he said, "I have a message that needs to be sent to Rome by the fastest possible means."

"By all means," said the bishop taking the letter. Weighing it in his hand thoughtfully, he considered Marlo for a moment. "Are you able to inform me as to the contents of this?"

"Absolutely," said Marlo. "His Majesty has just appointed Don John of Austria as Captain of the Seas and commissioned him to take action against the Algerians. We leave in less than a week."

"That is quick, especially for the king," said the bishop. "You said 'we.' I take it that you are going as well?"

"Yes," said Marlo, "and that is why this letter needs to be delivered as soon as possible. I won't be sailing from Cartagena for at least three weeks, and I expect to receive a reply from Rome."

"I assume that young Don John is your source for this information?" asked the bishop.

"Yes. I believe he told me as soon as he was informed of his commission."

"Very well, I will have this delivered by the fastest possible means. Someone will leave here within an hour. May God protect you and the young prince on this endeavor."

Chapter 12

June 1568

Marlo and Don John left Madrid in May, arriving in Cartagena on the first day of June. They had traveled the same road that Marlo and Father Andrea had used the previous summer. This time, the mild spring air and cool nights made the journey quite enjoyable. The green land, not yet having had time to turn brown from the dry, arid heat of summer added to the spirit of pleasant adventure. They traveled slowly, arriving in Cartagena with a small company of soldiers ten days after leaving Madrid.

The morning after they arrived, Don John and Marlo sought out Don Requesens. On presenting to the seaman the orders of the king, Don Requesens took them to the harbor and showed them the fleet. At Don John's request, they took a boat and boarded the flagship.

Marlo watched as the prince was shown around the *Capitana*. The young commander smiled excitedly as he surveyed his cabin. The cannon in the bow held his interest for some time.

Marlo was amused at the detail of decoration given to the *Capitana*. It was ornately decorated with gilded carvings depicting Jason and the Argonauts in their quest for the Golden Fleece. Fitting, he thought. Don John was a member the Order of the Golden Fleece. It would make sense for the ship he commanded to acknowledge that.

~~~

Returning to the city, Marlo left Don John and made arrangements for the stabling and care of his horse. He took his midday meal alone, and in the afternoon went back to Don Requesens' apartment to find out when Don John planned to depart. He was informed that the fleet would sail in the morning. As he was leaving, Don John saw him and called for Marlo to wait.

"There is a meeting with the chief officers tonight, after supper. I want you to be there."

"My Lord," said Marlo, "I have no real experience in naval matters."

"I know that," John smiled. "Yet you are a soldier, and you also are aware of the general situation of the Islamic threat. I would be glad
~~~

to have your thoughts on the decisions made after the meeting."

"I will be present, then," said Marlo.

~~~

That evening, six men sat around a table in Don Requesens' sumptuous apartment. Some were looking at their new commander with doubt, others with reservation. Only Marlo, who stood against the wall, had an inkling of what to expect. Don John leaned on the table, frustrated.

"So that's all we do?" he asked. "Let me remind you that if we do not stop the Algerians, we will not have enough grain for the coming winter."

"Yes, my lord," said Requesens. "We are aware of the necessity of success, but the best way to deter the pirate action is to be an escort for the trade fleet. That way we don't lose any of our goods, nor do we unnecessarily risk our ships. If an Algerian is still inclined to attack, then..." He shrugged. "We have the means enough to fight them off."

"Excellency," said Juan de Cordoba, "There is also the problem of Andrea Doria. He is currently providing protection to our shipping around Sicily. However, his fleet is too small to be effective. He also requests more men."

"How many ships do we have in port now?" asked John.
~~~

"Forty-seven, My Lord," answered Alvero Bazan, a veteran of many skirmishes with the Algerians. "I am of the opinion that we could easily send a third of them to Doria and still have a large enough fleet to accomplish His Majesty's orders."

"On that advice, we will keep thirty-three. Can we send Doria enough men so he can have full crews?"

"Yes, My Lord," said Requesens, "but that will leave us needing about five hundred to six hundred men."

"With the men we have left, could we still sail?"

"Yes, but we really won't be able to fight."

"In that case," said John, "we could always make sure we had at least five ships completely crewed."

"And the remaining ships?" asked Requesens. "How do you propose to use them? Just have them sail along and do nothing?"

"Not at all." John turned to his secretary, Juan de Quiroga. "Please draft a letter that can be sent to the governors of the major ports asking them to have men ready for us. We can plan our route to stop in at those ports and pick them up ourselves." John looked at Requesens. "Which garrisons could handle having reduced numbers?"

"Murcia and Seville, for sure, and possibly even Denia and Granada. If we were able to get at least a hundred each from them, our ships will be sufficiently crewed. We could pick up more at Gibraltar, I think."

"Draft letters to those governors, then," said Don John to Juan.

"That would take care of crewing the ships," objected Bazan, "that is assuming that the governors will provide enough men. How can we be sure of that? Most of the governors who have military garrisons in their provinces are not too ready to part with soldiers."

"His Majesty has given me the authority to enforce such a request. Now, regarding fleet movements, what would be advisable?"

"You have not commanded fleet operations, I understand, My Lord?" asked Bazan.

"This is my first," replied John quietly.

"Then in that case, I would recommend going first to some garrison along the Spanish coast. That way you can see for yourself what is involved in the coordination and movements of many ships at once. When we enter into battle, you might not have time to ask for our advice on fleet movement, and a working knowledge of naval maritime matters can mean the difference between victory and becoming a galley slave for an Algerian."

"That is good advice, My Lord," put in Requesens. "And as we will need replacements for some of the men sent to Doria, the port of Denia would be close, and yet give you sufficient time to get used to ship command." Marlo, at Requesens' gesture, came and refilled his wine glass. "It won't be long before you have enough experience to not have to rely on guidance every step of the way. Until then, you will need to avoid naval action if possible."

"Very well," sighed John. "We will commence operations. Don Requesens, when is the next trader leaving port?"

The burly, gray haired man pulled out some papers and glanced at the entries. "Well, the *Lucia* sails tomorrow for Sicily, and three other ships will be leaving today. I can have them wait so we can guard all four ships at once."

"Good. Any other scheduled departures?"

"Not for tomorrow, My Lord. However, there are two for Sicily in two days, four for Corunna the day after. And these numbers could change."

"Corunna bound ships, My Lord," said Juan de Cordona speaking for the first time, "only need to be escorted as far as Gibraltar. The Algerians have not troubled our shipping on the Atlantic."

"Yes, I had thought of that," said John. "See if those two bound for Sicily would be able to leave a day earlier. I want all those Sicilian bound ships to leave with the reinforcements for Doria. I do not like the idea of this fleet being spread out over multiple convoys." John rubbed his face in irritation. "If those two ships can't leave tomorrow, then hold the four scheduled for tomorrow's sail until the next day. But make sure that they all leave together. The ships being sent to Andrea Doria can run this convoy operation. Those bound for Corunna will have to strike out on their own. If they want protection, then they could wait and join us when we return from Denia. Do any of you see any problems with this?"

"That is a good plan, My Lord," said Requesens. He stood and bowed. "I will see to the ordering of the fleet. When will you want to set sail?"

"Tomorrow, if that is feasible."

"Quite feasible, my lord," answered Requesens. "I will make sure the fleet is ready."

"The *Capitana* goes to Denia. Let's hope everything is well there so we can get about His Majesty's business. If Requesens has his way, we might not encounter any pirates," said John after Requesens left.

Alvero Bazan stood as well and his aged face creased as he smiled. "Don't be too impatient. You have the genius to command. Once you learn about the complexities of naval warfare, you will be able to make you own decisions without having to follow the lead of Don Requesens. I will meet you on board." He bowed and the others left the room, leaving Marlo and Don John alone.

"Santiago," John sighed. "Marlo, the Algerian has grown too bold, thinking himself to be the hunter."

"That may be," answered Marlo. He realized that he had as much to learn about naval battle as the Royal Captain did. He poured himself some wine and sat down. "However, the king also has to keep the shipping from the New World safe. I don't think that this sudden rise in Algerian activity is a result of Spanish weakness. I am convinced that it is orchestrated. It would be too much of a coincidence that the Algerians raid your shipping at the same time the Moriscos seem ready to revolt while Selim is preparing his move on Venice. I rather suspect that if the pirates are not dealt with quickly, the king will not only be unable to deal with a future Morisco rising, but will also not come to the aid of Venice. And if Venice falls..."

"...Italy falls." completed John. "This is why I am frustrated. We are only exercising defensive maneuvers. At this rate, generations will pass before the Algerians are stopped, and by then it will be too late. We need to go on the offensive."

"But not before your time, My Lord," said Marlo. "The caution of Don Requesens has its place. The Algerians can't but help notice the presence of your ships in the Mediterranean. If they think that you are adopting a defensive posture, they could be lured into overconfidence. At that point, you can attack them when they are not expecting you to do so."

The Captain of the Sea grew thoughtful. After a moment, he stood. "Yes. I see your point. However, if Selim is indeed giving help to the Algerians as we suspect, then our mere presence could induce him to protect his ships. If he is indeed going to move against Venice soon, he will need, not just his fleet, but the Algerian fleet as well. But we should rest for the night. When the time comes, we shall strike."

"Good night, My Lord," said Marlo. He swallowed the rest of his wine and stood. "I pray that you can learn quickly all you need to. We don't have much time."

Outside the room, Alvero Bazan and Juan de Cordona were speaking quietly. They motioned to Marlo. "You seem more than just a servant. Nor do you act like the Captain's bodyguard. What's your role?" asked Cordoba.

"More of a witness," said Marlo. "His Excellency wants me to be around as someone to complain to. I have as little experience in naval matters as he does. I was formerly a member of the Swiss Guard in Rome."

"As a soldier, then, what's your impression of him?" asked Cordona.

"Young and enthusiastic, like myself. And willing to learn. However, I don't think it will be long before he will assert his authority. But not before he knows his business. I think he knows that responsibility."

"That's my assessment of him as well," said Bazan. "At twenty-one he is quite young for command, for sure. On the other hand, I get the distinct impression that he knows his limitations."

"If that's the case, he will be quite capable, in time," said Cordona. "Good night."

~~~

Marlo was awakened before dawn by one of the soldiers and given food. After eating, he went down to the quay and was rowed to the *Capitana*. In the growing light the ship began to gleam. When he climbed on board, John was already there. He was being shown about the ship by Alvero Bazan. When he saw Marlo, he motioned him to join them at the high peaked forecastle. Alvero was explaining to John the use of the three cannon.

"When we close with an enemy ship, we load these with shrapnel. These help clear the deck so the enemy can be boarded."

"I assume, by the way the guns are mounted, that they can only shoot forward?" asked John.

"Precisely, My Lord," answered Bazan. "When the ship is directly in front, at a reasonable distance, we can get off one or two shots for each gun. The length of the galley acts like a gun carriage, absorbing the force of the recoil. If these were mounted so they could fire to the sides, the galley would rock dangerously.
~~~

But since we can turn this ship with the oars quite rapidly, it doesn't really matter that these guns only fire in one direction. Then, once the guns are fired, we ram the enemy. But then we have to fight harder. However, we have very little chance of the enemy breaking free of us."

"So, we have to weigh which handicap we want?"

"Yes, My Lord."

John ran his hand along the barrel of the port side gun. "Do we ever use solid shot?"

"Sometimes," Bazan shrugged. "Common practice is to use solid shot at greater distance and try to pierce the ship at or below the waterline. As we begin to close with the ship, then we are too close. We can't depress the elevation enough for solid shot to strike the ship. Shrapnel does a bloody good job at clearing the decks, though."

"As you can see, Marlo," said John smiling, "I am having my first lesson. Guns I understand, and Don Quixada was fond of telling me, 'always start from what you know and then determine what you don't know.' My task is now to learn what it is I still need to learn."

"Then in that case, My Lord," answered Marlo, "I can't be of much help." He saw Don Requesens striding toward them. "I believe your lieutenant might be wanting a word with you."

"Your Excellency," Requesens said as he approached, "if you have a moment?"

"Good morning, Don Requesens," said John. He walked toward his lieutenant. "I am at your disposal."

"My Lord," Requesens bowed, "it is customary for the Captain of the Sea to address a few words to his officers and crew before we set sail."

"And we should be getting under way," finished John. "Captain Bazan, I will address the crew." As Requesens and Don John made their way to the high deck in the stern, Bazan spoke to the boatswain who blew his pipe. At the shrill call, the sailors assembled on the middle deck, while the officers arranged themselves behind Don John. The soldiers, with their muskets and polished breastplates and helmets, lined the gunwales.

Don John turned to the Franciscan priest who was accompanying the ship and knelt. The entire crew knelt also and received his blessing. Then Bazan stepped forward and called to everyone, "His Catholic Majesty, King Philip, the second of that name, has appointed as Captain of the Sea, his natural brother, His Excellency Don John of Austria, Knight of the Order of the Golden Fleece. The authority to command having been conferred upon him, he will now address the ship." Bazan stepped back and bowed to Don John.

"Spaniards and Christians in His Majesty's

service," began John, "Eight hundred years ago, Islam invaded our land, murdering its inhabitants and destroying the Church that had been planted in Spain. This horde swept over all of our homeland, except for one cave, where Pelayo and his handful of followers fought back and secured for themselves a small holding free of the rule of Islam. That small holding grew, and for seven hundred years, our ancestors fought to reclaim the land which had been stolen from them. They won it castle by castle, city by city, mountain by mountain, until once again, the cross of our Redeemer was replanted in every corner, in every city, in every town.

"Who has not heard of the glorious exploits of El Cid and his defeat of the Almoraverde Moors who had come from Algeria and threatened the Kingdoms of Leon and Castille? We also have not forgotten King Saint Fernando, and how he brought, for a time, the entire peninsula under the banner of the cross. And in our grandfathers' memory, the final reconquest of Granada by King Ferdinand. These men, and many whose names are forgotten, fought against great odds, and whenever they were in the greatest danger their faith was the strongest, and they were joined by Saint James, Saint George, and a host of angels. For God Himself would not rest until His land was returned to His care."

Marlo looked around him. The words of Don

John had brightened the faces of the soldiers and sailors.

"However, even as I speak," continued Don John, "Islam is preparing once again to fly the crescent over all of Spain. The same enemy is returning, for they will not rest until all the world turns towards Mecca in prayer and is bathed in the blood of Christians. We are called by our king to strike the first blow against them.

"In past years, Algerians have been attacking our shipping, hoping to interrupt enough of our food supply so that we suffer hunger and our people become desperate and welcome them onto our shores as saviors who will put an end to famine. But they will not bring salvation. Rather, they will molest our women, abduct our youth, murder our priests, slaughter our fathers, and enslave those who refuse to accept the words of Mohamed. By God's grace, this has not yet happened, and by His grace, we will not let it happen!"

The entire crew erupted in deafening shouts. "Santiago!" and "Viva Christo Rey!" reverberated through the harbor. Then, Don John raised a hand, and silence returned to the ship.

"Brothers, I am also compelled to tell you, that it is not Spain alone that is in danger. Rome is also. The Algerians are accomplishing two objectives with their piracy: to weaken us and to keep us occupied. If we are not successful, then Rome will be undefended, and the Turk will fly the crescent over St. Peter's.

"I was recently told a story of a simple farmer. When he heard about the threat to Spain and the greater threat to all of Europe, his reply was, 'I wouldn't worry too much. Saint Fernando will not let Islam overrun us again, as long as there is a Spaniard left to resist.'" Here, the men cheered and Don John had to pause again.

"And this I promise you: Spain will not fall. It will not fall because we remember. It will not fall because we are Spaniards, and we will do the task appointed to us, no matter how difficult. There will not be only one Spaniard left to resist; no, there will be thousands! Santiago! And at them!"

The men shouted the ancient war cry of Pelayo, El Cid, and Saint Fernando as loudly as they could. "Santiago! And at them!" reverberated off the deck, and moved across the water. "Santiago! And at them!" the sailors and soldiers from the rest of the fleet heard the cry and joined in. "Santiago! And at them!" again and again, until the entire harbor was ringing with sound, and the people on shore had to stop what they were doing to see what was happening.

Don John's standard was raised and the wind sent it streaming. The guns of the Castle of the Conception fired in salute. The war cry changed into cheers and Alvero Bazan ordered the sail unfurled and the anchor weighed. The oars dipped and rose as the *Capitana* began its progress out of the harbor. One by one, the ships of the fleet fired a salute to its youthful commander, set sail, and followed as the cannon smoke rolled across the water, diffusing the rays of the rising sun. The church bells began to peal. The crusade was going to the sea.

Chapter 13

June 1568

Marlo had cheered with the rest of the crew. Finally, the Spanish were doing something, and he was excited to see the first results of his efforts. While the alliance of nations that Pius the Fifth had envisioned had not yet been achieved, an ambassador had been sent to Italy, and now Spain was taking the necessary precautions to protect its trade. By keeping the Algerians occupied, Don John's fleet would prevent them from giving more aid to the Turks.

The *Capitana* sailed from the harbor and headed north. Don John ordered the ship to slow so the others could catch up. He signaled for the *Reya* to scout the waters ahead of them. The small, nimble ship glided past them, dipped her colors in salute, and sailed on. Marlo stood at the rail and watched the fleet form up behind and to the sides of the *Capitana*, the standards of the Spanish knights fluttering in the breeze.

Later that day, Marlo sat with Don John in his cabin. They had completed their meal and were recounting stories. John's association with the Royal Family had come as a surprise to him.

"I grew up thinking my name was Jerome. I always knew that I was illegitimate, but I had no conception that I was the son of Emperor Charles. When I was about twelve years old, I was brought to Valladolid and met King Philip. He was the one who told me that he and I had the same father and that my name was really John." The prince smiled sheepishly. "At first it was unreal. Not knowing my parents, I had dreamed that somehow I would find that I was part of the royal family and had been hidden away because of the embarrassment I caused. Finding out that that was indeed the case was exhilarating."

"Do you still think so?" asked Marlo.

"Not in the least," John shook his head. "Being the son of an emperor brings with it certain privileges and a guaranteed income. However, the *bar sinister* of a bastard son is indeed a bar. I can't inherit, nor do I enjoy the full privileges of a prince. Yet it is expected of me to fill all of the responsibilities of a member of a royal house. I find that I have to be better than a legitimate prince in all I do. Thus I am in command of this fleet. And I am answerable for its success or failure."

"That would be the same for any commander, wouldn't it?"

"For most commanders, yes," said John. "But a prince destined for a crown is easily forgiven any number of mistakes. The same applies to a reigning monarch. The only way to avoid this scrutiny is to enter a monastery."

"I believe you mentioned that you were destined for the Church at one time," said Marlo.

"Yes, I was destined for a religious life at first, but I was more interested in war, and my brother was eventually persuaded by Don Luis Quixada to let me pursue a military career."

"How do you expect to command this fleet?"

"By listening to those who know more than I do," said John standing. "But the evening is almost over, and I should be on deck."

Marlo followed him out of the cabin and accompanied him to the helm. Don John checked the course and made inquiries regarding the weather and the state of the ship and the fleet.

"I am told," said John to Marlo, "that we are traveling at just under twelve knots, with a favorable wind and the aid of the oars. That is, I assume, very good sailing."

"Do you know when we might reach Denia?" asked Marlo.

"I am also told that it will be sometime tomorrow afternoon. The oars will not be used at night, so we will be trusting the wind."

"Do you want me to accompany you when you meet the governor tomorrow?"

"I would greatly appreciate your company, but I don't need you."

"Then I will join you, with your permission," said Marlo, bowing formally.

"Permission granted," answered John. He left Marlo and spoke to Don Requesens, who then gave order for the Franciscan priest, Father Paulo, to be summoned.

Marlo watched as the sun set over the waters, the sails and masts silhouetted against the red light of the sun. At a signal from the *Capitana* the oars of all the ships were raised and held parallel to the surface of the sea. He turned around and saw that all of the sailors of the *Capitana* were gathered on the deck. Father Paulo was on deck. His voice broke the silence, "*Benedictio Dei Omnipotentis*." Marlo knelt with all of the men to receive the blessing. When he stood, the crew, at the request of Don John, sang the *Salve Regina* to ask for heaven's blessing on the battle about to take place.

After the hymn, Don John mingled with the men to see how they were situated and if they needed anything that he could provide. *This is how loyalty is won*, thought Marlo. *Let's see if he can command as well.*

~~~

The fleet reached Denia in the early afternoon the following day. The city had been held longer by the Christians and had lost much of its Moorish character. The Castilado was situated on the slopes of one of the hills that overlooked the city and was visible from the water—the home of the regional governor and the military garrison of the city.

Once the *Capitana* had anchored, a boat met them, containing representatives from the governor inviting Don John and his captains to the castle. There the governor would be pleased to hold a banquet in honor of the brother of the king and of his companions.

Don John replied that he would be grateful to meet the governor and that he would be bringing three companions.

Don Requesens ordered a boat lowered for himself and Marlo, while Don John and de Quiroga entered the governor's boat. Marlo's boat followed the prince. The six Spanish soldiers, with their armor polished and muskets beside them on the floor boards, quietly pulled at the oars. When the boat touched the quay, they leaped out and formed up behind Don Requesens and Marlo, who walked just behind their commander. They moved through the streets of the city, mostly ignored by the residents of Denia who were used to the frequent traffic of persons of rank from the Castilado.
~~~

Those who were near the Castilado's entrance, however, were surprised to hear the cannon fire in salute and see a detachment of the castle guard form up in the street and to see the governor step forward and kneel.

"Your Excellency," he said in loud and officious tones, "it is my singular joy to welcome here one whose honor and probity is known throughout the Spanish Empire. You are most welcome, My Lord Don John of Austria."

"My Lord Governor, Don Alfredo, right honorably have you welcomed me, and honored am I to receive your hospitality. The time has come for all true Spaniards to prepare themselves to defend the Cross, and for such a reason, am I making my visit."

"Come in, My Lord," answered the Governor. Marlo noted that the Governor had deliberately avoided making any comment on the reason for Don John's visit.

They were led to an elaborately frescoed reception room.

"My Lord," said the Governor, "please allow me to present my wife, Doña Marta."

A middle-aged woman simpered and curtsied. "A very great pleasure, Your Highness," said Doña Marta. "We hope you will grace us and remain several days."

"Not many days, My Lady," said John bowing. "I am compelled to be on my way tomorrow."

"We shall discuss this over dinner, Your Excellency." said Alfredo. "We have a modest banquet prepared. Not the best, but we didn't have time to prepare." He spoke the last word as if to reprimand a spoiled noble, thought Marlo.

Their hosts led the guests through a pair of arches with capitals reminiscent of Moorish architecture. The table was set and several people were already gathered. They were wealthy, and some were wearing their robes of office.

As they entered, a servant called, "His Excellency, Don John of Austria. His Excellency, Knight of the Order of the Golden Fleece, the Royal Governor of Denia and General of the Castle, Don Alfredo Munoz and his wife, Doña Isabel."

"How do you like that?" asked John under his breath. "I think that was a deliberate snub."

"He certainly is not skilled at diplomatic insults," answered Requesens. "He isn't subtle enough. His attempt at nuance is about as obvious as Señor Gobeli's limp."

"Let us be seated," said the Governor approaching them. They followed him. Don Alfredo placed himself at a large chair at the head of the table, instead of giving it to Don John and motioned for the prince to place himself to his right. Don Alfredo gestured for all to sit.

Several of the guests looked at each other,

unsure how to respond when Don Alfredo relegated the king's brother to the position of mere guest, and since Don John had remained standing, they hesitated in following the governor's example and sitting.

"My Lord," said John breaking the silence that had fallen about the table, "I most humbly beg your pardon, but it has come to my attention that I have neglected to inform you of the commission I have from my brother, the king. According to his good will, I am the Captain of the Seas and as such, the direct representative of the king in all matters pertaining to the defense of Spain's shipping and coastal cities. The trust and authority that His Royal Highness and his council have placed in me requires that I know, at once, the state of the garrison of Denia and what provisions are in place for its defense. I further require an accurate count of soldiers, attendants, and other personnel attached to this garrison."

As he had been speaking, the remaining guests had stood, and Don Requesens smiled slightly. Don Alfredo frowned. "This is highly irregular, My Lord. Such business is not conducted just as we are sitting down for a meal."

"Nor is it customary for a member of the Royal Family and an officer of the court to not have the chance to state his business," answered Don Requesens. "But if you will step over here, I will brief you in the particulars of

His Excellency's request in private." Don Requesens motioned for the governor to follow him away from the table.

"Señor Gobeli," said John quietly, "I'm afraid that I must ask you to forgo your meal. I would be more confident in the governor's report if he knew you were making your own assessment of this garrison. Señor de Quiroga shall accompany you. He will have the authority to obtain access to anywhere you need to go."

"I can eat later after I have completed my task," said Marlo. "I may even find out something useful over a glass of wine or two with some of the men."

"Good," said John, moving to the head of the table. He motioned to Don Requesens and the governor.

"Lord Governor," said John when Don Alfredo had returned to the table, "knowing how unexpected our arrival has been, and that you are busy with the affairs of the province, I have instructed Señor Gobeli to assist with the assessment of this garrison. If you would sign the letter that my secretary has ready for you, we can begin our meal."

Don Alfredo didn't respond, but signed the letter. "Let us sit," said John. This time, the guests remained standing until Don John had taken his seat at the head of the table first.

~~~
~~~

Marlo and Juan left the banquet hall and went out into the courtyard.

"Where should we start?" asked Juan.

"We will start by finding out where our six soldiers were quartered and find out from them where the officers on duty can be found."

Approaching the guards at the gate, Marlo smiled. "My pardons, but Don John asked me to check on his soldiers. He wants me to let them know how long they can be expected to stay."

"Well, Señor," answered one, "they have been given quarters in the south tower. I will show you."

"Thanks," answered Marlo. "What is your name?"

"Carlos Cordova, Señor,"

"Well, Señor Cordova, even though I attend His Excellency, I am not averse to sharing a skin of wine with you and your fellow."

"That would be generous, Señor," said Cordova, grinning. "I will let Colonna know."

"When do you get off duty?"

"At seven, Señor."

"There was an inn I passed on my way here, just down the road from the gate. I'll wait for you there." By then, they had reached the south tower, and Cordova opened a heavy door. He let Marlo and Juan pass through.

"Are there many soldiers here?" asked Marlo.

"About seven hundred all together, Señor.

Only about two hundred here at the castle. But there are several garrisons in the region."

"Why so spread out?" asked Marlo stopping and making a show of massaging his leg. "Wouldn't it make more sense to keep the larger concentration of soldiers here?"

"We have about four hundred down by the water, ready to sail if needed to repel any marauders. The trading season is just starting. The soldiers will soon be on convoy duty." Cordova frowned. "Your leg seems to be bothering you. Do you need anything?"

"It's nothing," said Marlo. "I was in a riding accident last year, and it hasn't healed properly."

"What happened?"

"I was exercising the horses with the Guardsmen and mistimed a jump. But I think we should move on. I would like to get back to the banquet as soon as I can."

"Yes, just this way," said Cordova.

They were led up a flight of stairs and into a large room. Around a rough table sat their solders eating their meal. "Thank you," said Marlo. "I will meet you and Colonna at the inn after seven."

"Very good, Señor," said Cordova.

After Cordova left Marlo greeted the soldiers and joined them at the table. "Tell me," he said, "do you know who the officers on duty are?"

"I believe that Captain Garcia is the officer

on duty now," said one of the soldiers. "If you want to see him, he is on the ground level. His office is next to the main entrance."

"Do you know if he is there now?" asked Juan.

"He was there a short time ago."

"How do you find things here?" asked Marlo.

"We can't complain about our accommodations," answered one of the men, "but it seems that the officers do not want us mingling with the soldiers."

"Is that unusual?" asked Marlo.

"Rather. Wherever I have gone, I always have been able to drink with the men off duty."

Juan looked puzzled. "Señor Gobeli, do you have any idea why this garrison is different?"

"Yes," said Marlo, "however, I think I need to look around before I speculate on the reason. Thank you for the information," he said turning to the soldiers. "I think we will be staying just one night." He stood and left.

They found Garcia's office, but he wasn't there. They made their way across the courtyard to the north east side to the stables. There they encountered a soldier leading a horse into the yard.

"Captain Garcia?" asked Marlo.

"Yes, but I have an errand to run for the governor immediately," answered Garcia, mounting his horse.

"If," said Juan, "it has anything to do with

making sure that we do not find out that the number of soldiers assigned to this garrison is about twice the size of what was reported you are too late. However, there is another task that the governor wants you to take care of." Juan handed the paper that the governor had signed earlier. Garcia read and shook his head.

"It says here that I am to accompany you on a complete inspection of our military readiness and allotment of soldiers. This is contrary to the orders I was given just a few minutes ago."

"I am aware of that," said Marlo, "but since these orders also come from His Excellency Don John, who has been tasked by the king to inspect the Mediterranean garrisons, they take precedence over any other instructions given at any other time."

"Very well," said Garcia dismounting. "Since we are near the stables, shall we begin there?"

Entering the stables, Garcia gave the reins to a stable hand. "I am staying here after all, Alonso. Stable the horse for me. This way, Señores," he added, leading Marlo and Juan through the rows of stables.

Marlo noted that the horses were well groomed and the stables were clean. "How many horses are there?" he asked.

"About one hundred," answered Garcia. "Some of them are for the wagons, others for officers and cavalry."

"How many animals in your other garrisons?"

"You know about them?" asked Garcia surprised.

"We know that there are others, yes," answered Marlo.

"We could field a cavalry of about two hundred fifty, and have enough horses for a complete supply train for a force of seven hundred. Plus, seventy remounts and horses for the officers."

"Impressive," said Marlo dryly. "His Majesty would be pleased to know that he has a small army here in Denia."

"Most of the soldiers are given naval duties. All of the ships would have to be in port for the small army to be of use."

"How many are not on sea duty?" asked Juan.

"As of noon today, we have five hundred soldiers ashore."

"I have seen all that I need to see here. Why don't we move on to munitions and ordinance?" said Marlo. Garcia led them from the stable and toward the north tower. A guard opened the heavy door. Inside were stacks of harquebuses, barrels of powder and bags of shot.

"Do you keep all of your powder here?" asked Marlo.

"No. Most of it is stored by the harbor. We keep enough here for guns of the castle and munitions for the men."

"This is just for the munitions?" asked Juan.

"Yes," answered Garcia.

"I have seen enough here," said Marlo. They left the storeroom. Standing outside, Marlo looked at the castle walls, noting the guns that he could make out. "We have used enough of your time," he continued. "Juan and I will just walk around the battlements and visit the soldiers' quarters. Can you show us where they are?"

After pointing them in the right direction, Garcia left. Marlo watched him go. The soldier did not go back to the stables but headed toward the governor's quarters.

"I think the governor is going to find out that we know more than we should," said Marlo with a smile. "It will be interesting to see how he reacts."

"How do you think he will react?" asked Juan.

"Either in a way that attempts to discredit what we have to report, or else he'll have to acknowledge that he has been building up his force here without the knowledge of the king."

"To protect Spanish shipping?" asked Juan.

"Well, that is what he will claim. However, I fancy that his main motivation might be the protection of his own wealth. The only thing that makes sense right now is that he is involved in trade himself. Whether that trade is honest or not, I will find out tonight."

"How?" asked Juan.

"With wine," answered Marlo.

~~~

After they had inspected the guns on the battlements they went to the barracks. There they found the soldiers ready to receive them, but information was not volunteered on what their shipboard assignments entailed. Marlo had expected that to be the case and was not surprised. When they returned to the Governor's quarters, they found Don John with Don Requesens.

"Ah, Marlo," said Requesens. "I trust that your inspection is complete."

"Not quite yet," answered Marlo. "I have to ferret out some more later this evening. However, we have some information for you."

"Let's have it, then," said John.

"Don Alfredo, I expect, is experiencing some difficulty about our unannounced arrival. We encountered the officer of the day watch, a Captain Garcia, who was in the process of leaving the castle on an urgent assignment. Needless to say, he wasn't able to complete that assignment."

"Could you be a little clearer?" asked Requesens impatiently.

"The crown has allotted three hundred fifty men for this garrison. Don Alfredo, however,
~~~

has about seven hundred, two hundred of which are currently at sea. It seems that he keeps only two hundred here and four hundred garrisoned by the harbor. This was what Captain Garcia was trying to prevent me from finding out."

"How did you find it out then?" asked John.

"Señor Gobeli, instead of seeking out the officer on duty," said Juan, "went to the guards at the gate and asked to be shown where your men were quartered. In the course of his conversation, he divulged the number of soldiers, prompted, I think, by the promise of free wine."

"What is the information you need?" asked John. "I assume that the wine has something to do with it?"

"The wine has everything to do with it," answered Marlo. "I expected the soldiers in the barracks to be told to keep their mouths shut before I had a chance to see them. But, the guard I spoke to hadn't received that information yet, and I am hoping that he won't have a chance to be told. What I need to find out is why Don Alfredo has need of the extra men. The only thing that makes sense is that they are used to protect shipping. If that is the case, I think the most reasonable explanation for the surplus of soldiers is that our esteemed governor is heavily invested in trade and is taking the steps to protect it. However, since he has not accurately reported the number of soldiers here, I wonder about the honesty of that trade."

"Do you mean piracy?" asked Requesens mockingly.

"Smuggling," answered Marlo.

Chapter 14

June 1568

The inn stood partway down the street from the main entrance of Denia's garrison. Marlo walked through the open door and took a table in an open alcove that overlooked the harbor. After ordering food from the maid, he took off his cloak and sat down. There were only a few patrons in the common room: an old man asleep in his chair, a couple of sailors finishing a meal. After a few minutes, the serving maid brought him wine, bread, and cheese. "Do you not have many customers?" he asked her as she put the food on the table.

"Right now we don't," the maid answered, wiping her hands on her apron. "In about a half an hour, some of the soldiers will be coming in from the Castle, and the sound of their jollity brings in people from the streets."

"Soldiers?" asked Marlo. "I am meeting two from the garrison here."

"This is where you should find them. Most of them pass through here during the week. If you didn't have that accent, I would have thought that you were one of them, yourself. Only off duty and more polite."

Marlo grinned at the maid. "We're not all that bad. But I'm glad you think I'm polite."

"Yes" The serving girl smiled. "I only wish that I could say the same about everyone else. They can get rude and the room gets loud."

"By the way, what is your name?"

"Lucia. My father owns this place."

"I'm Marlo Gobeli." Marlo leaned back in his chair and smiled at Lucia. "I think I shall wait for your soldier guests. Politely, of course."

Lucia smiled. "Señor Gobeli, I do think you are teasing me!"

"I'm polite remember? I can't tease you. And anyone seeing you wouldn't want to."

Lucia blushed. "I had better see about your room." She gave a slight curtsy and left.

Marlo smiled after her and began to eat. After he had finished his food, he leaned back in the chair and stretching his legs under the table, slowly drinking his wine.

Marlo had almost finished when the door of the inn opened, and Cordova and two other men entered, laughing and calling for Lucia.

When she came out from the back room, the men burst into a cheer.

"Lucia, my dear," called one. He was wearing a dark jacket, and his short beard was black. His hair was pulled back. "Come here." He put his arm around her waist and pulled her to him. "I waited all day to see you."

"Diego, get your hands off me," Lucia protested, struggling to get out of Diego's arms. "I won't serve you if you don't let go!" Diego only smiled more and pulled her tighter to himself.

"I would let her go, if I were you," called Marlo. He was still leaning back in his chair, and had a look of amusement on his face. "You are blocking my view."

Diego pushed Lucia away from him and moved toward Marlo, followed by his two companions. "What makes you think you can tell me what to do? You are not from here. Leave me alone, or I will make sure you won't bother anyone else!"

Marlo lifted the wine bottle off the table. "You can do as you wish Señor, but such beauty is best appreciated when seen from a distance. And I wouldn't want her to avoid this room. Come, sit, and let me buy you a drink. I already promised Cordova one. I have just come into port and had a wearing day running errands for the Captain of the Seas. I would like to have an entertaining evening." Lucia placed three more glasses at Marlo's table. Marlo filled them before refilling his. He stood up and held his glass up toward Lucia. "Señorita, I drink to you." He took a sip. "Please, I think these gentlemen would like to eat." He looked at the three men who were still standing and staring at him. "Your meal is on me also. Sit, and carouse!"

Diego took his wine. "As long as you don't get between me and the girl here."

"I will be gone tomorrow. I'll sing her praises and wish you all luck. But I'm not here to get in anyone's way. Please, sit and have a good time at my expense."

"Well, as long as you are paying." Diego sat followed by Cordova and Colonna, the other soldier Marlo had seen standing guard with Cordova. He drank his wine and held out his glass for Marlo to refill.

"Where are you from, if you don't mind me asking?" asked Colonna. He was shorter than Diego and wearing a light colored jacket. "You speak like a foreigner."

"Switzerland, by way of Rome," answered Marlo. "I used to be in the Guard. Then I injured my leg. So now I am sailing with Don John until I find something better to do."

"Galley service does not suit you?" asked Cordova.

"Poor food, terrible sleeping accommodations? I miss being ashore." Marlo decided to pretend that he would be interested in signing up for service here in Denia.

"You could join us here, Señor," said Colonna. "If you were in the Guard, you know how to fight, and you won't need to be trained."

Marlo ignored him. "Señorita!" he called. "Señorita," he said to Lucia when she arrived, "These men have endured the rigors of the castle all day: training, sentry duty, keeping their equipment in order. And they are thirsty. Could you bring us more wine?"

"I doubt they even did that much," said Lucia. "They complain every night how they never have anything to do."

"We always have something to do," said Diego. He leaned forward and grabbed one of her hands. He lowered his voice and leered. "I spend the day looking forward to seeing you, and that keeps me very busy indeed!"

"I know my father looks forward to your visits," said Lucia pulling her hand out of Diego's grasp. "You and your friends contribute a lot of money to our family funds. But I don't look forward to you." Lucia turned and started to walk away. As she left she looked back over her shoulder and said to the men, "But I don't dread your visits, either."

"That's my girl," shouted Diego. "You'll love me yet! Just hurry back with that wine. I'm thirsty!"

"I'm not your girl, or anyone's girl, for that matter. You need to learn from Señor Gobeli.

Ask, don't demand. I will be back with your wine and food."

"When I was sailing to Almeria we had a close call with the Algerians," said Marlo after Lucia left. "According to the captain of the ship I was on, this particular Algerian was rather bold. They came onto us only a few hours away from the harbor."

"Did you have to fight?" asked Cordova.

"No fighting, but it was a close call. They almost got us."

"You are lucky you escaped," said Cordova. "But what you say is nothing new. The Algerians have been getting bolder all year. There are more of them and they are attacking our shipping closer and closer to Spanish ports."

"Our shipping is never harassed," objected Diego. He drained his glass and held it out for Marlo to refill.

"What is your trick?" asked Marlo. "If I could tell Don John how to protect our shipping, then maybe I can remain ashore?" Before they could answer, Lucia came to the table with another bottle of wine. He took the wine from her and refilled his companion's glasses. Lucia set the food on the table and left. "Your health, Diego," he said, lifting his glass toward Diego.

"And yours," answered Diego. "You buy the wine and food, but leave the girl behind when you go. I could be friends with such a man."

"Then let's be friends for the night," said

Marlo. "Tell me, what is it like being posted here?"

"Pretty easy," answered Diego. "All we do is stand guard, and occasionally help to supply a few galleys."

"Galleys?" asked Marlo. "So if I remained here, I would still have to spend time at sea?"

"Not if you become one of Captain Garcia's men," said Colonna. "We just help provision them, that's all. The other garrison mans them."

"So that's why you are not bothered," Marlo chuckled. "Don Alfredo has his own galleys. He seems to be a careful governor. I think I just might stay here a while. So tell me," asked Marlo, refilling Cordova's glass, "Where have you served?"

"Just here," said Cordova, looking smug. "We work directly for Don Alfredo, so we get to stay here. The night duty can get annoying, at times."

"You certainly seem to be enjoying night duty right now."

"This is my kind of duty," Cordova giving Marlo a clap on his shoulder. "I could do without the other."

"What is so hard about standing watch at night?" asked Marlo. "I've done that a lot. It's merely boring."

"What's not boring," interjected Diego, "is being woken in the middle of the night to unload ships. I hate being a stevedore."

"At night?" Marlo laughed. "Now that is droll. Why would anyone want to unload ships at night?"

Cordova shrugged and drained his glass. "No idea. We just unload them, put the goods on wagons and carts, and see to it that the goods leave the city safely."

"Are all ships unloaded at night?" Marlo shook his head. "I would think that unloading during the day would be easier."

"Only the governor's ships," muttered Diego.

Marlo had some of the information he needed, and he spent the rest of the evening with the soldiers, singing, swapping stories, and enjoying himself. Well into the night, he paid Lucia and left the inn. He had found out what was going on.

~~~

Marlo rose early the following morning, washed and dressed, and went to Don John's quarters. When he knocked on the door, Juan answered. "Come in, Señor Gobeli. His Excellency expects you."

Inside Don John was seated at a table eating his breakfast. "Marlo," he said, "come and join me." Marlo sat down. Juan gave him a plate and served him. "So, Marlo," said John when Marlo
~~~

started his meal, "do you have any more information on your interesting theory? I must tell you that Don Requesens considers it rather preposterous."

"Regarding evidence, I have none," said Marlo. "However, I could make a more convincing case for smuggling based on what I was told last night."

"You interest me." John sat back and folded his arms. "Tell me what you were told."

"In the course of a rather congenial evening, I managed to steer the conversation to the various duties that are filled by the soldiers here. One of the guards told me that the soldiers are used to guard ships that come from the New World. It seems that several galleys would, at certain times, head out past Gibraltar, meet a small convoy of ships, and escort them safely here."

"And that is evidence of smuggling?"

"It is when one considers that the royal fifth is not paid from those ships."

"What?" John sat up. "How does Don Alfredo get away with that?"

"According to what I was told, Don Alfredo owns most of the ships that come to this port from the New World. When they reach here, they are unloaded at night. The goods and gold are brought here, unloaded at night, and then moved out of the city before daybreak. The soldiers never see anything of the cargo again, and they never see any royal officers. Nor are they aware of any shipments being sent to Madrid."

"So our illustrious governor is defrauding us?"

"So it would seem," Marlo shrugged. "I wonder if His Majesty's court is aware of Don Alfredo's trade activity?"

"Not that I am aware of," said John. "Do you know anything of it?" he asked Juan.

"No, My Lord," he answered. "That type of information is not usually given to me."

"What I don't understand," said John, "is why he needs all of the extra soldiers? Wouldn't the garrison here be enough to guard his ships?"

"Not really," said Marlo. "He can't use the three hundred assigned here. He has to be able to account for them at any given time. They are also not in his pay; thus their loyalty is to the king. The other three hundred fifty are paid by him. He is able to assure himself of their secrecy and loyalty."

"Yet they spoke to you," objected John.

"Not really, remember there was wine involved. And in the companionship of tavern stories, they were not as guarded in their speech as they should have been. Some told me of the meeting of ships from Gibraltar, others spoke about what happens to the goods here. Later information was furnished that no shipments were ever sent to Madrid. My questions were intermixed with stories and song, and I acted as if I was interested in joining the garrison here. They were just telling me what work here was like."

"Are you convinced of your theory?"

"Convinced enough that I would strongly encourage a real investigation," said Marlo.

"How about being convinced enough for me to use your information to our advantage?"

"As long as you didn't put yourself wrong by accusing the governor of particulars, yes."

"Very good," said John. He stood and placed his hand on Marlo's shoulder. "I expect you spent a good sum in wine. Let Juan know, and I will see you repaid. You go get ready to leave. I will confer with Don Requesens as to the best course of action. My ships are undermanned since we sent ships and men to Andrea Doria, and three hundred fifty extra men will make me quite satisfied."

Marlo stood. "I should dearly like to see you put the squeeze on our most honest and loyal of governors." He grinned. "Ferreting out information I am good at. And I would enjoy seeing it put to good use."

~~~

An hour later, Marlo stood to the side of Don Alfredo's study. Don John had taken the governor's desk. Don Requesens sat at his side, and
~~~

Juan de Quiroga stood nearby with a sheaf of papers. Don Alfredo sat across the desk from Don John.

"My Lord, I am afraid that I cannot provide more than a dozen men. The men assigned here are for the defense of the port, and not just from the Algerians. We need to ensure that trade goods are not molested by greedy malcontents."

"My Lord Governor," said John, "you know quite well that I am aware of the fact that the men you have stationed here are twice the number of men the king has assigned to this post. I would think that you would be able to spare significantly more than a mere dozen."

"Your Excellency," said Alfredo smoothly, "I have had to hire these men at great expense to myself and to the city. I need to have these men ready to come to the aid of trading ships at a moment's notice. There are times that I am left with fewer than a hundred men here ashore."

"However," said John, "the burden of protecting Spanish shipping is no longer yours. I have been assigned to that task."

"With all due respect," said Alfredo, "when you are near Tunis, or down by Sicily, you won't be here. And here is where the protection needs to be. The future of Spanish trade is at stake."

"I admire your zeal for protecting trade in which you have no chance at profit, as well as the fact that you spend your own money to do so. Would that more governors were so selfless." Don Alfredo sat straighter in his seat. "I hear that you even go so far as to protect American trade, even while it is still on the Atlantic and under no threat from Algerians."

"There is always the threat of English piracy, Your Excellency," said Alfredo.

"Yes," said John. He leaned forward and looked at the governor. "It seems to me that you are acting above and beyond the interest of your office. What motivates you in your overwhelming concern for the wellbeing of Spain?"

"Your Excellency," Alfredo shifted in his seat. "I love Spain, and I would think that, in protecting my interests, I am providing valuable service to the king."

"What do you love more, Spain or your own interests?" John's voice was quiet and he seemed almost bored.

"Spain, of course," Alfredo bowed slightly in his seat. "I only desire the security of the interests of the king."

"I see." John held out a hand to Juan. His secretary handed him a sheet of paper covered with close writing. The prince scanned it, placed it face down on the desk and clasped his hands over it. "My Lord Governor, this is a most interesting paper. I wonder if you can explain why His Majesty's court knows nothing about your trade with New Spain?"

"Trade? How could I have trade?"

Juan handed another sheet of paper to Don Requesens. "Don Alfredo, I have information about the Royal Fifth not being paid," said Requesens.

Marlo gaped. *How did Juan get that information?* The commander's secretary had claimed earlier that he knew nothing.

Requesens took another sheet of paper. "Dates, ships, type of cargo." He reached for another bundle of papers. "Names of galleys used to escort trade vessels to port and of their commanding officers."

They are making this up, Marlo realized and tried not to smirk. Don Alfredo shifted in his seat, took out a handkerchief and wiped his face. He opened his mouth, and then closed it without saying anything.

"Well, My Lord Governor," said John, "what have you to say about this?"

"You don't understand," said the Governor. He swallowed and wiped his face again. "I am merely involved in trade. And helping to protect other traders, as well."

"Helping by defrauding His Majesty of necessary funds? Funds he could have used to protect all of his interests?"

"My Lord, I meant no harm," protested the governor.

"You meant no harm to yourself, I'm sure," said Requesens. "But what about the harm to

His Majesty's fleet by refusing us needed men?"

"I only did what was best. You don't know the conditions here. I do." Alfredo looked defiant.

"I think we do," said John quietly. He turned to his secretary. "Señor de Quiroga, take down a memo and prepare a report for His Majesty informing him of the extent of the fraud." He turned back to the governor. "It won't be long before His Majesty's agents will be able to express to you the gratitude you deserve."

Don Alfredo turned white and slumped in his chair. After looking at the governor for a few moments, John spoke again to his secretary. "Make sure that his Majesty is fully informed that Don Alfredo has been so conscientious that he has even taken upon himself the onerous task of managing the funds from the royal fifth by adding and training three hundred fifty men. Add further, that Don Alfredo, realizing that there are still funds remaining, volunteers to continue to pay the men, even though they will no longer be under his direct administration."

"Your Excellency!" protested Alfredo. "I can't afford that. This will place me in debt!"

"You are already in debt," said the prince. "However, even when this operation is over and you no longer have to pay the salaries, you will still be in debt to the king. He might forgive that debt, though. You have been only interested in Spain's economic wellbeing, after all." He stood. "I will take three hundred fifty of the men you have here in the castle and at the garrisons near the harbor. We leave today." John walked to the door followed by Marlo and Juan. "Don Requesens, will you oversee the transportation of the soldiers to the ships?"

Requesens nodded and followed John out. At the door, he turned to the governor. "I will need to speak to the officers that you are sending in thirty minutes. Don't forget," he added, "His Majesty expects prompt delivery of the Fifth from this day forward."

Outside, Requesens caught up with his commander. "That was well handled, My Lord."

"Will you strip him of his governorship?" asked Marlo.

"There is no need," smiled John. "He will behave from now on. I will leave that headache to my Royal Brother."

"He might not like that headache," said Requesens.

"No, I don't think he will," answered the prince. "But it's not my fault that he is the king."

~~~

Several hours later, Marlo was leaning against the starboard rail of the *Capitana*. Don John was standing next to him. They were watching the men from Denia as they were
~~~

rowed to their assigned ships.

"So far, they seem completely equipped," said Marlo, looking at a boat that passed near to them. "They all have breastplates, helmets, and weapons. They also seem disciplined."

"With Don Requesens overseeing the operation," answered John, "it isn't likely that we would get anything else."

"What do you think will happen to the governor?"

"Him? Less than he deserves. My brother will probably act upon my suggestion and consider the cost of equipping and paying the extra soldiers as part of the Royal Fifth. However, he will probably have to pay the rest."

"Is he likely to remain as governor?"

"Probably not, but that is not my decision." The prince pointed to a boat that was heading toward them. "Here comes my lieutenant. We will weigh anchor soon."

Don Requesens climbed up the side of the *Capitana*, saluted, and walked over to his commander. He was smiling. "The men are aboard, Your Excellency."

"How do you find them?" asked John.

"They seem disciplined. If I may suggest, it would probably be for the best if we take our own men and spread them evenly through the ships, using as many of our own officers as possible. Since the men from Denia have been trained and are paid by Don Alfredo, I am un-

comfortable with the idea of them being concentrated on just a few ships. Separating them
will reduce the likelihood of desertion or insubordination."

"Make it happen," John nodded. "Do you
want to make the arrangements now or at our
next stop?

"Now will be preferable," answered Requesens. "The sooner the soldiers get used to
their new officers, the better. And if I can make
another suggestion, since this fleet is untrained, we should put it through maneuvers at
Santa Pola. Sometimes, Algerians will use that
island as a temporary base of operations, striking at our trade from a secured location. We
can conduct maneuvers, while seeing if any pirates happen to be there as well."

"And for me to learn about fleet maneuvers," added the commander. "Very well." John
looked about the harbor. "When will we be able
to depart?"

"In an hour, Your Excellency," answered Requesens.

"Then, give the order when we are ready.
We make for Santa Pola."

After the soldiers had been evenly distribut-
ed among the ships, Don Requesens spoke to
Alvero Bazan. Bazan shouted out a few commands, and a soldier fired one of the bow guns.
The Captain of the Sea's standard rose to the
top of the mast and broke in the wind. The an-

chor was raised, and the *Capitana* maneuvered its way out of the harbor.

Once out of the harbor, the fleet headed due south against a contrary wind. Marlo spent most of his time in the bow of the ship. The smell of the unwashed, sweating prisoners was too strong for him to remain in the stern. He lounged against one of the bow guns as the fleet continued its way through the afternoon of that day. At night, after the stern lanterns were lit, he laid down for the night, using a coil of rope for a pillow. He stared at the stars as the ships moved slowly through the moonless dark. He drew up his cloak and slept.

The next day was Sunday. After sunrise, mass was celebrated on those ships that had chaplains. Meanwhile, the ships continued their slow journey south.

After mass, Marlo watched as Don John and Father Paulo moved along the catwalk among the prisoners, bringing them water and food, Father Paulo speaking to those who were Catholic.

When the commander returned to the deck, he gave orders for the sails to be unfurled, as the wind had shifted in their favor. "Pass the order to the rest of the fleet. We will use sail alone, today, unless oars are needed for a ship to keep up with the fleet," he told Captain Bazan. "Since today is Sunday, we will give even the prisoners a day of rest."

"Yes, My Lord." Captain Bazan passed the orders and the signal flags rose.

"Señor Gobeli, will you accompany me to the bow?"

Marlo and John made their way to the front of the ship. As they passed the prison hold, some of the oarsmen cheered. The boatswain unfurled his lash.

"You are to remain silent!" he shouted.

"Let them be," said the prince. "Today is the Lord's day. We will relax some of the restrictions on them, and they will serve better as a result."

"Yes, My Lord," answered the boatswain doubtfully, but he did furl his lash.

"There is Don Requesens frowning at me," said John looking back when he had reached the bow. "I know practice is to try to think of the prisoners as only a means of propulsion. I can't do that. Most of them are Catholic, even the criminals. Some of them are volunteers. And I am reminded of our own people, captured, and worked to death in the galleys of the Turks and Algerians."

"It is unfortunate that we need them," answered Marlo. "In the army, we forget about misery such as this. Except those of us who have reason to remember."

"Not our captains. They forget about and ignore the hell that exists in their ships. Though how they can do that with the stench is beyond me."

"The Knights of Malta are bothered, and they do something about it. Whenever they reach an anchorage, they wash the galley prisoners and even flood the hold to flush out the filth."

"That might be something to try. I don't know if I can get my captains to do that. After all, the galley has been used for thousands of years, and they won't see the reason to change a system that has worked well all this time."

"When do you expect to reach Santa Pola?" asked Marlo presently.

"Tomorrow morning. We will sail at this leisurely rate today and tonight. Captain Bazon tells me that we will approach the island from the east."

"What are the chances of finding Algerians there?"

"Not great," John shrugged. "According to Requesens, they don't have a permanent base there. It is just a staging ground, and the trading season is only just beginning. However, we might just get lucky," he added hopefully.

~~~

"My Lord, Santa Pola has been sighted," Captain Bazan said.

"Don Requesens," said John, "please keep me advised of the best way of doing things. I would like to form the fleet into a posture most
~~~

suited to trap any pirates who might be sheltering on the island. It seems to me, that if the fleet split into three groups, the two flanks approaching from the north and south, with the third group in the center, we could cover the escape routes."

"Very likely, My Lord. However, that might be difficult, separating the fleet into independent groups when they are not yet practiced in working together."

"Is there a way to set the fleet up so that order could still be given if need be?"

"Yes, if we form a crescent, with the horns pointing toward the island. If we see any activity on a particular side of the island, we can send ten ships from that horn ahead."

"Good," said John. "Signal our intention for that formation, and that Cordona and Andrade are each to coordinate the wings. I would like them to command ten ships each. The remaining ships will be formed in the center with the *Capitana*."

"At once, My Lord." Requesens hurried off to give the orders. "Stay here and learn with me," said John to Marlo.

A gun fired and the signal flags were hoisted. The oars of the *Capitana* moved backward, slowing the ship. On both sides, the ships lined up with the flagship, raising flags to signal acceptance to the Commander's orders. When the ships had formed a line, Cordona and Andrade signaled their ships to move ahead, and the line of ships, over two hundred feet long, curved inward on both ends toward the island. When the crescent was formed, another gun was fired from the *Capitana* and the entire formation moved toward the island.

On all the ships, soldiers lined the sides, standing at attention, the matches of their muskets smoldering. Don John left the stern and inspected the soldiers and the prisoners. Moving toward the bow, he looked at the formation. "Don Requesens, signal Cordona to straighten his formation," he called. He left the bow and headed back to the stern.

Santa Pola was no longer a dark smudge in the horizon. Marlo could make out the waves on the shore and the green of vegetation. There was no sign of any ships.

"Don Requesens, I don't see any sign of pirates here," said John.

"No, My Lord. Though there could be some on the far side. Then again, they might not be here."

"Would it be feasible to send Cordona and Andrade to circle the island?" asked the prince.

"It would," said Requesens. "However, the movement of the ships may not be as neat as one would desire."

"They need the practice, anyway," said John. "Let's do it."

"Very well, My Lord." In a minute, the bow

gun spoke again and another set of signals was hoisted. "The order has been given, My Lord," said Requesens when he returned. "They just await your signal to break off."

The island was drawing closer. When they were about a thousand yards from the western point Don John ordered the *Capitana* to hold its position and for the other ships to move on. The gun fired yet again, and the two wings of the crescent broke free and moved alongside the island.

"I don't know what to hope for more," said John to Marlo, "that we find some Algerians, or, considering we have an untrained fleet, that we find nothing."

"At this point, I would prefer nothing, My Lord," answered Requesens.

The two groups rounded the west side of the island, passed each other and headed back toward the *Capitana*. "They signal that there is nothing, My Lord," announced Captain Bazan.

When the ships joined the flagship, Cordona shouted to John. "No ships, Your Excellency. But there are a few structures that are unoccupied near the southern anchorage. It seems that the Algerian pirates still use this island."

"My Lord, those structures might make good targets for a firing exercise," suggested Requesens.

The fleet formed a line and moved south. Then, led by the *Capitana*, the ships in single file circled north and headed toward the anchorage and the abandoned buildings on the shore. When they were two hundred yards from the shore, all three guns fired. The *Capitana* jerked, and a cloud of smoke rolled back toward them.

"Hard to the starboard!" Bazan shouted. The starboard oars moved backward in the water, while the port oars continued their normal movement. The *Capitana* spun and headed down alongside the western side of the line of ships. The guns of the next ship fired, and it, too spun and followed in the *Capitana's* wake.

Marlo watched as each ship fired and moved out of the way. About half the shots struck, sending wood, stone and dust into the air. After the last ship had fired, only small portions of the walls remained.

"This was a good demonstration," said John at Marlo's elbow. "The ships seemed to be well handled, even with the new men."

"Most of the new men just stood along the sides with weapons at the ready, My Lord," said Requesens from behind them. "However, I agree with your assessment. The ships were handled well."

"Is this all?" asked Marlo. "It was over rather quickly."

"We should practice the forming of a line of battle from our normal sailing formation, as well as the rapid change of direction of that line of battle," answered Requesens.

"I suppose that means I should practice that," smiled John. "Let us resume our sailing formation on a southerly heading, and from there conduct the rest of the maneuvers. That way we can still maintain a heading for Cartagena."

"Very good, My Lord." Requesens moved ahead to speak to the signal man.

"This, Marlo," said John, "I fear, is going to be anti-climactic after the excitement we just had." Don John turned toward Don Requesens. "Don Requesens, I would like to make sure the prisoners are given a brief rest and water before we resume."

Requesens looked surprised. "Your Excellency, we have protocols for keeping them watered and changing out those who are so exhausted; besides, you let them rest yesterday."

"Nevertheless, I want them rested. I have watched them ever since we have begun this mission. They have little comfort. I don't want to tempt God's anger by adding more misery to what they already suffer. They will have a brief rest and sufficient water. Make sure that happens on the other ships as well."

Chapter 15

June 1568

"The exercises went remarkably well, I thought," said John. He refilled his glass and offered the wine to Requesens.

"The precision of ship movement needs some improvement. However, I think the exercise was good." Requesens wiped his mouth and sat back in his seat. He put his napkin down next to his plate. "If you will excuse me, My Lord?"

"Yes, thank you," said John. Requesens stood and left the cabin. Don John sighed. "He is a good at fleet command, but he can be overly critical, at times."

"I think the maneuvers were well handled," said Marlo. "That was the first time I have seen a large fleet put through its paces."

"You are not saying that just to please me,

are you?"

"Not by any means. I was impressed at how the fleet was able to move as if it was one unit. The gunnery exercise was impressive. And guns I know."

John grinned. "The noise, the smoke, the flying rubble. One ship after another. Yes, that was exciting. I hope that this isn't the only time we get to use the guns. We need some action against a real enemy."

There was a knock on the door, and Juan de Quiroga looked into the cabin. "Your Excellency," he said, "there is a ship heading toward us."

"What kind?" John stood.

"She seems Spanish, and they are pulling hard at the oars."

"I will be right there," said John buckled his sword belt. "Let's go see what she wants."

On deck, Marlo and Don John stood in the stern and watched the ship draw closer to them, its oars dipping in and out of the water rapidly. As the galley drew closer, the oars were held suspended over the water. Just as the galley drew abreast of the *Capitana*, its sail was furled, and the galley slaves dropped the oar blades into the water, pulling backward to slow the ship to match the speed of the *Capitana*.

"What ship?" called Bazan.

"The *Francesca*, out of Santa Pola." came the reply. "This is Captain Guzman. Is this the fleet commanded by Don John of Austria?"

"I am Don John."

"Your Excellency, I have a message for you. If I may come aboard?"

"Come, and welcome," called John. A line was tossed to the *Capitana* and the *Francesca* was tied up alongside. Guzman climbed across the gunwales and was escorted to the deck.

"Your Excellency," said Guzman saluting Don John, "we received word that you have been sent to harass the pirates who have been disrupting our trade."

"That is correct, Captain," answered John.

"I have information that might interest you, then," said Guzman.

"Very well, let us go into my cabin. Don Requesens and Señor Gobeli, if you will join us?" Don John led the way into the cabin. He gave Guzman his seat and stood with his hands clasped behind his back. Don Requesens and Marlo stood by the door. "This must be of some importance," said John, "you were pulling hard to get to us. By the way, how did you know where we were?"

"The island of Santa Pola is just a few miles from the port of the same name. We heard your gunnery exercises and sent a ship to investigate. We arrived after you had left. That was a beautiful scene of destruction you left behind." Guzman grinned. "That should make any Algerians who come there a little nervous."

"That was the intention," said Requesens. "You said that you had an important message?"

"Let the good captain have a chance to get to his point," said John. "He only just arrived." He turned back to Guzman. "Unfortunately, only the buildings were on the island. I was hoping to encounter the pirates themselves. Destroying buildings can be exciting, but unless the Algerians are dealt with, they will just rebuild."

"It was comforting to know that His Majesty is doing something, regardless," said Guzman. "That island has almost effectively halted our shipping. The Algerians will wait there and go after ships that try to enter the harbor. We have a few war galleys, but they are not enough to guarantee safe arrival of trade ships. When they return and find their shelters are nothing but a pile of rubble, they just might hesitate. I think you have given them notice that their pirating days are over."

"I hope so, but I doubt it," said John. "As long as we are of different faiths, our shipping will continue to be harassed." He went over to cabinet where the wine was stored. "Would you like some refreshment? You must have pulled hard to get to me."

"No thank you, Your Excellency," answered Guzman. "I would like to get back to Santa Pola before nightfall." John returned to the table and sat. "We had word that you were sent to hunt and harass the Algerians, and three days ago, a ship straggled into port. It had been badly knocked about, and the prisoners were spending their time bailing water, rather than rowing."

"So you know where the pirates are?" asked Requesens.

"Not really. This galley was part of an escort for a couple of ships that came from the African coast. They were set upon shortly after they had passed the Straits of Gibraltar."

"I assume the trade ships were taken?" asked John.

"Yes, the pirates had close to fifty galleys, and they cut out the trade ships. One of the escort galleys was sunk, the other taken. The *Gloria* was furthest north. She was hit several times by cannon fire, and her captain determined that he couldn't fight off fifty galleys. He had the wind to help the oars. By nightfall, the pirates had ended their chase, and he managed to limp to Santa Pola."

"Fifty pirates. Near Gibraltar," said John. "Is that usual?"

"If you had seen the state of the *Gloria*, you wouldn't doubt the captain's story," objected Guzman.

"No, I don't doubt the story," said John. "It is the size of the fleet that is unusual. The Algerians tend to work in small groups. Fifty ships sounds like a war fleet."

"It is a war fleet," said Guzman "and it wasn't an Algerian fleet. These were galleys of the Turkish navy. Ochiali commands them."

"Ochiali?" asked John.

"He is a renegade Christian," said Requesens, "and probably the most brutal of Selim's captains, and has developed a reputation exceeding that of the Algerians. They only take the ships and turn the captives into galley salves. Ochiali just slaughters everybody. He usually operates in the eastern Mediterranean. I have never heard of him in the west."

"With a fleet of fifty ships, he could effectively trap and destroy every ship that attempts to pass through the Straits," said John. "The American and African trade will be shut down."

"And the Indian trade, as well, Your Excellency," added Guzman. "Once the African ships were safely delivered to port, the escort was supposed to head back into the Atlantic and meet the East India ships. They are due any week now."

"I think, Don Requesens, we will just stop at Cartagena long enough to see if the soldiers from Murcia have arrived. I will write to His Majesty and set out for Gibraltar." He stood. "Captain Guzman, I am grateful for that information, and if you find out anything else, send the news to Cartagena. It will be forwarded to me from there."

Captain Guzman stood and bowed, "I wish you success in your hunt. We in Santa Pola will pray for you."

"Please, do." John's face was stern. "There is more at stake than just our shipping, and your news confirms it."

Outside, the sun was close to setting. Captain Guzman went back to the *Francesca* and, turning, she began to head back to Santa Pola. The wind was against her so she only used her oars. Don John stood at the stern rail and watched her depart.

"Señor Gobeli," he said, "it seems that the Holy Father's assessment of the crisis was accurate. I believed you before, but to have it confirmed..." the prince broke off.

Marlo didn't respond. The storm threatening Europe was beginning to batter against a divided Christendom. The presence of a Turkish fleet in the western Mediterranean could only mean one thing: Spain was about to be inundated.

"We need to find him, Marlo." John broke into Marlo's thoughts. "We need to find him fast. And we are running out of time."

~~~

The coast of Spain slipped past them. They were moving with the wind blowing from the southwest. Between the sails and the oars, the fleet moved swiftly toward Granada under blue
~~~

skies and clear nights. Cartagena was three days behind them, and they were drawing close to Almeria.

Their stop at Cartagena had been short. Close to a hundred soldiers from Murcia had been waiting for them, but when spread out over the fleet, the fighting force of each ship had only been increased by three. At Almeria, Don John hoped to find more soldiers, and even send to Granada for a detachment to be sent to Malaga.

In Cartagena, Marlo had found a letter from Father Veraccio requesting that Marlo remain with Don John and report on the effectiveness of the Spanish navy and the conduct of Don John. The letter also verified the news of Captain Guzman. Ochiali had recently been appointed the Pasha of Algiers and was indeed at sea with a hundred Turkish ships.

When he had informed Don John, the Captain of the Sea's only response was to express concern about the disparity of forces. He was confident that the superior weaponry and firepower of the Spanish fleet would reduce the advantage of Ochiali's superior numbers. He was concerned, however, that any victory over Ochiali would be at the cost of a large number of his ships.

Along with Don Requesens, Don John's first goal was to find Ochiali. Requesens was of the opinion that the pirate had divided his fleet, and if that was the case, the Spanish fleet could attack the Turkish fleet with close to equal numbers. But Ochiali had to be found first.

~~~

At the evening of their third day out of Cartagena, the fleet put into Almeria. Don John and Requesens went at once to the governor and requested reinforcements. They returned in the morning with news that there would be fifty more men to be added to the fleet. Since it was Sunday morning, the soldiers would not arrive until the afternoon.

"We still need more men, My Lord," said Requesens, as he, John, and Marlo were heading back into the city to attend mass. "Fifty soldiers are negligible in a fleet this size."

"I am quite in agreement," said John. "I wonder if we could get more from Granada itself?"

"That comes with a risk, My Lord," said Marlo. "The reduction of the size of the garrison in Granada could put the citizens in real danger if the Moriscos do rise."

"The soldiers could be returned after the sailing season ends in September," said Requesens. "If the Moriscos are of a mind to rebel, as unlikely as that is, they won't without help from Selim. The soldiers would be back before such help can arrive."

"How far is Granada from here?" asked John.
~~~

"Almost eighty miles, My Lord," said Requesens. They had reached the church. John stopped and considered.

"Señor Gobeli, would you be willing to ride as fast as possible to Granada?"

"Yes, My Lord."

"Well, let me think on it. I will let you know after mass."

~~~

When mass was over, they left the church. Outside, John turned to Marlo. "Get yourself a horse and everything you need. Meet me at the governor's house. I will have an official request written up for you to hand to the Alcayde of the garrison at Granada."

"At once," said Marlo. He went down to the ships and asked to be rowed to the *Capitana*. He boarded the flagship and went to Don John's cabin. His secretary, Juan de Quiroga, was inside.

"Juan, I need to get my sword and cloak. Don John is sending me to Granada with a request for more soldiers. And could I have ten *escudos*? I need to get a horse immediately, and I may have to buy it."

Juan went to the chest where the fleet funds were kept, counted out ten *escudos* and gave it to Marlo. "If you would just sign here," said Juan. Marlo signed his name on the ledger. "I hope you have a safe journey," said Juan as
~~~

Marlo was leaving.

"Safe, and fast. I don't know where I will meet up with the fleet again."

"Either here or Malaga, I would assume. *Vaya con Dios*." said Juan.

"*Vaya con Dios*," answered Marlo, and he hurried out of the cabin.

Marlo climbed back into the waiting boat and was rowed back to the quay. Leaping out of the boat, he hurried into the city and found a stable where he was able to purchase a horse. He led the horse to the governor's house. Don John and Requesens were outside waiting for him.

"Señor Gobeli," said John handing him a sealed letter, "give this to Inigo Lopez de Mendoza, the Marquis of Mondejar and the Captain-General of Granada. This is a request for at least two hundred men. When you receive his answer, ride as quickly as you can to Malaga. That also is about eighty miles from Granada. We should be there with the fleet."

"I assume I wait if nobody is there?" asked Marlo.

"Yes, and let me know how long it will take for the Captain-General to have the men at Malaga."

"Well," said Marlo getting on his horse, "if all goes well, I will be in Malaga in a week." He spurred his horse and rode away.

Four days after setting out from Almeria, the *Capitana* and the rest of the fleet put in at Malaga. Since the day was drawing to a close, Don John elected to remain on board until the following morning. After he ate his supper, he stayed in his cabin and continued his report to the king. King Philip had requested detailed and regular reports, and since he was the king, a request was to be understood as a polite way of phrasing a direct command.

After writing for an hour, he was interrupted by a knock at his door.

"Come in," he called.

"My Lord, there is a boat approaching." John put down his quill as Juan entered his cabin. Don John stood and followed his secretary out of the cabin.

He joined Requesens on deck as Captain Bazan greeted a stocky man who had just climbed aboard. "Do you know who he is?" he asked his lieutenant.

"No, but I assume we will find out," answered Requesens dryly.

"You are blessed with the gift of the obvious," smiled John.

"Your Excellency, allow me to present Don Fillipe. He commands His Majesty's garrison here in Malaga," said Captain Bazan. Don Fillipe bowed.

"Welcome aboard, Don Fillipe," said John.

"This is Don Luis Requesens, my lieutenant."

"I am pleased to make your acquaintance, Your Excellency," said Fillipe. "We received your request for more soldiers a few days ago. I have the honor of giving you eighty men."

"That is good news, indeed," said John. "Why don't you come below and take some refreshment."

"Wine for the guest, if you please," said John to Juan when they had entered the cabin. "How is the trading situation in Malaga?" he asked Fillipe.

"Not that good. Most of the ships are afraid to leave port. About a week ago, a small village about twenty miles south of here was raided by Turks dressed as Algerians. They burnt every house, killed all the elderly, and took everyone else captive."

Don John put down his wine and stood. He went over to the porthole and looked out across the harbor. "How many?" he asked quietly.

"About fifty dead," answered Fillipe.

"And captured?"

"About a hundred. Every boy and young maiden. And anyone else who could pull an oar."

"Did you find out how many ships or who the captain was?" asked Requesens.

"No. Those who escaped could only say that there were a lot. Of one thing they were certain: these were not Algerians."

"Ochiali," said Don John harshly. He was oppressed with the thought that if he had come in this direction instead of toward Denia, this raid would not have happened. Guilt gave way to a smoldering rage. He returned back to the table, his eyes hard. "Don Fillipe, we will take those men now. Sometime soon, there may be more soldiers arriving from Granada. If you would be so kind as to put them up until we return. I was planning to wait for them, but I am going to hunt down that monster."

"My Lord," said Don Requesens after Don Fillipe had left, "can I offer some advice?" They were back in Don John's cabin. Don John was looking at the charts and trying to figure how far Ochiali could have sailed in a week.

"Please, do," said John without looking up.

"My Lord, I would caution you. Don't let your anguish over the sufferings of Ochiali's victims prompt you to hasty action. This sort of thing happened a couple of years ago here in Malaga. It is part of the danger of living on the coast."

"Has years of active service made you numb?" asked John in surprise. "Just because something terrible happens frequently doesn't make the suffering any less for those who have to undergo it. Do you think that those poor victims stood philosophically by while their friends and relatives were slaughtered? Do you think they just shrugged their shoulders as they were made captive thinking that this was just part of life?" John's voice grew harsh and loud. "No! A thousand times, no! Don Requesens, they are Spanish. They are Christians. They had hopes and joys. They loved and lived. And now those still alive are living through hell! The able bodied pulling oars, and no tenderhearted captain to give them rest and water. The girls will spend the rest of their young adulthood being violated. And imagine the terror that is twisting some poor father as he is chained to an oar while his daughter is carried away before his very eyes."

Don John went toward the window. He rested his hands against the bulkhead. "No, Don Requesens," he continued in a low voice, "I will use everything in my power to find those barbarians, and when I do, I will use all the knowledge and expertise of my officers to destroy them." He turned around and stared at Requesens. "As long as I am Captain of the Sea, I will not rest until our waters are rid of that monster."

Don Requesens stared at his commander. In the few weeks that he had known him, he had never seen Don John angry. He opened his mouth to remonstrate and then closed it.

"Don Requesens, I am sorry," said Don John. "That was uncalled for. And no, I don't think you are unmindful of the sufferings of our countrymen. It's just...those poor people." John sighed and sat down at his writing table. "Being angry will not drive this menace from these waters. Tell me, what should we do?"

"Your Excellency," said Requesens, "I am sure that no apology is needed. You are correct regarding the suffering of Ochiali's victims; however, I have learned that being philosophical about it enables me to function. There is so much misery inflicted by evil men, and if I allowed myself to feel the full weight of it every time, I would go mad."

"Then it is a good thing you are here to keep me under control," said John with a small smile. "And speaking of being controlled, what controlled and calculated measures shall we take?"

"Well, I tend to think that Ochiali will make for the East Indian fleet. It is probably very likely that he is waiting outside the Strait of Gibraltar. I would recommend that we head for Gibraltar, and if they have not seen the Turkish fleet, send a ship over to Cueta and see if they have."

"And if Ochiali's whereabouts are unknown?"

"The head out into the Atlantic and escort the Indian fleet to San Lucar. Afterwards we can return to the Mediterranean if we have no news."

"Very well, let us go to Gibraltar. However, Señor Gobeli has at least three or four days before he arrives here. I would like a couple of fast ships to bring him to Gibraltar."

"The *Reya* is the fastest we have. I will leave her and another ship here. And My Lord," Don Requesens stood and broke his usual gravity with a feral grin, "Let's go find that Son of Belial and send him back to the hell from which he was spawned."

Chapter 16

June 1568

Marlo was startled awake by the sound of horses. Rolling onto his side he saw four men, mere silhouettes in the dim moonlight, riding down the road toward him, and he could tell they were wearing turbans. *Moriscos! They had better not find me*, he thought. Quietly, he gathered his cloak and sword and crawled into the brush.

He was in the hills southeast of Granada, and still a day's journey from the city itself. The two days of travel had been without incident, and he had found a place to sleep the previous night. He had ridden hard after that and was nowhere near anyplace to stay when night fell. So he rode a little way off the road and tethered his horse near a small stream that flowed between two hills. Now he was preparing to flee.

The riders drew closer, and his horse whickered. Realizing that the Moriscos would probably find his horse, Marlo began to work his way upstream. Turning back, he saw the four riders stop. One of them dismounted and walked quietly toward Marlo's horse. The rider had only moved twenty paces off the road before he stopped and motioned to the other three. They dismounted and draped their reins over some branches and joined the first.

Marlo went on his hands and knees and slowly began to crawl around to the north of them. Carefully feeling for sticks that might break under his weight as he moved, he continued to watch the four men.

One of them saddled Marlo's horse while the other three searched the area where Marlo had been sleeping. After searching for a little longer, they gave up, not being able to track Marlo in the night.

By this time, Marlo had only moved about thirty paces toward the road. He stopped moving. Two of the men, one of them leading his horse, had gone upstream, and now they were heading back to the road. Instead of going back downstream, they made for the road by the shortest way. Their path would lead them right past Marlo.

Marlo quietly put down his cloak, and prepared to leap. The two men came closer. Then they were right next to him. Marlo leapt out from behind a bush and slammed a fist into the face of the nearest man. He dropped. The other man gave a shout of surprise and raised his hands. Marlo lashed out with his foot and kicked the man in the side of his knee. The man leapt back and then jumped on Marlo, shouting something in Arabic.

As Marlo fell backward, he tucked his head forward and drove both of his knees up. His right caught his opponent in the stomach. Marlo hit the ground and rolled backward over his shoulders. Kicking out his legs and shoving with his hands, Marlo threw the man off. He rolled to the side and drove his foot against the man's temple. The turban softened the impact, but it was enough to stun him. Marlo grabbed his sword, leapt up, and threw his foot into the stirrup of his horse. He swung himself into the saddle, kicked the horse and shouted.

The other two men had reached their horses. One was already mounted, but the other started toward Marlo when he heard the sound of the fighting. He tried to grab at Marlo as the horse moved past. Marlo kicked out with his left foot and drove the man off. Reaching the road, he clapped his heels against the horse's flanks and galloped back toward Almeria, with a turbaned rider in pursuit.

Marlo bent low over his horse's neck and urged him onward. He remembered that he had ridden through a small village about five miles before he had stopped for the night. Looking back over his shoulder, he saw the other rider about five horse lengths behind. He urged his horse again and galloped recklessly through the night.

~~~

It was still dark when Marlo rode into the village. His pursuer had given up the chase after a few minutes, but Marlo still kept checking the road behind him. Riding up to the little village church, he dismounted and brought his horse around to the back. He took off the saddle and tied the reins to a fencepost. Inside, he lay down in a corner and went to sleep.

He woke to someone shaking him. When he opened his eyes, he saw a priest leaning over him. "What are you doing here?" he asked. His voice was stern. "This is not an inn."

"I was set upon by four Moriscos," answered Marlo. "I came here to escape because the houses were all dark."

"Is that your horse in the back?" asked the priest. Marlo could not tell if the priest was satisfied with his explanation.

"Yes, Father. I can go move it."

"I don't know if your story is true or not," said the priest. "There are too many renegades coming and going. I would be satisfied if you just took your horse and left."

"Could I get some water first?" asked Marlo.
~~~

"There is water in the village well. You can get water there."

Marlo genuflected and left the church. The priest followed him to make sure he got his horse. Marlo saddled the animal and led it back to the street. When he reached the front of the church he turned to the priest. "You mentioned renegades earlier, Father. Have you been having problems with them?"

"The last few months have been one continuous problem," answered the priest. "From Moriscos preaching rebellion, to vagrants like you. Travelers have been waylaid on the roads, and I have been told that those who openly proclaim Islam are left alone. If you are an honest traveler, I would recommend that you find lodging in normal fashion."

"I will remember that, Father," said Marlo. "And I apologize for causing you any worry." He walked away leaving the priest standing on the steps of the church. He found the well and drew water for the horse. Then he refilled his water skin and ate some food. After he rode out of town, he continued on his way. He kept careful watch as he rode, but he saw nothing of the four men who had woke him the previous night.

~~~

The streets of Granada were crowded when he rode into the city that evening. He was sur-
~~~

prised at the number of men who were wearing the Moorish turban. He had seen a few men wearing their traditional garb last year, but now he saw many more people openly dressed in Moorish attire and speaking in Arabic. It was obvious that conditions had deteriorated since his last visit, and he wondered about the Montoyas. In spite of the late hour, he decided put off his errand to the Captain-General and visit Señor Montoya and Maria.

Riding up to Señor Montoya's shop, he dismounted and rang the bell. He grinned in anticipation of Maria's reaction to his unannounced presence and half hoped that she would be the one to open the door. She wasn't. Instead, a gray-haired man in plain attire greeted him. It was Carlos.

"Can I help you?" he asked.

"I think you can, Carlos" said Marlo. "I visited Señor Montoya and his daughter last summer, and I was invited to call on them if I ever passed through Granada. Would they be available?"

"Señor Gobeli! Of course. Come in."

"Thank you, Carlos," said Marlo, following the servant through the door. He stood off to the side of the hall as Carlos closed the door. "Tell me, how are Señor Montoya and Maria?"

"They are well, Señor," answered Carlos. "Wait here, and I will announce you." Marlo watched as Carlos walked down the hall and knock on Montoya's study. The door opened and Marlo heard the low murmur of voices.

"Marlo!" called Montoya as he stepped out of his study and hurried over. "I was never so pleased in my life! Come in, come in. Carlos, can you care for Señor Gobeli's horse?"

"Si, Señor." Carlos took the reins from Marlo and led the horse around the side of the house.

"Let us go into my office," said Montoya leading Marlo into the house. "Did you just arrive?"

"Yes, I just got here," answered Marlo. "I left Almeria three days ago, and I will probably be leaving tomorrow."

"I hope you didn't ride out of your way," said Montoya. He opened his office door and motioned for Marlo to enter. "Come, sit down."

"No, I was sent to Granada with a message for the Captain-General. Once I deliver it, I will have to reach Malaga as soon as I can." Marlo sat and stretched out his legs.

"Since you just arrived, I assume you haven't found a place to stay?"

"No, not yet. I thought I would stop by here first."

"I'm glad you did, Marlo, and I insist that you spend the night here. The last I knew was that you were heading off to Cartagena. What brings you back?" said Montoya.

"After Cartagena, I traveled to Madrid as a bodyguard for an envoy from the Holy Father to propose the formation of an alliance against the Ottoman Empire."

"How did that go?"

"Not as well as I had hoped. His Majesty seems overly cautious, but Father Andrea, the envoy, did return to Rome with a minister from the king to discuss the matter with the Holy Father," answered Marlo.

"And you? What are you doing now?"

"I am sailing with Don John of Austria who is in command of thirty-three ships. He is trying the Algerians back to their harbors. I should think that your shipping will be safer this summer."

"I hope so," said Montoya. "Have you eaten yet?" he asked.

"Not yet," said Marlo.

Montoya stood and rang a bell. Carlos opened the office door.

"Carlos, could you bring some supper for Señor Gobeli? He hasn't eaten yet."

"Right away, Señor," said Carlos

"And tell Maria that I need to see her, but don't tell her about Señor Gobeli." Montoya winked at Marlo. "We will just let her be surprised."

"Of course, Señor," said Carlos shaking his head.

"How is your business faring with the unrest?" asked Marlo after Carlos left.

"The unrest, as you call it, has not been a

problem. I have had no difficulties from any malcontents, and I doubt if things are as bad as you thought last year."

"My impression in riding through this region was that they were worse," said Marlo. "That is one of the reasons I stopped by. I wanted to see if you and your daughter were safe."

"I appreciate that, but you needn't have worried," said Montoya. There was a quiet tap on the door. "Come in," called Montoya.

Marlo stood as the door opened. Maria entered and stopped. She gasped and her face flushed. "Good evening, Señorita," said Marlo with a smile. "I hope my presence is not unwelcome."

"My dear," said Montoya, "Señor Gobeli is on an errand for Don John of Austria. He is with the fleet that is hunting the pirates."

Maria smiled courteously. "I hope you are successful in that, Señor Gobeli, because you are quite successful at making unannounced visits."

"I am sorry, Señorita," said Marlo bowing slightly.

"My dear," said Montoya, taking Maria's hand, "Señor Gobeli stopped here first, even before carrying out his commission from Don John, because he wanted to see if we were safe, though he need not have worried. He even came here before finding a place to stay." Maria looked at Marlo. The mischievous smile that she was used to seeing was gone. In its place was a serious concern that surprised her. His clothes were stained from travel, and the sleeve of his jacket was ripped. He looked exhausted.

"I am sorry, too," said Maria. She had been surprised at Marlo's presence, and was surprised again at the extent of his concern. "You do look worn out. Sit down, and let me get you something to drink."

"Carlos is taking care of that," said Montoya.

When Carlos entered he was carrying a tray with meat, fruit, and bread. He set the tray on Montoya's desk and poured wine for Marlo. "Carlos," said Montoya, "Señor Gobeli will be staying here tonight in the guest room. Can you see that it is ready?"

"Si, Señor." Carlos bowed and left the room.

"Señor Gobeli, why are you with the Spanish fleet?" asked Maria. "I thought you were working for the Holy Father."

"I still am," said Marlo. "Rome wants me to report not only on the conditions here in Spain but also on the actions taken by the king against the Algerians." He picked up a piece of bread and turned to Montoya. "Speaking of which, I do not share your optimism about the peaceful intentions of the Moriscos. Everything that I have seen in this region in the last few days shows that the unrest is becoming public. I fought with four men wearing Moorish garb last night."

"Did they hurt you?" asked Maria.

"No, thank God," said Marlo, "they were hunting for me and were spread out. I managed to outride the only one left in any condition to ride. I spent the rest of the night trying to sleep on the floor of a church."

"Papa, don't you think that these Moriscos might just mean us harm?" asked Maria. "Attacking travelers does not seem like they are peaceful."

"There may be a few who are taking advantage of the situation," said Montoya. "However, that doesn't mean that the majority of them are seditious. There have always been bandits."

"Señor Montoya." Marlo put down his food and looked at the merchant. "Selim has made his most vicious admiral the Pasha of Algiers. Ochiali is doing everything he can to ruin Spain. It is not by chance that Ochiali is the new Pasha. Right now, he has a large fleet in the Mediterranean, hunting for Spanish trade ships. We have already heard of one fleet that was demolished. No, the threat to Spain is not just a minor concern. Selim is trying to keep the king occupied by sea, and there is some evidence that he has promised to help an uprising here. The public display of Moorish attire in the streets of Granada only shows that the Moriscos are confident that they will not be punished for breaking the king's laws. There has to be real reason for that confidence."

"That reason may just be that nothing has been done to them," said Montoya. "The Moriscos I have spoken to all claim that they wish us well, and are very polite when they do business with us. No, I think that your concern doesn't reflect the situation. I do appreciate your thoughtfulness, however."

Marlo changed the subject. Señor Montoya seemed convinced in his assessment, and Marlo felt too exhausted to debate him on that point. He finished his meal and talked about his winter in Madrid and his experiences with the Spanish fleet.

"You are probably in need of rest," said Montoya after Marlo had finished his meal. "Let me show you to your room."

Marlo stood gratefully and, after saying goodnight to Maria, he followed Montoya out of the room and down the hall. "This is it," said Montoya, "if you need anything, just ring that bell. I hope you will have time to visit a little tomorrow before you leave."

"A little," said Marlo, "but I do need to reach Malaga as quickly as I can. The fleet is waiting there for me."

"Well, get your rest, then," said Montoya.

Marlo thoughtfully watched Montoya move

down the hall. He hoped that he could be able to persuade the merchant that he needed to leave Granada soon. And if he wouldn't leave, he should at least send Maria away. He went into the room and closed the door.

He had only just sat down to take off his boots when there was a gentle tapping on the door. He stood and opened it. Maria was standing outside wearing a shawl.

"Señor Gobeli?" she said. "Can I talk to you outside?"

"Of course," said Marlo. He stepped out of the room, closed the door, and followed her down the hall and out of the house. Maria led him to the rear of the house and into the small garden courtyard surrounded by a delicate colonnade with Moorish arches. Maria walked to one of the benches and sat. Marlo stood to the side and looked down at her. Her features were shadowed in the gathering dark.

"Señor Gobeli," she said looking at him, "I am grateful for your concern for our safety, but there is a reason why my father thinks that there is no risk for us to remain." She looked away. "Shortly before you left last year, a man, one of the Moriscos in the mountains, came here. You were out of the house at the time. He bought all of my father's wool. This man assured my father that the Moriscos only went to the hills to be able to practice their culture and lifestyle. He said that they don't wish us ill, and have no intention of rebelling."

"I remember you father telling me about him," said Marlo quietly. "Do you believe those assurances?"

"I don't know," said Maria, "but my father does. I am uncomfortable whenever that man speaks to me. I wonder at times what he is up to."

"You make it sound as if you have encountered him more than once."

"The first time was on the street and he gave me too much praise. He has come here often, to buy food and wool. Each time he asks to see me, and each time he makes me uncomfortable. My father doesn't see it, and he doesn't even get suspicious at the amount of grain this man buys."

"I assume this Morisco has a name?" asked Marlo. "I wonder if he is one of the renegades I met in Juviles."

"He calls himself Farax."

"No, I didn't encounter anyone of that name."

"Marlo, what is going to happen?" Maria looked up at him, her face reflecting the moonlight. "It is not just me, but some of my friends have also had unpleasant encounters with Moriscos. I dare not even leave the house except with my father. Why can't he just see what is going on?"

"I don't know," said Marlo. "Have you told

him about Farax?"

"No. I am afraid he would just consider it my imagination and dismiss it."

"I think you should. And tell him about your friends, too. You say that Farax has been buying a lot of grain?"

"Far more than he would need for himself. And a lot of wool, as well. He has become our most reliable customer."

"That might be it," said Marlo. "Your father doesn't have a financial motive for leaving, and since this is also his home, he doesn't want to go someplace else. I think that if his concern for you gets great enough, he will leave."

"And if he stays here?" asked Maria. "What will happen to us?"

Marlo sighed. "Señorita, I would like to comfort you and say that all you would need to do is remain indoors and you will have nothing to fear. But, I can't. When I was here two years ago, I had to go into the mountains to find people openly practicing Islam. Now, I see Moorish attire in the streets. I hear Arabic being used in public. This morning, a priest told me that travelers are often waylaid, and only those who proclaim their attachment to Islam are allowed to pass by unmolested. You need to explain your distrust of Farax to your father."

Maria wrapped her shawl tighter around her shoulders and hugged herself. She was almost regretful that Marlo was so candid. If anything, her anxiety had increased. "How much longer do we have?" she whispered.

"I don't know, but I will do what I can to encourage your father to leave here. I will come back when I am no longer needed with the fleet, probably sometime in winter. When we return to Madrid in September, I will see if Don John can find out anything from the king, and I can send that to your father."

"Oh, thank you," said Maria standing. Marlo's promise of help eased her fear a little. "I feel so alone. You won't forget?"

"How could I?" Marlo smiled. "I have been worried about you ever since we parted company. All winter, when His Majesty seemed to be doing nothing, I was concerned that the Moriscos would start trouble. Keep your courage up. I promise that I will return."

Chapter 17

June 1568

The morning after his visit with Maria and her father, Marlo delivered his message to the Captain-General of Granada and was told that no soldiers were available. Disgusted, Marlo rode hard to Malaga to deliver the news to Don John. When he arrived, Don John was no longer there.

However, the *Reya* was still in the harbor and Marlo had himself rowed out to her. Captain Morales informed him that Don John had received news of Ochiali being seen near Gibraltar a week ago, had gone to try to find him, and that Marlo and the *Reya* were to proceed to Gibraltar as soon as possible. Marlo retuned to shore and sold his horse. In the evening, the *Reya* set sail for Gibraltar.

The run to Gibraltar was uneventful, and

when they arrived there they found the fleet five days gone. Captain Morales was given written orders from Don John to proceed immediately to Puerto Santa Maria and wait for the fleet's return. Leaving Gibraltar that day, the *Reya* had a difficult passage due to the strong current in the Strait. Reaching the Atlantic, the galley headed north. He and Morales arrived at Puerto Santa Maria to find that there was no news of the fleet and had no idea how long they would have to wait. Marlo wondered what Don John was doing.

The Captain of the garrison at the Castle of Santa Maria gave him a place to stay, and the following morning, Marlo walked along the harbor, speaking to the captains who were ashore. None of them knew where the fleet was. Most of them, in fact, had no idea that Spain had a galley fleet of that size on patrol. After a fruitless morning, he returned to the castle and asked for the use of its library. He could at least read while waiting. He would enjoy the chance to rest.

~~~

"Señor, the fleet has been sighted." Marlo looked up from his book and saw Captain Morales.

"How long before they are anchored?" asked Marlo.

"About thirty minutes. I don't know about
~~~

you, but I am glad that we didn't have to wait more than a day."

Marlo closed his book and returned it to its place on the shelf. "Let's go meet them."

Captain Morales and Marlo left the library and made their way out of the great castle that overlooked Puerto Santa Maria. They walked through the narrow streets and down to the harbor. When they arrived, the fleet was entering the harbor. "Wait here," said Captain Morales. "I will get someone to take us out to the *Capitana*."

The guns of the castle spoke in salute. From the bows of the *Capitana*, Marlo saw a puff of smoke, followed a few seconds later by the sound of the flagship's answering salute. He adjusted his sword and waited for Captain Morales.

Marlo heard Captain Morales calling: "I have a boat!"

He walked quickly to where the captain was waiting. "Over there," the captain indicated. They went over the waiting boat and climbed in.

"All right, Señores," said the boatman. He pushed the boat away from the quay. With a little grunt, he began rowing to where the *Capitana* was dropping its anchor.

The little boat worked its way through the galleys. Marlo heard his name called, and saw Captain Cordona waving. "I see you have returned to us," he called.

"Until I am sent away again," Marlo called back. He was gratified by Cordona's greeting. It did feel as if he was returning to where he belonged. While his work for Father Veraccio was rewarding, he had missed the camaraderie of the Swiss Guard. It was with a feeling of satisfaction that he climbed onto the *Capitana*.

"Señor Gobeli." John was waiting on deck. He clasped Marlo's hand. "I hope your travels were as uneventful as mine."

"Not completely uneventful, My Lord," said Marlo bowing. "Yet not as successful as you would like."

"Come into my cabin. You can tell me the bad news there." John led Marlo and Requesens below. "How did you make out with the Captain-General?" he asked after they sat down.

"Not that well, My Lord," answered Marlo. "He was bothered by your request. Not because he felt that you were asking for something for which you had no right, but because of the situation in Granada."

"What is going on there?" asked Requesens.

"The unrest is growing. The Moriscos are getting bolder. They have taken to wearing traditional garb and speaking Arabic in direct violation of His Majesty's law. Travelers are being molested outside the cities. I even tangled with some."

"You don't seem to be injured," commented

John.

"No, I managed to escape and spend the night in a church. However, unrest is growing. Some of the Moriscos are claiming that they have no intention of violating the king's peace. I don't believe that. They are breaking the law in public and have even taken to banditry on the highways. That doesn't sound peaceful to me."

"But that might not mean that they want war," said Requesens.

"The Captain-General is not so optimistic. I delivered your request, My Lord. He hasn't refused completely, but he did ask me to convey his wish that the request be reconsidered. The garrison in Granada is down to a few hundred soldiers, and he feels that these will not be enough to quell a rebellion. If he supplies you with the number of soldiers requested, he will only be left with a handful. That might embolden the malcontents."

"That is something to consider," said John. He looked at Requesens. "What would you recommend?"

"The Moriscos may be a problem, but Ochiali needs to be dealt with at once. In order to have our ships up to full fighting compliment, we have to reduce the coastal garrisons. I would recommend that we find out exactly the number of men needed to have full fighting forces on each ship. Based on what the captains tell us, we can decide how many men we can afford to take from Granada."

"Very well," said John. "Could you see to it?"

"Yes, My Lord." Don Requesens stood and bowed.

"Something must have kept you from waiting for me at Gibraltar," said Marlo after Requesens had left.

"Did Captain Morales tell you about the village Ochiali sacked?"

"He told me about it, yes," answered Marlo. "He also indicated that Ochiali might be near Gibraltar. Was he?"

"Are you afraid that you missed out on something?" asked John with a smile.

"No. I was just hoping that you had chased him away."

"We saw nothing of him." John shrugged. "The day after we left Almeria, we saw a merchant galleon. The captain informed us that the Indian fleet had already put in at San Lucar. But he had no knowledge of pirates. It seemed as if Ochiali was not inside the Strait of Gibraltar. I wondered if he was out in the Atlantic waiting for the Indian fleet and missed them completely. Gibraltar had no news of the pirates, and neither did Cueta."

"Where did you go after that?"

"Rio del Oro. When we put in at Cadiz we were informed that the pirates were rumored to be in that area. No sign of them." John sighed. "Marlo, we have been at sea for three weeks, and there is no sign of that fleet. We hear stories, but nobody knows where Ochiali is. The king sent me out to drive them back to port, at the very least. Sailing aimlessly about will not accomplish that."

"What else can we do? It is not like we can conjure Ochiali to wait outside of Gibraltar for us to come and fight him."

"I would like some action. Something that will let him know that we are on the hunt and that we will fight."

"Well, if I think of something, you will be the first to know," said Marlo. He stood and stretched. "If you don't mind, I think I will go out on deck." John nodded and Marlo left the young commander staring at a map.

~~~

The following morning the fleet put out to sea. Don John, after reviewing his men, had sent a message back to the Captain-General insisting that two hundred men to be sent as soon as possible to Malaga instead of the four hundred originally requested.

After the fleet left harbor, Don John noticed that Marlo was in earnest conversation with Captain Bazan. They had a map and were discussing something quietly. Marlo eventually rolled up the map and made his way along the catwalk and climbed up the ladder to the upper
~~~

deck. He was smiling as he approached the captain.

"My Lord, I have something for you," he said.

"Let's go into my cabin then, Marlo," said John. He led Marlo into the cabin and removed the porthole covering to let in the midday air. "What do you have?" he asked turning around.

Marlo closed the door. Moving Don John's books to the end of the table, he rolled out the paper. It was a map of the straits of Gibraltar. He placed books and a candle stand on the corners of the map to hold it down. "Here," he said placing his finger on a point on the south side of the straits to the west of Cueta.

John bent over the map and looked at Marlo. "What am I supposed to be seeing?"

"An opportunity."

"For what?"

"For action," said Marlo with satisfaction. John looked puzzled. He bent over the map again. After a moment he straightened.

"Marlo, must you be so vague? What in heaven's name are you talking about?"

"You remember how you were complaining that you have done nothing but sail since we left Cartagena on the third of June?"

"Yes, go on."

"Do you remember the current that flows through the Strait?"

"Yes."

"Do you also remember the Algerian castle on a cliff overlooking the southern side of the straits?" John nodded. "Well," continued Marlo, "what I have is an opportunity for you to take it. I am sure that the authorities in Cueta would be pleased to no longer have this fortress as a threat."

The prince looked at the map again. "I agree to that, but how do you propose to get our men up to the castle? I remember quite clearly that it was on a cliff. Or do you propose that we build trebuchets and throw the men up there?"

"Nothing so drastic, my lord, though the idea is entertaining. Look here. This fortress, Fagazas I think it is called, sits on a small promontory. On the east side, there is a small inlet. I was asking Captain Bazan about the geography there, and I am sure it can be done." Marlo pulled out his dagger and used the point to show his plan. "The cliff ends here. Over here, the shore is steep, yes, but it can be climbed with ease. I remember, and Bazan confirms this, that there is a gradual slope leading up to the southeast side of the castle."

"Marlo, you are a God-send," said John. He rubbed his hands and picked up a jug and a glass. "Now, do you have the details of how we could do this?" He poured wine into the glass, gave it to Marlo and filled one for himself.

"No," said Marlo. "I am only a trained soldier. Give the proposal to Bazan and Requesens.

They should come up with something."

"I will, and right now." Going to the door, he opened it. "Juan, could you give my regards to Captain Bazan and Don Requesens and ask them to join me?" Closing the door, he went back to the map. "You mentioned the current earlier. Why?"

"With the current, we could move the ships, under cover of night, into the inlet without the noise of the oars or the use of the sails. If there is any kind of light, the sails will be easily seen from the castle."

In few moments there was a knock at the door, and Captain Bazan and Don Requesens entered. "You asked for us, my lord," said Requesens.

"I did," answered Don John standing. "Come here and look at this map with me. Marlo, can you repeat what you told me?"

"This fortress of Fagazas, here," began Marlo pointing with his dagger. "It is on a cliff. However, and you confirmed this for me earlier, Captain, on the southeast side of this promontory, there is a little inlet where boats could land. From there is an easy climb up to the castle. If we use the tides, we could come past the castle and into the inlet without visible sails and in complete silence. The element of surprise would be on our side."

"Well, gentlemen," asked John. "What do you think? Is something like this feasible?"

"More than feasible," answered Requesens. "Captain, are you sure that soldiers could make it to the castle?"

"Yes, the beach is steep, as well as the hill," answered Bazan. "However, the soldiers would easily be able to walk up the slope. I've been in the area a few times, and there are no obstacles. They should be able to make it without attracting attention. How they storm the castle is another question."

"The castle is not protected by a moat, and it only serves to keep our ships away," said John.

"Yes, but how will they get in?" asked Marlo.

"If I may, My Lord," said Requesens. John nodded. "Fagazas is fortified facing the sea. If I remember correctly, the sides away from the sea have low walls. Grappling hooks and rope should enable our men to scale the walls, especially if they approach the walls where fewer sentries are posted. There even might be an entrance in the back that could be forced."

"Good," said John, "but the real problem will be to get enough men over the walls before the sentries find out we are there. If they find out too soon, we still could be repulsed."

"My Lord," interjected Captain Bazan, "split the fleet. Send the landing party ahead utilizing the current, and then have the other half follow at a distance with sails and oars so we are noticed. We could use the oars to halt us in the current and shell the fort. The landing crew

will be able to reach the rear of the castle un-
noticed."

"If you think that is a good plan," said John
to Requesens, "determine who will lead the attack, and which ships will fire upon the fort.
Can you have that ready for me in in an hour?"

~~~

In less than an hour, Requesens returned to
the cabin. "My Lord, I have the fleet division
for your approval." Don John took the paper
and frowned as he looked over it.

"I was planning on leading the landing party," he said.

"Your Excellency," said Requesens cautiously, "as the Captain of the Sea, or Admiral if you
will, your position is to oversee the operation.
You will not be able to do that if you are
ashore. That is why you have officers. They do
the work for you, so you can step back and see
the entire operation and make decisions accordingly. What if Ochiali swoops suddenly on
the fleet that is bombarding the castle, and the
landing needs to be aborted? If you are ashore,
you won't be aware of that development and
won't recall the landing crew."

"But I see that you have assigned the landing to yourself? Shouldn't you be here too?"

"Not necessarily," answered Requesens. "If
you tell me to stay, I will have to. However, the
soldiers assaulting the castle will expect either
~~~

you or myself to lead the attack, and since your position is here with the fleet, that leaves the command of the assault to myself."

John sighed. "I can't argue with that. Very well. When does the current begin to flow in past Gibraltar?"

"Shortly after midnight, My Lord."

"Good. Make all the necessary arrangements." Requesens bowed and left. Don John sat. "I hope this works, Marlo."

"So do I, My Lord. However, I would like to go with the landing party," said Marlo.

"By all means." John stood and opened to the cabin door. "Let us go up. And you need to get yourself a breastplate and helmet if you are going into a fight. Go get yourself armed."

On deck, Don Requesens was in the process of sending messages to Cordona and Aliende. He turned to Don John and saluted. "My lord, I am sending extra soldiers with Cordona as well as with eight other ships. You will have fifteen ships, including the *Capitana* for the bombardment. Once the ships are ready, I will go over to the *Miguel*."

"Not alone," said John.

"My Lord, your place is here," objected Requesens.

"I didn't say I was going. Señor Gobeli wants to join the landing party. Let me know how he does. I know he has been trained as a Swiss Guard, but I have no idea how he conducts himself in action."

"Of course, my Lord," said Requesens. Marlo returned to the deck with breastplate and helmet. "We will board the *Miguel* in about fifteen minutes, Señor Gobeli."

"I am ready," answered Marlo.

The sun was setting when Marlo boarded the *Miguel*, the last rays turning the gathering clouds red. Cordona welcomed Don Requesens and Marlo and ordered his ships to make their way south toward the Strait of Gibraltar.

They rounded Gibraltar just before midnight, and making use of the slack in the tidal current, positioned themselves along its southern shore. After midnight, Cordona was informed that the current was beginning to flow into the Mediterranean, and he moved the fleet away from the shore and ordered the oars to be stowed.

The current grew stronger as the Atlantic tide flowed through the twelve-mile gap of the Strait, into the Mediterranean. The ships, carried along by the moving water, glided silently past the shore.

~~~

Don John watched the *Miguel* move into the darkness. The *Capitana* held its position on the western opening of the strait. The sky was dark, and the moon, half way to full, was hidden behind the clouds. Captain Bazan moved
~~~

the fleet away from the shore and waited.

Ten minutes after the ships with the landing party had vanished, he began to move into the strait, carefully studying the dark shore, watching for the castle.

~~~

Marlo stood at the bow of the *Miguel* watching the silhouette of the castle slip by. The oars were shipped and the soldiers stood along the gunwales, silent. Aside from the slap of the water against the ships and the occasional creek of the tiller, the fleet was noiseless. He watched the dark shadow that was the cliff, and noticed that it began to deepen. He carefully made his way back to the stern, where Cordona stood by the tiller.

"Captain, we are passing the promontory," he whispered.

"Bring the ship fifteen degrees to the starboard," he whispered to the helmsman. The *Miguel's* bow swung slowly toward the south and the fleet began its quiet progress into the inlet.

~~~

"My Lord, it is time. Would you like the honors of the first shot?" Captain Bazan was smiling.

"Yes, I would," answered John. He moved to the bow, greeted the gunners, and stood by the starboard gun.

"Back oars," called the captain. The oars pushed against the water. The helmsman swung the ship toward Fagazas. When the bow was pointed toward the castle, Don John touched the match to the gun. It belched fire and smoke with a roar and was answered by the other two guns. The *Capitana* shuddered with the recoil. Guns spoke from fourteen other ships, throwing fire and smoke toward the castle. Bazan straightened the course of the *Capitana* and the gunners worked feverishly to reload.

"Fire when ready," said John, and he moved to the stern to join Captain Bazan. The ship swung about again and fire and smoke shot out a second time towards the castle.

~~~

The *Miguel* rounded the promontory just as the sound of cannon fire erupted from Don John's ships. Looking up at Fagazas, Marlo could see the flashes of the answering Algerian guns. Smoke rose over the castle, illuminated from below by the red fire leaping forth from the cannon. He could even feel the thundering roar of the castle's guns.

"Get the oars out!" he heard Cordona call.

"What is it, Captain?" asked Marlo.

"The current is too fast. We need to use the oars or else we will overshoot our landing."
~~~

The oars splashed into the water and the prisoners leaned against the current. The *Miguel* shuddered as the oars fought the rushing tidal current. The helmsman hauled on the tiller, trying to force the ship to move against the current.

"Hard to port!" shouted Cordona. Don Requesens hurried from where he had been waiting to disembark.

"What are you doing?" he called.

"The water is too swift! We are not going to make our landing, even with the oars. I am trying to prevent us from being dashed on those rocks!"

Don Requesens looked to where Cordona was pointing. The *Miguel* was moving, almost sideways, towards the rocks on the eastern point of the inlet. "Call off the operation," he called. A gun in the bow fired and the ships following the *Miguel* turned and began to force themselves back into clear water.

~~~

The *Capitana* had to turn more than ninety degrees to the starboard in order to bring her guns to bear. Already they were approaching the promontory, and when the helmsman pushed on the tiller to straighten the ship, the force of the current drove the ship toward the rocks. Captain Bazan shouted for the port oars to be stilled while the prisoners on the star-
~~~

board side pulled on theirs. The rocks drew closer.

"Point the bow in that direction," he called to the helmsman, pointing to the northeast. "And pull on those oars," he shouted to the boatswain. Slowly the *Capitana* pulled away from the rocks.

Behind them, the rest of the fleet still fired and struggled against the moving water. Don John saw that the castle was now behind them. Water fountained just behind the *Capitana*. The cannon on the fort were firing.

"We can't turn and fire at them again, My Lord," said Bazan. "We have done what we could. The current is moving too quickly, and it is impossible to row against it."

"Move out into the strait, out of range of the guns," John ordered. He looked behind him. Smoke wreathed the castle, and the cannon fire flashed red in the gloom. There were no more shots directed against the *Capitana*, but the ships behind him were still in danger. As he watched, the mast on the *Reya* shuddered and slowly toppled into the water. The drag of the sail and the mast in the water strained against the lines that were still attached to the ship. The *Reya* began to list as it was pulled around rapidly toward the rocks.

Chapter 18
July 1568

The *Reya* continued to swing around her downed mast, her list increasing as the ship was inexorably dragged by the dead weight in the water. Soldiers scrambled to the *Reya's* port side and feverishly hacked at the tangled rigging. Swinging axes, swords, and knives they severed the lines, and the ship sprang upright and slowly began to correct her course. Her oars were useless since the falling mast had broken most of the port side oars. Another galley moved close, tossed a line to the *Reya* and began to help tow her out of danger, leaving the damaged mast and sail floating in the water. Moments later, the damaged oars were thrown overboard, and her starboard oars were redistributed between both banks of rowers. Though the *Reya* was missing half her oars, she was able to move again under her own power.

The *Capitana* had moved past the promontory. Don John stared toward the inlet to see if there was any sign of the landing party. There was none. They passed the eastern end of the inlet, and John saw dark shapes on the water ahead.

"I think that is the rest of the fleet," said Captain Bazan. "It doesn't seem as if they were able to land. The current must have been too strong for them."

A light showed from one of the dark ships. "Ahoy! This is the *Miguel,*" called a voice.

"This is the *Capitana,* is everything alright?" shouted Bazan.

"If you call a failed mission alright, then yes," came the answer.

Don John went to the rail and peered into the gloom. "Don Requesens, the *Reya* has lost a mast and most of her oars. We need to put in someplace to repair her." Don John saw the *Miguel* begin to glow. He looked behind him, and halfway up the western sky, the moon shone through a gap in the clouds. The water glowed silver, revealing the rest of the fleet.

"It's a good thing the moon waited, My Lord," came Requesens' voice. "Was anyone lost on the *Reya?*"

"I have not yet ascertained that."

"We should put in at Peñon de Velez. We should be there before the afternoon," added

Requesens.

"Very good," said John. "You and Señor Gobeli stay on the *Miguel* for now. You can return to the *Capitana* at Peñon de Velez."

Don John returned to his cabin, lit a lantern and looked at the map. Peñon de Velez was a small island fortress off the coast of North Africa. With the *Reya* being towed, the fleet would reach Peñon de Velez by midmorning.

When dawn came, John ordered several galleys to give a few oars to the *Reya*. Captain Morales was able to cast off the tow-line and keep up with the fleet. The night's action had only injured a few prisoners, and aside from not having a mast, the *Reya* was still seaworthy.

When they reached Peñon de Velez, the prisoners were brought on the deck of the *Reya* to begin clearing away the wreckage. Tangled and damaged lines were cut, and the stump of the old mast was lifted out of its seat and cast overboard. Don Requesens went around the fleet and gathered extra lines. He sent men to the shore to look for a suitable mast or a tree if no masts were to be had.

~~~

"My Lord, if you don't mind, I would like to visit that castle." Marlo stood next to Don John after the ship was anchored. He and the young prince were looking at the fortress of Peñon de
~~~

Velez. It was a built on a small mountain sticking out the water of the harbor. The shore of the harbor itself was lined with fishing vessels and houses on the western side. To the east, a flat plain curled around the bay. Even though the mainland was nominally part of Algerian territory, the island fortress was impregnable to assault. Any force that would try to land and storm the island would have to climb up cliffs and craggy slopes, exposed to cannon and musket fire from the fortress walls. The fortress itself would also prevent Algerian ships from putting into the harbor. "I am intrigued by the fact that Spain is able to keep this harbor even though it is completely surrounded by Algerian territory," he added.

"Go satisfy your curiosity," smiled John. "I would like to join you. I miss the feel of solid earth and stone beneath my feet." He shrugged. "Later, perhaps. I have to see about the repairs to the *Reya* and write my report to the king."

"Oh, the woes of command," said Marlo with mock sympathy. "There are times I am glad I wasn't born into the nobility. I get to escape such headaches."

"If you are not careful, I will demote Requesens, put you in charge of the fleet, and retire somewhere where I can comfortably watch you make a fool of yourself!" John chuckled. "And I think that would be a most entertaining thing to watch."

"It probably would be," agreed Marlo, "There is a very good reason you are in charge, and I will never be." Marlo grinned suddenly. "But it has its perks. I get to go on a carefree jaunt up to that castle and not be bothered by reports and repairs."

John shook his head. "Captain Bazan," he called, "can you come here for a moment?"

"Yes, Your Excellency," said the captain moving toward them.

"I need you to arrange transportation to the island. This young man is to go to the castle. There he, I hope, will drown his impertinence with wine and song."

"Young?" laughed Marlo. "From one youth to another. However, I shall do my best to comply and leave my impertinence at the bottom of a bottle of wine."

Shaking his head, Captain Bazan left them and ordered the boat to be readied. "Do you think we shocked him?" asked John.

"Him, no," answered Marlo, "Don Requesens, on the other hand, would be appalled."

"Yes, he would be," John nodded. "Can you just hear him? 'It is not good for the men to see such displays, My Lord. You are the brother of a king and the son of an emperor. What would His Majesty say?'" Don John took on the dry, gravely tones of his lieutenant.

"Leaving our levity aside," he said after a moment, "I am grateful that you are going. I would like to know about the state of the garrison there, and what sort of recommendations I should make to the king, if you would be willing to give me your impressions?"

"Of course, My Lord."

"Let me write a quick letter of introduction," said John. Marlo followed the prince as he went into his cabin. The prince took a sheet of paper and wrote for a few minutes. Then he folded and sealed it.

"Please give this to the alcayde," he said. Marlo took the paper, bowed and went back on deck. He went to the side and climbed down into the waiting boat. "Why don't you see if they have a spare mast so we don't have to find one ourselves," called John as the boat pushed away from the ship.

"I will find out," Marlo called back.

At the island, Marlo stepped ashore, thanked the sailors who had rowed him out, and walked up the path to the fortress. At the gate, he presented the letter from Don John and asked if he could see the alcayde of the garrison. The guard looked at the seal on the folded letter and handed it back. "This way, Señor," he said.

The fortress was like a walled village; a well-fortified walled village. The stone buildings inside the walls were stout enough to withstand any attack, and the walls themselves were easily accessed from any of the buildings. The only real danger was from a naval bombardment, but Algerian galleys were not large enough to carry the huge guns needed to do any real damage to the walls.

Marlo was led to the center of the fortress, to a wide building that was surmounted by a tower, the top of which, Marlo surmised, commanded a view of the entire harbor and surrounding shore. Inside, Marlo was introduced to Don Garcia, the Alcayde of Peñon de Velez.

"His Excellency, Don John of Austria, Captain of the Seas, sends his greetings. He wishes to have the opportunity to call on you at your earliest convince. He sends this letter by way of introduction," said Marlo, giving Don Garcia the letter.

"Thank you," answered the alcayde. He broke the seal and read the contents. "Please inform your commander that he is more than welcome. I can attend to him whenever his duties permit."

"That won't be for a few hours, at least," said Marlo. "One of our ships lost a mast during an exchange with the Algerian fortress of Fagazas in the strait just to the west of Cueta. He also needs to prepare a report for His Majesty. Since I am not officially under his command, I decided to come ashore and feel the ground beneath my feet. Needless to say, I am rather intrigued at how you are able to keep this fortress on an island not two hundred yards off the Algerian coast."

"Unfortunately, I don't have a spare mast here," said Garcia, "so I can't help you there. There are fishing boats in the village that might have one the right size."

"Don John's lieutenant is checking that out. Won't taking one of the fishermen's masts hurt his trade?"

"Not really. They can fell another tree and make one. As long as they are paid for it, they won't grumble much."

"I'll mention that to Don John when I return," said Marlo.

"Why don't you sit and have some refreshment." Garcia pointed to a chair and asked a servant to bring some food and wine. "I assume you would like a little something to eat?"

"Some real food would be a treat," answered Marlo. "I still haven't gotten used to ship fare." The servant returned with wine, water and a platter of fruit and meat.

"You came just at the right time," said Garcia. "I was about to eat myself, and I have nothing pressing to attend to. I tend to think that your interest in how we survive here is also shared by Don John?" he asked with a slight smile.

"True, enough. His Excellency, as part of his assignment, is inspecting the garrisons located throughout the western Mediterranean, and, as long as I was visiting, he asked me to give him my impressions."

"Our garrison is rather small,' said Garcia. "We have a hundred fifty soldiers, and that is sufficient to repel marauders who attack the locals on the mainland. While the shore is nominally part of Algeria, it is essentially under our control. We buy fish from those who live there. The Algerians don't like that, and every now and again some local tribe attacks them. We fight them off."

"How often does that happen?" asked Marlo.

"About two or three times a year."

"Do they ever attack the castle?"

"Once in a while, but they don't have the naval support. If their galleys were gathered, then they could, but piracy is more profitable. So the ships just keep at that."

Marlo finished his food and wiped his fingers.

"Since you have eaten, is there anything else you would like to see?" asked Garcia.

"I would like to visit your armory and take a look at your fortifications, if you don't mind."

"Of course." Garcia stood and Marlo followed him out of the room.

They went outside and to a low building. "The soldiers live in here," said Garcia. "The armory is attached. This way they can arm themselves quickly when there is need." Inside he introduced Marlo to a short man who was sitting at a desk sorting paperwork. "This is Captain Gonsalvo. He can show you around."

Gonsalvo stood and greeted Marlo. "You must be from the fleet," he said.

"Yes," answered Marlo. "The commander, Don John of Austria, wants me to report to him of the state of your defenses. His Majesty has asked him to report on the current conditions of the Spanish garrisons, especially those in close proximity to the Algerians."

"Well, you can't get any closer," smiled Gonsalvo. "What would you like to know?"

"He would like to inspect the armory and outer defenses," said Garcia. "Let him see anything he needs to." He turned to Marlo. "Señor, I am pleased to have made your acquaintance. Please send my regards to His Excellency, and inform him of my readiness to wait on him." With that, he left.

Gonsalvo led Marlo into the armory, and Marlo made note of the number of weapons and the supply of powder and shot. Afterwards, he and Gonsalvo went up onto the outer walls.

The guns were concentrated toward the harbor and the sea and were in good condition. The fortress would not be easily taken, he surmised, especially since there was little room on the island for a force to land. Even if an attacking force did land, there was no protection from the cannon.

After his inspection, Marlo thanked Gonsalvo. As he was preparing to leave, a bell began to ring. "What is that?" he asked.

"That," said Gonsalvo, "means that Algerians have been sighted on the shore. They are going to make yet another attempt on the fisher-folk. Though why they are doing that when your ships are here is beyond me. If you will excuse me, I have to get to my men."

As he was speaking, soldiers were already filing into the courtyard, slinging ammunition pouches across their shoulders and adjusting their helmets. "Do you mind if I join you?" asked Marlo.

"I see that you have a sword. Do you know how to use a musket?" asked Gonsalvo.

"Yes, I was a member the Swiss Guard in Rome. I can fight."

"Then come on, get yourself a weapon." Marlo ran back into the armory, grabbed a helmet and a harquebus. Throwing an ammunition pouch over his shoulder, he ran back to join the thirty soldiers leaving the fortress.

The soldiers jogged toward the shore where there were several boats moored to a stone quay. They took up the oars, cast off, and began to pull for the mainland.

Marlo saw that there were about a hundred marauders in the plains to the east of the fishermen's huts. They broke into a run when they saw the boats.

"They don't give up," said Gonsalvo. "See, they are trying to prevent us from landing. They won't succeed; we have too much of a head start."

The boats quickly reached the shore and the men leapt out. Forming up behind Gonsalvo, the soldiers ran inland. Once they were off the sand, Gonsalvo ordered the soldiers to line up. Marlo loaded his weapon and joined the line. He blew on his match and raised the musket. He looked down the barrel, his eyes watering from the acrid smoke of the slow burning match. The Algerians ran across the plain toward him, their white and brown robes flowing about them.

The marauders kept no formation as they charged, and they were shrieking and brandishing their swords. They came closer, and still there was no order to fire.

Marlo nervously readjusted his match and raised his weapon again. The heat of the sun no longer bothered him. His entire attention was focused on the whirling mob that drew ever closer.

"Fire!" shouted Gonsalvo.

Marlo pulled the lever. The match dropped into the pan, and for a second nothing happened. Then the gun jumped in his hands. Explosions rang out to both sides of him and a cloud of smoke blocked his vision. But not before he saw at least ten of the marauders stagger and fall.

He pulled the match and re-primed the pan. He poured a measure of powder into the barrel and rammed home a ball. Blowing on the match, he reset the action. Alongside of him, the other soldiers raised their weapons again. The marauders had almost reached them.

"Fire!" shouted Captain Gonsalvo again. Again, Marlo's vision was obscured by smoke. Then the marauders were on them.

His ears ringing from the gunfire, Marlo desperately swung the butt of his musket up in front of him and caught an Algerian on the chin. The Algerian fell backward and collapsed. Marlo dropped his gun, drew his sword, and parried a blow that was aimed at his head.

Around him the high-pitched cries and ululations of the marauders mixed with the cries of "Santiago" and "Castille" from the Spaniards. Marlo stumbled, his foot dropping into an unseen depression in the ground. An Algerian, seeing him fall, screamed and leapt at him. Marlo raised his sword. The Algerian landed on him, impaling himself.

Marlo threw off the bleeding and gasping body, stood, and attacked three Algerians who had just overwhelmed the soldier next to him. Catching them unawares, Marlo passed his sword between the head and shoulders of one of them. He managed to stab another before he was noticed. The unwounded Algerian swung and swiped at his legs. Marlo jumped over the sword, spun to his right and slammed his left elbow into his opponent's face. He felt and heard the crunch of breaking bone, and the Algerian collapsed. Engaging the Algerian he had already stabbed, he ran his sword again through the marauder's chest. Before he could withdraw his sword, Marlo felt a weight crash into his back, and was driven to the ground. He felt a prick on his right side, as the point of a dagger glanced off his breastplate.

He bunched his arms and legs together, leapt up and backwards. He heard an exploding gasp in his ear as he landed on his assailant. Rolling off, he stood, kicked the marauder in the head, and picked up his sword.

Looking around, he saw that most the marauders were dead or dying. However, all the Spanish soldiers were engaged with at least one, and the battle had moved away from him. Leaping over a writhing body, he stumbled, caught his footing, and ran to rejoin his companions.

~~~

At the sound of musket fire, Don John looked up. Before he could leave his cabin, his secretary, Juan de Quiroga burst in.

"My Lord, there is a skirmish on the beach!"

Don John ran on deck. The castle rose on the hill above the harbor, and past the island, he
~~~

could see gun smoke drifting from the shore. Cries and the clash of steel echoed over the water. Through the smoke, he could see a line of soldiers preparing to fire again at a charging mob of Algerians.

"Don Requesens!" he shouted. "Get the soldiers into boats. At once!" Without waiting for a reply, he ran back into his cabin and put on his breastplate and helmet. Grabbing his sword, he ran back onto the deck. Already, the soldiers were jumping into the boats. Paying no heed to the cries of protest from Requesens, he leapt into the nearest boat. As soon as it was full, the soldiers pulled at the oars.

"Give it everything you have," said John. "Quickly now."

The men pulled hard at the oars, and the boat quickly reached the beach to the east of the battle. Once beached, John led his men at a run toward the fight. The sounds of steel against steel and the cries of those fighting grew louder. "Let's move," he shouted, kicking up sand as he ran.

~~~

An Algerian loomed in front of Marlo. Marlo struck him down, the marauder's defiant shriek turning suddenly into a gasping gurgle. Another group of marauders rushed over the plain and set against the southwestern body of the Spanish. Captain Gonsalvo was surrounded.
~~~

Marlo ran around the press of men to come to the captain's aid.

Gonsalvo was desperately defending himself from six Algerians and had already killed one by the time Marlo arrived. Marlo cut one down, and was beset by another, a tall muscular man who beat down Marlo's guard with a violence that drove him back. Marlo lunged, and his sword was casually swept aside. He recovered in time to block a blow that would have trimmed his head just below the ears.

Marlo found himself slowly giving ground. Realizing that he was being driven toward the fallen bodies, he moved to his left as the marauder swung down with his sword. Blocking the blow, Marlo, aware that his left leg had caused him to stumble several times during the battle, planted it firmly on the ground, hoping that it wouldn't give out on him. While the Algerian was still recovering from Marlo's sudden change of direction, Marlo lashed out with his right foot and caught his opponent directly on the knee, bending it sideways. The Algerian staggered, and Marlo plunged his sword into the Algerian's throat. Letting the body fall off the length of his sword, Marlo turned and went to help his captain.

But it was too late. As the marauders broke into retreat, he realized that there was no helping Captain Gonsalvo.

Chapter 19
July 1568

Don John came closer and saw close to three dozen Spanish fighting furiously against twice their number. By the bodies of the dead Algerians, he could tell that the fight had originated near the shore and then moved across the field. He paused to let his men form up. "Santiago, and at them!" he cried, and the fifty soldiers with him shouted and charged toward the fray.

The Algerians saw the charging Spanish and fled. John proceeded toward where several soldiers were gathered around a fallen man. One of them, bloodstained and covered with sweat, looked up at his approach. It was Marlo.

"I am afraid you came too late to help Captain Gonsalvo, here." Marlo stood and took off his helmet and wiped the sweat from his face. "I am glad you came, though. We were hard pressed."

John watched the Algerians disappear into the hills. He considered following them, but decided that it would be folly. The Algerians knew the territory and would easily elude his small force. He sighed and looked again at Marlo. The right side of his shirt was wet with blood. "How seriously are you injured?" he asked.

"Injured?" asked Marlo. John pointed at Marlo's side. Marlo lifted his right arm and looked bemused with the stain on his shirt. "I am not sure," he said.

"Sit down," ordered John, forcing Marlo down. He helped Marlo remove his breastplate and lifted Marlo's shirt. "I need a clean piece of cloth and some water," he called. One of the soldiers handed over a handkerchief and a water skin. John moistened the cloth and cleaned the blood off Marlo's side.

"Just a small gash," said John when he could see the wound. "It looks like you were only pricked and the point of whatever it was glanced off of a rib. We will put a pad over it and keep pressure on it." He put a clean cloth over the wound and bound it in place, wrapping a long piece of cloth tightly around Marlo' chest. "There, you will be fine a few days," said John when he had finished.

"Where did you learn the healer's art?" asked Marlo as he lowered his shirt.

"Don Luis Quixada," said John. "He insisted

that I learn, not just to be able to care for myself if there was no surgeon present, but to help others. 'A knight should know all about battle, including its aftermath,' he used to say quite frequently."

"You have just made me a believer in that philosophy," said Marlo with a chuckle. "It looks as if the soldiers are preparing to return to the castle. We should probably join them."

"We should." John led the way over to the boats. The bodies of Captain Gonsalvo and a fallen soldier were already in one boat, and the other soldiers were climbing into the remaining boats. Don John sent his soldiers back to the *Capitana*, and crossed over to the island fortress with Marlo.

After paying his respects to Don Garcia, Don John returned the *Capitana* with Marlo. There he found Requesens waiting for him.

"Your Excellency," said Requesens quietly, "I need to speak to you. Could we repair to your cabin?"

John nodded and the two disappeared. Marlo watched them leave and wondered what was afoot. *Probably something to do with the repair of the* Reya, he mused. He settled himself down in the bow, back against one of the cannon. His side was sore, but he was relieved that he had not needed stitches.

Now that he was seated, he found himself to be exhausted. The combination of the thrill and terror he had felt in the battle faded, leaving him lethargic. He relaxed with a satisfied contentment.

The battle had been a test. In spite of his training, he had never been involved in a pitched battle. He had always handled himself well in small frays, but had always wondered if he could retain his self-control when faced with the prospect of being overwhelmed by superior numbers. While he had been nervous, he had not only stood his ground, but had fought well. He smiled and closed his eyes, aware of nothing but the warmth of the sun and the silencing of a nagging doubt.

~~~

He was nudged awake. Opening his eyes, he saw Juan de Quiroga leaning over him.

"His Excellency needs to see you, Señor," the secretary said.

Marlo stood and stretched. He smoothed out his jacket and followed Juan to Don John's door. Juan opened the door, stood aside, and motioned for Marlo to enter.

He stepped inside and the door was closed behind him. "You wanted to see me, My Lord?" asked Marlo.

"Yes," John put away his papers and sat up straight. He was serious. "Señor Gobeli, I would like you to answer this: what in God's name were you doing getting involved in that skir-
~~~

mish? You had no right to unnecessarily risk yourself."

"Your Excellency, I am a soldier."

"But you are still in the service of Rome! You have a greater responsibility than any other soldier in this fleet. You cannot neglect that. Would you be serving the Holy Father by getting yourself killed for no other reason than that you wanted a good fight?"

"Your Excellency, yes I have to serve Rome, but can I sit by and let innocent people be attacked for no other reason than that they provide fish to the garrison in the fortress? My Lord, the defense of the weak is a cause for which any soldier should take up arms."

"Yet if you have a responsibility that outweighs that, you can't put that responsibility in danger unless there was no other option. If you were killed, it would complicate the formation of the papal alliance. Even though you are on detached service, I know you are still making regular reports about this fleet, and I let it happen because I realize the gravity of the threat. This alliance needs to happen, and you were foolish to get involved in that fight. There are soldiers in the castle who deal with this on a regular basis. They saw the marauders and responded. There is also a fleet full of soldiers here. There was absolutely no need for you to risk yourself."

"With all due respect, Your Excellency," said

Marlo, "I think I am missing something. There was no 'need' for me to be part of the landing party when we attempted to take the castle last night. And the same reasons that kept you out of that landing party, My Lord, should have kept you from leading the reinforcements to-day."

"As the commander of this fleet, I don't have to justify my actions to you," said John. His voice was hard. "And as for being part of the landing party that was something different. And Don Requesens was instructed to keep an eye on you." John stood and clasped his hands behind his back. "Señor Gobeli, I must ask you not involve yourself in any conflicts for the duration of this cruise. This ship is not likely to see action; the role of the flagship is to stay out of conflict and direct the rest of the fleet. So as long as you remain with this fleet, you remain with this ship, and as long as you remain with this ship, you will not be risking your duties to the Holy Father. I trust you can live with that?"

"I understand, Your Excellency," said Marlo. He stared straight ahead, his eyes focused on nothing. "May I have Your Excellency's leave to withdraw?" John nodded and Marlo made a stiff bow, turned, and walked out of the cabin.

Don John sat down and rubbed his face. He found that he was shaking. He had just given a friend a tongue-lashing and had not enjoyed it. There were sides to military command that he found onerous. He leaned back in his seat and sighed.

He knew what Marlo was feeling. When he had returned from his rescue, Don Requesens had proceeded to admonish his commander. And he had not been gentle. Requesens had made it plain that John's action in leading the reinforcements had been unnecessarily rash. His duty as the commander of the fleet was to keep himself safe in order to direct the action of everyone else. Requesens even had a letter from the king ordering him to prevent his half-brother from doing anything rash. Even though he recognized the wisdom in Requesens' words, the correction had not been easy to swallow.

He stood and made his way out of the small cabin and onto the deck. He nodded to Captain Bazan's salute and went over the rail to check on the repairs on the *Reya*. The damaged mast had been cleared away, and the crew was in the process of stepping the new one. He guessed that the *Reya* would be ready by sundown, and the fleet could resume its patrol in the morning.

He looked around the *Capitana* and saw Marlo leaning against one of the bow cannon. When Marlo noticed Don John looking at him, he turned his head. John sighed inwardly. He had hoped the Marlo would take the correction like the soldier that he was.

The sky was hazy when they left Peñon de Velez. Don John ordered the fleet to proceed east along the coast of North Africa. He hoped that the presence of the Spanish fleet would draw Ochiali into the open.

Marlo and John still had not spoken, and the young commander wondered what was going through his friend's mind. He paced the deck, occasionally looking toward the bow where Marlo had resumed his place among the forward guns. *Maybe I should have spoken to him as a friend and not as an officer*, he thought. He shrugged inwardly and looked to the coast of Africa, now only a dark smudge along the southern horizon.

At midday Captain Bazan came to his cabin. "My Lord," he said, "the *Miguel* signals that they have sighted two corsairs with a captured merchant vessel."

"Prepare to give chase," said John. "I will be on deck in a moment." Bazan left and Don John stood. He buckled on his sword and went on deck.

"Where are they?" he asked Bazan.

"Almost due east, according to the *Miguel*. We can't see them yet, and the *Miguel* is holding back just enough to keep them in sight."

"Bring us up to the *Miguel*," said John.

Bazan called out to the boatswain, and the prisoners began to pull harder on their oars.

The *Capitana* moved forward through the fleet, closing the distance with the *Miguel*. John went along the catwalk and climbed high in the bow. When he arrived, he saw Marlo standing at attention. "Good afternoon, My Lord," said Marlo formally.

"Good afternoon," answered John. He looked at Marlo, trying to read what the young man was thinking. "It seems that we may have found some sign of the pirates, at last."

Marlo nodded. "I saw the signals from the *Miguel*." He stepped aside and motioned for Don John to move forward. John glanced at Marlo and stepped onto the bowsprit. Holding onto the bowline, he peered into the eastern horizon.

He could see nothing until they drew alongside of the *Miguel* and Cordona indicated a point just off the port bow. John could make out the sails of three ships. Two ships had the lanteen sails of galley ships, and the third was square-rigged. They were heading southeast. John nodded and turned to Requesens, who was standing behind him. "Maintain our position and keep those ships in sight, but don't let the rest of the fleet come any closer. I don't want those ships to realize that they are vastly outnumbered. Have Cordona and ten ships move toward the north. When they are in position, give orders for the fleet to give chase. No signaling with cannon until we are sighted."

John remained watching the ships while Requesens gave orders to Cordona. He watched as the *Miguel* dropped back and began to move toward the north.

"My Lord, they have turned due east," Marlo called.

Don John turned away from the *Miguel*. His quarry had indeed altered course. The ships were now moving directly away from the fleet.

"Don Requesens," he called, "we will commence the chase, but keep Cordona to the north of us."

The boatswain blew his whistle, and the prisoners pulled even harder on their oars. Behind the *Capitana*, the rest of the fleet began to gather speed.

"What do you make of those ships?" John asked Marlo.

"Very likely Algerian corsairs with a captured merchantman, My Lord," answered Marlo.

"I hope they lead us to the main fleet."

"Unlikely, My Lord. They were probably escorting the merchantman to port. Based on the direction they were traveling, Ochiali's fleet is somewhere to the north of us. That is assuming that those two corsairs were part of a fleet and not acting independently."

"Thanks," said John wryly. "So I chase these two ships and leave Ochiali at large. And even if I do capture them, they may not have any information about the location of his fleet."

"We won't know until they are captured, My Lord," said Marlo.

"No, we won't," agreed John. "Let's pray that we can catch them, then." He looked at the three ships on the horizon. It did not seem as if the fleet had closed the distance at all. "I need to go order the *Reya* and some of the faster galleys to move on ahead."

"Of course, My Lord," said Marlo.

Marlo moved along the catwalk before turning again to watch the corsairs. He was glad that the pirates had been sighted since it gave him an excuse to hold a normal conversation with Don John. His irritation at being treated as a common soldier had only lasted for a little while, but he had not known how to resume normal discourse with his friend. He had been reminded of something that he had begun to forget: Don John was in a position of authority, and Marlo also realized that he had allowed himself to become resentful to John's admonishment just as he had been resentful to those of his old commander. He had argued with them both times. And both times, he had been wrong to do so.

He had also been thinking about his tendency towards risk. Following the Moriscos into the hills and spying on their camp had been a thrill. It also had been dangerous. Joining the battle on the beach had been the same. And he admitted to himself that while following the Moriscos had been necessary, joining the skirmish had been foolish. Don John had been right to correct him.

Marlo looked back for a moment and watched as the *Reya* eventually caught up with the *Capitana* and slowly moved past. The ships on the horizon were no closer, and Marlo hoped that the *Reya* could catch up with them. Behind him, he could hear the crack of the boatswain's whip as the prisoners were urged to greater efforts.

The fleet slowly drew closer to the three ships, and Marlo could just make out figures on their decks. By the time the *Reya* with the three other fast ships had moved a mile ahead of the fleet, Marlo figured that the corsairs now knew they had an entire fleet chasing them. He stood on the bowsprit and stared intently at the ships. He realized that his surmise had been right. The corsairs had moved ahead of the merchantman.

Leaping off the bowsprit, he ran along the catwalk and climbed up onto the stern deck. "My Lord," he called, "The corsairs are abandoning their prize!"

"Let us hope the *Reya* can keep up with them," said John.

"My Lord," said Requesens, "it would be inadvisable to let the ships get so far ahead that we will not be able to give them aid. What if they are led into the rest of the fleet and we are too far away to prevent their capture. It would be good to make sure that they do not go beyond the horizon."

"That makes sense," said John. "I don't like it though." He sighed. "Very well, recall them when you think they have gone far enough."

He walked over to Marlo and stood quietly looking at the fleeing ships. "It is frustrating," he said after a moment. "There is a fleet of ships out there. We keep hearing about them, and when we finally see a couple of pirates, we can't catch them."

"It is part of the hunt, My Lord," said Marlo, "and besides, Ochiali is probably trying to avoid meeting us in battle. According to the reports, his ships are actually Ottoman ships, not Algerian. Selim probably doesn't want Ochiali to risk them. They are needed for the eventual move against Venice. If we keep pursuing and making our presence felt, I think that Selim will eventually recall the fleet."

"That only provides a temporary solution," said John. "I don't want to do this every year. I want to find and destroy them, now."

"If you do this every year," said Marlo, "you will eventually meet him and then you can have your wish fulfilled. However, I don't think that Selim's fleet will be on this side of the Mediterranean next year. Once he begins his move on Cyprus, he will be using those ships to prevent Venice from sending reinforcements. I think that Ochiali is trying to cause enough chaos that your ships will be held back just in case Ochiali takes to the sea again."

Don John looked out at the corsairs. Since they had abandoned the merchant vessel, the pirate ships had moved ahead quickly. He could see that they were moving faster than the fleet. They even seemed to be moving faster than the *Reya*.

"Don Requesens," he said, "recall the *Reya* if she has not engaged the corsairs by the time we reach the merchant."

"Very good, My Lord," said Requesens.

The merchant was still sailing away from them, but the fleet was gaining. At Captain Bazan's suggestion, the *Capitana* fired a single shot to her starboard side. After a moment, the ship lowered her sails and waited for the fleet.

John watched as soldiers from the *Miguel* crossed to the waiting ship. They climbed over the gunwales and moved the Algerian sailors to the bow.

"My Lord," said Bazan, "Cordona signals that the ship is secure."

"Thank you Captain. Don Requesens, will you take Señor Gobeli with you and see what you can find?"

"Yes, My Lord." Requesens bowed and joined Marlo at the bow as the *Capitana* moved forward. Just before she made contact with the merchant ship, the prisoners pushed against their oars, halting the galley. Don Requesens and Marlo jumped across the gap between the ships.

Cordona was onboard and saluted Requesens. "Welcome aboard the Spanish ship *Rosa*," he said. "Don Requesens and Señor Gobeli, allow me to introduce you to Captain Salinas."

"Thank you for the rescue, Don Requesens," said Salinas. The captain was short and stocky. His lined face was creased with a smile. "I was sure that we were destined to end our days pulling oars for the Ottoman Empire."

"These were Turks?" asked Marlo. "We thought they were Algerians."

"They were Turks," answered Salinas. "At least those who herded me and my crew into the hold and manned my ship were."

"How is your crew?" asked Requesens.

"No one dead, God be praised," the captain shrugged. "There was no fighting. What could we do against fifty ships? They closed in on us and we just surrendered. The Turks placed us in the hold."

"Fifty?" asked Requesens. "Is that an accurate count?"

"That is a guess. It could be more, but not less. There were a lot of ships in that fleet. It was quite a bit larger than yours."

"When were you captured?" asked Marlo.

"Yesterday evening," said the captain. *We can't be far from them*, thought Marlo. The trip out through the Strait of Gibraltar had been a waste of time. Instead of going west from Almeria, the fleet should have gone south and east. Marlo shook his head slightly. If the *Reya* had not been damaged, they might have met up with Ochiali.

Requesens gestured toward the prisoners in the bow. "Is this all of them?" he asked Cordona.

"Yes, we checked the entire ship."

"We will divide these among our vessels. They can pull oars for us."

"Will there be enough room for them?" asked Marlo.

"There should be,' said Requesens. He went over to the gunwale and waved to the *Capitana*. "Come, Señor Gobeli, let us report to Don John."

The *Capitana* approached, and Marlo and Requesens crossed over to her. Don John was waiting for them in the bow. Marlo was silent as Don Requesens made his report. He was thinking about where Ochiali might be. "My Lord," he asked when Requesens was finished, "Ochiali can't be far from here. Could we take a look at your charts?"

"Do you have yet another idea?" asked John.

"Possibly, though I can't guarantee that it will be any more successful than my last one."

"Well, I am willing to hear you out." John led the way to his cabin.

Inside, he pulled out his chart of the chest and spread it out on the table. "So, where do you think Ochiali is?"

"My Lord, Captain Salinas was here when he was captured," Marlo pointed to a location between Peñon de Velez and the Spanish coast. "He was sailing from Cadiz to Sicily, which is why he was not keeping to the coast. The corsairs were heading for Algiers. They were escorting the captured ship, and probably had orders to meet up with the fleet somewhere."

"We were not told that," said Requesens.

"No, we were not," said Marlo, "but it is a logical surmise. Those corsair galleys were Turkish, not Algerian. But that really matters little. What we do know is that Ochiali was here yesterday evening. If those galleys were to rejoin his fleet, I doubt that he headed back toward the strait. It more probable that he headed due east."

"The Balearic Islands," said John.

"That would make sense, My Lord," said Requesens. "These islands, especially Mallorca, have been used by the Algerians for shelter. They are nominally under Spanish rule, but His Majesty does not have the naval capabilities to keep the Algerians away."

"Don Requesens," said John, "I believe you are mistaken about the naval situation. His

Majesty does have the navy. I think it would be a good to set our course for Minorca."

"The likelihood of finding Ochiali there is slim, My Lord," said Marlo. "This was just a surmise on my part."

"Don't downplay your analytical abilities, Marlo," John smiled. He placed his hand on Marlo's shoulder. "This is the only indication we have of where Ochiali might be. Until we have concrete information, we have to follow every lead, however slight." He placed both hand on the table and leaned over the map. He looked up at Marlo. "Besides, it will be Ochiali's fault if he is not there, not yours."

Marlo and Don Requesens chuckled and took their leave. On deck, Requesens spoke to Captain Bazan about setting course for Minorca. Bazan shook his head. "We won't be heading for Mallorca for a little while," he said.

"Why not?" asked Marlo.

Bazan pointed to the northeast. There the sky was filling with tall white clouds. "We are in for a storm. We need to look for a sheltered cove. Otherwise we will be severely tossed about and the fleet will be separated. Mallorca is going to have to wait."

Chapter 20
July 1568

"Shelter?" asked Marlo. "Those clouds look harmless."

"That is a big storm brewing, Señor," said Bazan. "The air is still and hot, and getting hotter by the minute. The heat and those clouds indicate a large storm. We should find someplace where the fleet can shelter from the worst of it. If that storm is a large as I think it is going to be, then there is a good chance of ships being swamped and the fleet being driven apart."

"I will inform His Excellency," said Requesens. "Meanwhile, determine where we can go."

After Requesens had left them, Bazan said, "Let us see, Señor." He opened a chart. "We are here. Here," Bazan stabbed a finger at the map, "is the creek of Trifolques. It is under the control of the king."

"Will it be protected?" asked Marlo.

"Of course. The city of Melilla controls the entire region. And quite securely, at that."

"That was not what I asked," said Marlo, "though it is good to know. I meant is it protected from the weather?"

"Somewhat," answered Bazan. "The mouth is wide enough for the fleet. The worst of the swells will not reach us. The wind and rain will still buffet us quite a bit, but it will be a lot better than being at sea."

"Could we head back to Peñon de Velez?"

"We wouldn't reach it in time. Trifolques is only a couple of hours away. Peñon de Velez is at least half a day's sail. The storm would reach us before we could get there."

Marlo nodded and looked at the clouds building in the northwest. They were larger. He moved along the catwalk and went among the bow guns. The light wind was still to their backs, and it was beginning to blow fitfully. He wiped his brow. The air was rather hot and moist.

An hour later, the wind died down completely, and the sails were furled. The prisoners continued to pull at their oars, racing against time. The clouds continued to move toward them from the east, turning to deep shadow the sea below. The wall of clouds turned from white to gray, flecked with orange from the western sun. Marlo opened the top of his shirt. The air seemed hotter and very humid. He looked back to the stern. Don John was pacing the deck and frequently glancing toward the building bank of clouds, halting to speak to Bazan.

"Will we make it, Captain?" he heard John ask.

The captain's lined face turned to the youthful commander with a grin. "We might be tossed about a bit before we get there, Your Excellency, but I think we will be anchored by the time the real blow sets in."

John looked at the sky again. "Somehow I rather think you are looking forward to this."

"I wouldn't say that, My Lord." Bazan winked.

"I hope that the weather is not up to your expectations, Captain." John shook his head and resumed pacing the deck.

The sky to the east grew darker. The fleet rowed in the still air with their sails furled. Soon, the wind began to blow, this time from the northeast. In a few minutes, the breeze turned into gusts. The sea grew choppy, and the ships rocked in the contrary swells, making it harder to keep the oar blades moving in rhythm. As the wind increased, salt spray blew into the ships every time the bows crashed into a wave.

Marlo carefully made his way back to the stern. He was wet from spray, and the shifting deck made it difficult to walk. He found it awkward to keep his balance. Just as he was congratulating himself for not being seasick, the deck dropped suddenly. He stumbled. Grasping a line, he saved himself from falling, but in doing so, he found himself looking at a prisoner on the port side of the ship. To Marlo's dismay, the prisoner was in the process of being violently sick. Marlo gasped, his stomach suddenly queasy. Sweating, and with his mouth suddenly watering, he turned and crawled on. He made it past the rowers and to the starboard gunwale.

Afterwards, he knelt down, breathing deeply, looking at the horizon and tried to think about something else.

"Are you alright, Marlo?" He heard Don John ask. He felt a hand on his shoulder. "You didn't hurt yourself in that tumble back there?"

"No, I'm fine," answered Marlo. "At least I will be in a minute." Breathing slowly, he pulled himself upright. "I was only a little sick."

"Just hang in a little longer. Captain Bazan says that Trifolques is in sight. We will be anchored within thirty minutes."

"At least the rain has not started yet."

"As for that," said John gesturing to the east,

"the rain will be here very soon. Look." Marlo looked and saw the gray wall of rain ahead of them. "We won't get into the mouth of Trifolques before that reaches us, but Captain Bazan assures me that we will be safely anchored before the worst is upon us."

The fleet slowly moved east against the wind. When the ships turned south to head into the sheltered cove, the storm swells started to rock the ships from side to side. The oars moved intermittently, the boatswain calling the rowers to stop whenever a swell interfered with the movement of the oars.

As the *Capitana* moved into the cove, the rain began. Captain Bazan sent a sailor into the bow to make sure that the ship did not run aground. In the bay, the swells were smaller, and the galley made its way deeper into the sheltered water with greater ease.

When the anchor was dropped, the *Capitana* swung around, its bow facing the wind. Marlo looked back and watched the rest of the fleet come to anchor. In a few minutes the entire fleet was swinging on their anchors. Sailors moved about the galleys to secure them for the duration of the storm.

~~~

The rain and wind drenched the ships for almost two entire days. The prisoners and soldiers fared the worst. While the officers were
~~~

able to take shelter in their cabins, the others had to endure the wind and rain without any shelter. When the ships had first anchored, the soldiers had tried to use a sail as a type of wind and rain break without success. Even though the mouth of Trifolques was sheltered from the worst of the storm, the wind was still too strong, and the canvas kept collapsing. For two nights the soldiers hardly slept. Whenever Marlo looked out of Don John's cabin, he saw groups of men huddled under pieces of oil-cloth, shivering together in the cold.

After the rain had passed, John ordered the fleet to remain at anchor to give both the prisoners and the soldiers a chance to rest. Relieved soldiers took off their wet clothes and went to sleep for the first time in two nights.

~~~

The next day, Don John went to pay his respects to Don Lara, the governor of Melilla. He was gone most of the day, and it was not until the following morning that the fleet was able to resume its patrol, leaving the mouth of Trifolques and heading east on a calm sea. Don John kept the fleet in sight of the African coast hoping to intimidate the Algerians with a show of force. The fleet rowed all morning with no sign of any Algerian ships. At midday, he gave up pacing the deck of the *Capitana* and invited Marlo below.
~~~

"How was your visit to Melilla?" asked Marlo as they entered the cabin. "You were there longer than I expected."

"It seems that most of our provincial governors are inept," said John when he and Marlo had seated themselves and begun to eat. "Don Lara of Melilla was of the same class as Don Alfredo."

"Another case of smuggling, My Lord?" asked Marlo.

"No, but just as selfish." John paused and sighed. "The inspection of these governors and garrisons was long overdue, it seems."

"What did you find?"

"Fraud," answered John. "After what was a pleasant conversation with Don Lara, I sent Juan to look around. He came back to me with complaints from the garrison that the soldiers had not been paid for several months. Don Lara was using any imagined slight of conduct to dock the soldier's wages. In fact, he had a third of the garrison incarcerated as they were unable to pay fines that he had levied on them."

"What did he do with the money he was withholding from his men?" asked Marlo.

"Increasing his prestige with the nobles in the city."

"So, I assume that is why you spent all day there?"

"Yes," John sighed. "I had Juan going through Don Lara's accounts, and I insisted on interviewing many of the men. Fortunately for the soldiers, Juan was able to determine how much pay was defrauded."

"Did Don Lara have sufficient funds to pay the men when you were done with your investigations?"

"Just enough. I made sure that the men were paid before I left. With these governors more concerned about themselves than the security of the Spanish trade, it is no wonder that the Algerian has grown bold." John shook his head. "I had to remove Don Lara from his position. He no longer commanded the respect of his men. I appointed an acting governor, and now I have to give this problem to my Royal Brother."

Marlo leaned back in his chair. "Besides dealing with greedy governors and pirates we can't find, this has been a rather tedious cruise. What do we do now?"

"Don Requesens advised that we continue along the African coast for a couple of days, and then head north to Mallorca. If your guess is correct, we should find Ochiali somewhere around there." There was a knock on the door. "Come in!"

The door opened and Juan leaned into the cabin. "My Lord," he said, "two ships have been sighted to the east. Captain Bazan thinks that they are the same ones that we pursued the other day."

"Very well," said John standing. "Inform Captain Bazan that I will join him presently." Juan bowed and left, closing the door behind him. "Well, Marlo, you were just complaining about another tedious cruise. It looks like we should have some ship action, after all."

"Not to reduce your enthusiasm, My Lord," said Marlo, "but if they are the same ships we chased the other day, we probably won't catch them. They were faster than even the *Reya*."

"Your encouragement is most heartening, Señor Gobeli," said John dryly. "Why don't we go on deck and see if we can't prove you wrong."

Marlo followed Don John out of the cabin and onto the deck. The sea was still calm, and the breeze was still too light for the sails to be of any use. The *Capitana* was flanked by the *Reya* and the faster ships of the fleet.

"What do we have, Don Requesens?" asked John.

"Two ships, my lord," answered Requesens. "They were sighted a few minutes ago. I took the liberty of having the faster ships join us—in case you desire to give chase."

"Very good, Don Requesens. What is their bearing?"

"They are heading directly away from us. I think they know we are here."

"Give chase then," said John. "Maybe we will get lucky this time." The *Reya*, complying with

Don Requesens' signal moved ahead with the three faster ships.

"Let's pray that the wind gets stronger," said Requesens. "We may be chasing those ships for a while."

"The wind will also help them," said Bazan. "I just hope our oarsmen have more stamina."

The distance between the *Reya* and the *Capitana* slowly increased. The rest of the fleet spread out behind the *Capitana*, the calls of the boatswains urging the rowers to greater efforts sounding out over the still water.

By mid-afternoon, the corsairs were two dark specks on the horizon. The *Reya* had managed to keep pace with them and was now several miles ahead of the rest of the fleet. Don John joined Marlo, who was leaning on the center bow cannon.

"What do you make of the chase?" he asked Marlo.

"Well, my lord, they seem to be keeping close to the shore. I wonder if they are looking for a safe harbor to dart into."

"That might be dangerous for them," said John. "Bazan is confident that the wind will pick up soon, and if we chase them until after nightfall, they might miss their safe haven altogether."

"Let's hope they don't lead us into the arms of Ochiali's fleet in the night," said Marlo.

"They won't. We will go slowly during the

night, and move a little further north. The night promises to be clear, so we should be able to see any waiting ambush in time to avoid it."

~~~

Captain Bazan was accurate in his prediction. Around five in the afternoon, the breeze picked up and blew in from the west. Sails were unfurled throughout the fleet, and they were able to close on their quarry. By the time the breeze reached the corsairs, they had been able to close the distance by a couple of miles. Once the corsairs had unfurled their sails, though, the fleet again lost distance.

By the time night fell, the pirates were beyond the horizon. Don John ordered the rowers to stop, and the ships were quiet, except for the slap of water on the sides and the occasional murmur of muted voices. A lantern was hoisted aloft on the *Capitana.* A light showed briefly in the distance.

"Was that the *Reya*?" asked Marlo.

"Yes," answered Requesens. "She is acknowledging our signal to break off the chase. We will join them shortly."

After an hour, a light appeared in the bay beyond, and the *Reya* slowly became visible in the starlight. Don Requesens ordered the fleet to proceed eastward using only the sails.

During the night the wind grew stronger, and the fleet moved north to avoid running
~~~

aground. Other than the sound of the water, the ships remained silent. Lanterns were not lit, and the lookouts were changed regularly in order to remain alert for any sign of ships to the north and the east.

~~~

In the morning, after the prisoners were fed, the oars were employed and the fleet turned southeast back toward the African coast. Don John ordered the fleet to form up to the north of the *Capitana* to cover as large an area as possible.

"Señor Gobeli," said John later in the morning. "I fear that those ships did not slow down during the night."

Marlo looked about the water from where he was sitting on the gunwale near the tiller. "No, I don't think they did."

"We probably should have kept going," said John with a sigh.

"That might not have helped," answered Marlo. "Those ships were faster than us. They might have outrun us no matter what we did."

Ahead of the *Capitana*, the shore bent north into the sea. The fleet was forced to turn northeast to avoid running aground against the rocks.

"My lord!" called the lookout as they rounded the point of the cape, "there is one of the ships! Off the starboard bow, against the
~~~

rocks."

Marlo could just make out the ship in the distance. It was not moving, nor were its sails up. "It seems to have run aground," he commented.

"So it has," said John. "And it looks like it is abandoned."

"Are we going to leave it and try to find the other?"

John was silent for a moment. "No," he said, shaking his head, "if it is indeed abandoned, then the galley slaves were probably left behind. Besides, I want to find out where that ship came from." He left Marlo's side and went to talk to Captain Bazan.

The *Capitana* drew closer, and Captain Bazan ordered the musketeers to load their weapons. Soldiers lined the starboard side of the ship and watched for any movement on the grounded galley.

"Stop oars," Captain Bazan called, and the *Capitana* glided toward the ship. There was no sign of movement.

"Drop the anchor!" Bazan shouted.

The anchor splashed into the water and set. The *Capitana* swung around and strained at the rope. Six other ships joined them.

From each of the ships, boats were lowered so that soldiers could climb into them. They rowed slowly towards the wreck. The first touched and soldiers climbed aboard, swords drawn. Marlo watched as they began to move across the slanted deck. One of them gave a shout, gesticulated to the other boats, and leapt back into his own.

"What could be wrong?" asked John.

"I'm not sure. There can't be anything dangerous. Only that one boat is returning, and fast."

"Your Excellency," called the soldier when his boat finally reached the *Capitana.* "Your Excellency." The soldier paused. His face was pale. "Your Excellency," he gasped a third time.

"What is it, Miguel?" asked John. "What is wrong?"

"The prisoners. God help us, the prisoners! We need a priest."

"Father!" shouted John. The Franciscan priest was already moving toward the side of the ship to climb into the boat. "Wait!" called John. "I'm coming."

"Your Excellency," protested Requesens, "It might be a trap. You can't be putting yourself at risk like this."

"The soldiers have the ship secured. The chances are slim of there being a trap, and if there is something wrong with the prisoners, I need to see it."

"But, My Lord," Requesens began.

"Are you coming, Marlo?" called John, ignoring his lieutenant's protestations. Marlo leapt into the boat, and it began moving toward the galley.

"Now, Miguel," said John quietly, "tell me what is wrong."

"Those barbarians," began Miguel. His voice was hoarse. "They left the prisoners. Dead."

The boat touched the side of the ship, and the rowers grabbed the ropes and held it steady. Don John climbed into the galley, followed by Marlo and Miguel. The deck was slanted, and Marlo walked with care toward the center, where he could look down into the lower decks. He only walked a few paces before he stopped short, his gasp echoing that of the young commander.

"Dear God!" said John.

The galley slaves were draped over the benches and each other. They were covered in blood.

"God have mercy," he whispered.

Together, Don John and Father Paulo climbed down into the hold.

Most of the prisoner's throats had been slit. A few were decapitated. As they moved closer, they heard a groan.

"Quick!" shouted John. "I think at least one is still alive!"

"How can we find him?" asked a solder.

Marlo went to one of corpses. "We move the bodies onto the deck. Here, help me with this one."

One body at a time, the dead slaves were

lifted out of the hold and lined up on the deck. As they moved toward the other end of the hold, the groans got louder, and they were able to determine that more than one prisoner was still alive.

"Father, come here," called Marlo. "I found one." He bent over a young man, emaciated and scarred about the chest with welts. He was bleeding from a wound in his side. The slave opened his eyes as Marlo tried to staunch the wound. "*Per favore*," the slave gasped in when the priest bent over him.

Father Paulo made the sign of the cross over him and then gave him some water. Marlo ripped off part of his shirt, wadded it, and pressed it against the slave's wound. "Help me get him up onto deck," he called.

Assisted by two soldiers, Marlo and Father Paulo carried the man onto the deck. They laid him down, and gave him more water. When Don John joined them, his clothes were stained with blood. "Who did this?" he asked.

The wounded man looked at John and shook his head. Marlo repeated the question in Italian.

"Ibrahim," he whispered.

"Were they Turks or Algerians?" asked Marlo.

"Turks."

"Were you part of a fleet?"

"Yes."

"Do you know who commanded it?"

"Ochiali." The slave closed his eyes.

Marlo stood. "They were from Ochiali's fleet," he said.

Don John's eyes were hard. "God help him if we catch him. By all that is holy, this is unspeakable! To murder the galley slaves?"

"This killing is just Ochiali's way of letting us know that negotiation is no longer possible."

"Negotiation," said John with disgust. He walked back toward the hold.

~~~

Only twenty-three of the hundred and two slaves were still alive, and most of those were near death. Don John had more boats brought over, and the living were sent back to other ships.

"What are we going to do with the dead?" asked Marlo.

"We are going to give them a decent burial at sea," answered John.

When they returned to the *Capitana*, they were met by Don Requesens. "Did you find out where the ship was from?"

"Yes. Ochiali," answered John. "And pass the word. I want any information that we can get from the rescued prisoners. We need to find this monster."

"Yes, my lord." Don Requesens bowed and left.
~~~

"Come," John turned to Marlo. "This is a grisly job, and it is not over yet. But I need to clean up. The bastards," he hissed. His face was stern and angry.

Marlo followed him into his cabin. "Sit, my lord," he said. He closed the cabin door and opened the cupboard. Taking a glass, he filled it with wine and gave it to Don John. "Drink this. It will do you good."

John drank the wine down. "We still have to bury the dead. That is the least we can do for them."

"And the injured?" asked Marlo.

"We will bring them to Denia. That is closest to the Balearic Islands."

By nightfall, all the dead were shrouded and placed on the decks of ten of Don John's ship. On the wrecked ship, there was little else to be found. All the cargo had been carried off, the powder barrels emptied, and the food removed. Marlo guessed that the Turks had used the galley slaves to move the cargo to the undamaged vessel, and then slaughtered them.

The next morning, they were thirty miles off the coast of Africa. Don John ordered a halt. On each ship carrying the dead, a priest gave the Catholic burial service, singing the *Libera Nos* of absolution and sprinkling them with holy water. Then, one by one, the weighted bodies were cast into the sea.

Chapter 21
July 1568

Six of the wounded victims died on the way to Denia. Each evening the fleet paused to drop at least one body into the sea, and Marlo wondered who they were. Their families would never find out what had happened to them.

Contrary to his usual practice, Don John used the fleet prisoners in rotation through the nights, and even kept the prisoners at the oars in spite of favorable winds. The fleet was able to reach Denia in three days.

Don John remained aboard as Marlo and Don Requesens oversaw the transportation of the wounded. When the seventeen wounded galley slaves had been safely brought ashore and arrangements made for their care, Marlo returned to the *Capitana* while Don Requesens went to the governor to make sure the victims would be able given transportation to their homes when they had recovered. He was gone for three hours.

Dusk had fallen when he returned to the *Capitana* and knocked on Don John's cabin door. Requesens was smiling as he entered.

"Well, that is quite satisfactory," he said with a chuckle.

"What might that be?" asked John.

"Remember Don Alfredo?"

"Too well. That is one reason why I stayed on this ship. If I had landed, I would have had to pay my respects."

"You would not have seen him if you had gone ashore. Remember how you made him continue to pay for the extra soldiers he hired but didn't remove him from his post?"

"Yes," said John.

"Well, no sooner did His Majesty receive your report than Don Alfredo was summoned to Madrid. Don Rivera, the new governor, happened to be with the king when he read your report. Apparently His Majesty laughed heartily. The manner of forcing him to continue to pay the soldiers' salaries amused him greatly."

"Well, I am glad he found it entertaining. I didn't," said John.

"Don Rivera seems a decent fellow, and he promised to make sure that the victims would be able to return to wherever they came from, if they choose."

"Good," John stood. He opened a chest and pulled out a map and spread it out on the table. "Now, I would like to depart in the morning. Will we be able to reach Mallorca within a day?"

"Yes," said Requesens. "We could even split the fleet and send one part to the north of Ibiza and the other smaller islands while we keep to the south. We could meet up again on the western side of Mallorca."

"Make those arrangements, then. In the morning we resume our hunt."

~~~

"These are the jewels of the Mediterranean," said Don John pointing to the island of Mallorca ahead of them. "The Balearic Islands are probably the closest to paradise this side of heaven."

"Then it is a shame that the king lets the Algerians entrench themselves here," said Marlo.

John smiled. "Marlo, one day you are going to make a disrespectful comment like that at the wrong time and find yourself clapped in irons." He shook his head. "For your own good, I should make sure you are never around the king or anybody else who could be in a position of punishing you for your impertinence."

"But then you would have to refrain yourself from placing me in the nearest dungeon you can find," said Marlo. "I have been told that I
~~~

have no respect for superiors."

"Well, you are going to have to control that impulse for a while." John indicated the island ahead of them. "Do you know what place that is?" he asked, turning to Bazan who was standing at the tiller.

"That is Cuidadilla, My Lord," answered the Captain.

"I assume it is under Spanish control?"

"That is the strongest fortification the king has on these islands. The Algerians leave this place alone, tending to land on the other side of the island."

"We should ask them about Ochiali, My Lord," said Marlo. "The alcayde there should know if he is in the area."

"We can send a ship or two in to find out, Your Excellency," suggested Captain Bazan.

"It might be best if I went personally," said Don John. "Asking about Ochiali will give me an excuse to check on the state of the garrison stationed here."

"Are you sure you want to do that?" asked Marlo. "Remember what happened with the last garrison you inspected?"

"No, I really don't want to. But I should," answered John. "Captain Bazan, inform Don Requesens of my intention to visit that castle, and have the fleet wait in readiness in the harbor." Bazan bowed and went below.

Mallorca grew tall and green as the fleet approached. Cuidadilla was situated on a rock that overlooked the harbor, the guns on its walls were a deterrent against hostile ships.

The *Capitana* left the fleet behind and moved deeper into the harbor. Once she was anchored, Don John and Marlo climbed into a boat with Requesens and were rowed to the quay. Stepping ashore, they followed the road that led up to the castle.

At the castle gates, they were met by a lieutenant who led them inside. Passing through the courtyard, the lieutenant led them through a colonnade and into a room, open on one side, overlooking a small flower garden.

"If you will wait here, Your Excellency," said the lieutenant, "I will inform Don Mendoza that you have arrived."

In a few minutes Don Mendoza entered the room. His elderly face was creased with a smile of genuine pleasure. "Your Excellency, we heard that you were commanding a fleet to fight back against the Algerians. How do you find sea life?"

"As well as one could expect," answered John. "We actually have only seen a couple of pirate galleys. We hear rumors of a large fleet, but we can't seem to find it."

"Whatever you are doing, it seems to be working," said Don Mendoza smiling. "This summer has seen the least pirate activity in a while. Most of our Sicilian trade ships never see an Algerian ship, and none have been attacked for the last month."

"Have you had any reports of Algerians here in the Balearic Islands?" asked Requesens.

"We were told of one galley near Majorca," answered Mendoza, "but that is all. Usually they will raid coastal villages, but not this year."

"And no news of any large fleet of Algerian or Turkish ships?" asked John.

"This is the first time I have heard of them," said Mendoza frowning. "Though we generally don't hear of what is going on in the rest of the Mediterranean. If I do hear anything of that fleet, I will send the information on to you."

"We would be most grateful," said John. "You can contact me in Cartagena. If I am not there, the Captain-General there will either send it on to me or make sure I receive it when I return."

"Consider it done," said Mendoza. "Now, would you like some refreshment? One of the reasons I enjoy being stationed here is the cuisine."

"We would be honored," said John. "And at the same time, you can update me on the current state of the garrison here."

"Of course." Mendoza stood. "We can discuss that while we eat."

~~~
~~~

"That was a relatively painless inspection," commented Marlo as they were being rowed back to the *Capitana*. "Don Mendoza seems to have everything in control."

"Including his kitchen," chuckled John. "I think he took more pride in the quality of his food than in the morale of his soldiers. But you're right. He seems to be a capable commander for that garrison." The boat touched the *Capitana* and Marlo took hold of the line. Don John climbed aboard, followed by Requesens and Marlo.

"Do you plan to continue patrolling these islands?" asked Requesens as they walked toward the stern.

"What is your opinion?" asked John.

"That there would be no reason not to." Requesens shrugged. "The next time an Algerian landed to raid a village, they would probably hear of us. That would make them a little less anxious to venture into waters we control."

"Then we should continue with our plans," said John. "Though it frustrates me that we never seem to be able to find that fleet."

"We do seem to be chasing their shadow," said Requesens. "Though I wonder if that is because they are running from us."

"Let's hope they are running, not raiding," said John grimly. He looked back at the receding castle. "Let's hope they keep running all the way back to Constantinople – and sink just before they get there."

For two days the fleet patrolled the Balearic Islands. Circling Mallorca, they went northeast to Minorca. There were no signs of pirates on either of the islands, and Don John gave the order for the fleet to set course for Barcelona.

The harbor of Barcelona was busy. Merchant ships filled the southern area of the harbor. Some were unloading their cargoes, and others were preparing to sail. On the opposite side of the harbor, fifteen galleys were being rigged and mounted with cannon. Five of the galleys were without masts. The *Capitana* anchored near them.

Once ashore, Don John went to the governor's palace. After paying his respects to the governor, he went to his room to prepare his report for the king. As he worked, there was a knock at his door.

"My Lord." John looked up. Juan was standing at the door. "I have a letter for you from Andrea Doria."

John put down his pen. "Thank you, Juan," he said. He took the letter from Juan and opened it after his secretary left. The letter was short and dated eight days earlier.

> *Your Excellency,*
> *On the twelfth of this month, I received*
> *word of a large fleet of Turkish ships near*

John put down the letter and went to the door. "Juan," he said, "Please convey my regards to Don Requesens and request that he and Señor Gobeli join me as soon as possible."

Returning to his desk, he folded up the report he had been writing to his brother. He could complete it once he had decided what to do about Doria's intelligence.

"Your Excellency," Requesens said as he and Marlo entered, "your secretary indicated that you needed us at once."

"Yes," said John. "This was just delivered." He handed Requesens Doria's letter. Requesens read it quietly and handed it to Marlo.

"So Ochiali is finally located," said Marlo handing the letter back to John. "That is where he went. The Adriatic."

"Waters that are usually controlled by Venice," said Requesens shaking his head. "This is not good."

"How so?" asked John.

"It means that Selim is confident that his fleet has nothing to fear from Venice. And the fact that Venice seems to be doing nothing about it indicates that he is right."

"What is Selim trying to accomplish?"

"Possibly intimidation, my lord," answered Requesens. "Possibly extorting concessions from Venice."

"My lord," said Marlo. "If Selim is seeking concessions then he is probably trying to put Venice off guard. All indications are that Selim is gearing up for war, and Rome has received no information to the contrary. If this European alliance can be prevented, then Venice will have no allies when she is attacked."

"That is possible," agreed Requesens.

"Then what should we do?" asked John.

"My Lord," said Marlo, "we have chased that fleet all summer. We have seen nothing but devastation in its wake. Now that we know where it is, we should move against it. Even if we can't engage it, we can at least chase them back home."

"While Señor Gobeli's overall idea is good," interjected Requesens, "those waters are Venice's to defend."

"Yes," said John. He leaned forward. "However, this is an opportunity to secure Spain's position. Action against that fleet would make the Algerians far more cautious."

"Then I would recommend reinforcing Doria, My Lord," said Requesens. "If he has a large enough fleet, he can move against them when they leave the Adriatic. That way the pirates see our resolve not to tolerate any more of their activity, and Venice receives no insult."

"How many ships could we send?"

"There are at least ten ships here that are almost ready for sea, and the king has ordered them placed at your disposal. Those, plus half our fleet. We could easily send twenty-five ships to Doria and still have reasonable numbers with which to protect our trade."

"Very well," said John. "Let us send twenty-five ships under Cordona right away. Could you see to it?"

"At once, My Lord."

"Make sure Cordona knows that he will be under Andrea Doria's command. I will write to Doria telling him that Cordona is to be used for action against Ochiali's fleet. Once that fleet has been attacked and driven back to Constantinople, Cordona is to return with his ships."

"At last," said John to Marlo after Requesens had left. "We have him."

"What are your plans now?"

"I am going to the shipyard to get those ten ships ready for sea. Then I should go to Cartagena and see if my Royal Brother has any instructions for me. But first, I need to finish this report to him."

"I can't help you there," said Marlo.

~~~

The following afternoon, Marlo was walking among the warehouses. Casual conversation with the dockhands and merchants indicated that the trading season had been moderately trouble-free and that most of the grain had made it into port.

This is good, he thought. *Both the pope and the king will be pleased with these results.* Turning a corner, he saw Juan de Quirroga running down the street.

"Señor Gobeli!" he called when he noticed Marlo. "Come quick. Don John wants you at once."

"I am on my way," Marlo responded. He moved through the streets and up to the palace. Once inside, he went to John's apartments, knocked, and entered.

John was standing by the window, his hands resting on the sill. He glanced toward Marlo, gestured to a chair, and turned back toward the window. Marlo kept quiet. He saw that something was bothering the prince. Eventually the prince turned around and sat down with a sigh.

"What is the problem, my lord?" asked Marlo.

"Don Carlos has died." John sighed. "I know
~~~

he was not the best of people, but he always treated me with consideration."

"I'm sorry for it, then," said Marlo. "That leaves Spain without an heir."

"Spain was already without an heir. The king judged him unfit to inherit, and the Spanish empire is probably better off without him; he was nothing like his father. But still, I am going to miss him."

"Will you be heading back to Madrid?"

"That depends on what the king wants. We should return to Cartagena immediately, though." John turned to walk out of his room. "Could you find Juan and tell him that we will be departing in the morning. Then find Requesens and tell him that I want to see him in an hour."

"Where are you going?"

"To the church to have a mass said. I will be back within the hour." John turned and left the room.

Marlo went to Don John's study. Juan was copying out the Captain's recent report to the king. He looked up when Marlo entered. "Good evening, Señor Gobeli."

"Juan," said Marlo. "Don John wants to sail to Cartagena in the morning."

"I assumed that would be the case," said Juan. "I am completing a few necessary things first, then I will make sure his gear is transferred to the *Capitana*."

"Good. Do you know where I can find Don Requesens?"

"I think he is in the shipyard. Two galleys are being outfitted, and he wants to make sure everything is in order."

"Thank you," said Marlo. "I need to tell him that Don John needs to see him in an hour. If he stops by, could you let him know?"

"I will tell him," answered Juan.

Marlo left Juan and walked his way down to the shipyard. He walked along the docks. He found Don Requesens supervising the placement of cannon on one of the ships. "Don Requesens?" he called.

"Just a moment," answered Requesens. He spoke to the workmen and then joined Marlo on the dock. "These two ships will be ready tomorrow evening, and another two the next day. What do you need?"

"Don John needs to see you. He just received word that Don Carlos has died."

Requesens was silent for a moment. "Very well. I know he was friendly with the prince. I will be there."

~~~

An hour later, Marlo and Don Requesens joined Don John in his apartment, who received their condolences with composure and thanked them. "I assume you need to return to Madrid?" asked Requesens.
~~~

"I should," answered John. "Even though Don Carlos was no longer the crown prince, he was still my brother's only surviving son. I am sure the king would wish me to return as soon as I could."

"I would agree with that," said Requesens.

"I plan to leave in the morning, and sail to Cartagena. I will take the road to Madrid from there. You shall command for as long as I am gone or until the king appoints someone else."

"What about Doria?"

"Send Cordona and the ships to him as we had planned. I trust your judgment."

"Very well, My Lord," said Requesens. "I must congratulate you on a good first command. You did well."

"That may be," said John, "yet it bothers me is that I was not able to finish what I had set out to do."

"You did well, my lord," repeated Requesens.

"I appreciate that," said John. "But we did not meet the pirates, and we are retreating, leaving the sea uncontested."

"Your Excellency." Requesens walked over to Don John and put his hand on his shoulder. "You have done what was expected, and I have been proud to serve under you. You are rather young, in fact the youngest Captain of the Sea ever, and there were others who had experience and would have been the more logical choice. But your conduct during the last few months has shown that His Majesty knew what he was doing when he gave the command to you. Instead of being arrogant, you clearly recognized your weaknesses. You asked for advice, you listened to the voice of experience, and above all, you were able to make sound decisions. You don't need me anymore. You have learned how to command and I would consider it my honor to serve under you again.

"And as far as the pirates are concerned," continued Requesens before his commander could interrupt, "you have succeeded. Yes, there were no significant battles. But the Algerian ran from you. The Turks ran from you. You were sent to make the waters safe for Spain, and you did just that."

Don Requesens paused and stood tall. He looked into Don John's face for a moment. "Your Excellency," he said dropping to his knee and placing his right hand on his chest. "You are a true Spaniard and bear the mark of El Cid. You have succeeded and have shown yourself to be the best of men. May God preserve you."

"That was unexpected," said John after Requesens had left.

"But not undeserved," added Marlo. "I could have told you the same thing a long time ago."

"Both of you have a gift for flattery." John shook his head. "But I don't do well with flattery – it makes me uncomfortable. I wish I felt that I deserved Don Requesens' praise. I still feel like I don't know what I am doing."

"We don't ever get rid of the nagging doubt. For some, that doubt is buried, and for others that doubt paralyzes."

"Which one would you say I am?" asked John.

"Neither," said Marlo firmly. "Your doubt forces you to seek advice from those who have more experience. And I do have to agree with Requesens. You have made the Mediterranean secure for Spanish trade. Spain will not starve this year. And you have possibly given Selim doubts about the advisability of trying to reestablish Moorish rule in Granada."

John was silent. He looked out the window at the ships in the harbor. Most of them were his, but trade ships were coming in laden with grain. Commerce had been good for the merchants, and every ship that escaped molestation from the Algerians added to the financial security and well-being of every Spaniard dependent on the goods and grain those ships carried. He turned back to Marlo.

"What are your plans now?" he asked.

"I will return to Madrid with you, if I may," answered Marlo.

"I would be glad to have you with me," said John. "I expect we will stay in Madrid until the spring."

"As for that, I only plan to be in Madrid for about a month. Then I need to go to Granada."

"Why?" asked John.

Marlo looked at his friend, and then out the window. "There's a promise I need to keep."

Chapter 22
September 1568

September eighth was a special day for Maria. It was the anniversary of her baptism, and she had always attended mass to commemorate it. This might be the first year she would not.

Maria lay in bed trying to decide. Her father would not go. She had asked him the previous evening. In spite of her fears about traveling through the streets of Granada without an escort, Montoya had encouraged her to go to mass in the morning. She wanted to, as she had been at home far too much the last few months. In fact, aside from going to mass on Sundays with her Father, she had not left the house at all.

Maria pulled up her legs and rested her chin on her knees. *What sort of unpleasantness would happen?* she thought. Dirty looks and leers from the younger Morisco men. Insults from the more hateful. None of these would actually cause her physical harm. She would be embarrassed, yes, but no real harm would come. Surely in the streets no one would offer violence?

Throwing back her bedcovers, Maria climbed out of bed and began to dress. Since it was her baptismal day, she put on her favorite dress: dark red accented with black edging at the hem and around the cuffs. White silk, embroidered with roses, cascaded down her chest. Her father had purchased this dress for her two years ago, and she always wore it on special occasions. She thought it highlighted her luxurious dark hair. This was her special day. She would wear her special dress. She would go to mass.

Draping a shawl around her shoulders she left her room. She found her father in his office going over the accounts with Carlos.

"I am going to mass," she told him.

"Good girl," said Montoya. He stood and walked over to her. He took her hands and kissed her. "My beautiful one," he said smiling down at her, "go to mass, and when you get back, I have something special for you." Maria kissed her father on his cheek and turned to leave. "Don't forget to say a prayer for me," he called after her.

"Of course," said Maria smiling. "I always

pray for you at mass. I will be back soon."

Maria hesitated at the steps of her house, her anxiety clamoring to be heard. She looked down the street and saw that there were quite a number of people going about. Many of them in Moorish attire, but most of the people were wearing normal Spanish clothing. *Well, it seems safe enough*, she told herself and stepped into the street.

She was not bothered as she walked the half-mile to the church. Some of the young men looked at her as she passed, but none of them were unpleasant. Nobody approached her, and when she reached the steps of the church, she looked back and saw that nobody was following her either. Feeling relieved and a little ashamed at her concern, she entered the church, made the sign of the cross with holy water, and prepared herself for mass.

During mass, she felt herself relax. Maybe she had been a little foolish in her fears. What if her father was right? She hoped that Marlo would be returning to Madrid soon, and that he would find out what the king thought about the Morisco situation. She prayed that he would not forget his promise to send that information to her father.

After mass, she lit a candle for her mother before leaving the church. When she stepped outside, she was surprised to see a crowd in the square. Two men were standing on the edge of a fountain. One of them was Farax. She gasped and darted back into the church, not wanting him to see her. Keeping the door ajar, she could hear Farax shouting to the crowd.

"I tell you, Selim has promised to send his army! The Sultan is not unaware of our suffering, and suffers with us."

"How can you be sure of that?" a voice called out.

"This man here has been sent by the Sultan. Ibrahim was sent to personally assure us of the Sultan's desire to assist us. Not only that, Ibrahim, as an experienced officer of the Turkish military, is here to guide our efforts and help us prepare for the time when we will throw off our oppressors and take back our lands!

"In our hands, Allah's holy sword will restore us to our heritage. No longer will we be prevented from using our language. No longer will the Christian peasant denounce us to the Inquisition. Our property will be safeguarded, and the customs of our fathers restored."

Maria sagged against the doorpost. She knew she shouldn't have come to mass alone, and now Farax was stirring up the mob in the square, the same Farax who knew where she lived.

"People of Granada," continued Farax, "do not loose heart. If Allah has allowed these tribulations, it is because we have not been faithful. We have acquiesced to acting as Catholics in order to be left in peace. Such hypocrisy is disgusting in Allah's sight, and He has turned His wrath against us to purify our intentions. Yet, now the time of His wrath is spent. No longer does He desire our oppression; He is anxious for our service.

"Long ago our fathers came to this land and found it a paradise inhabited by a rude and uncultured people. They brought the message of Allah to this very soil. They built cities, universities, and a culture that had never before been known in these parts since the old Roman Empire. We liberated the people from the darkness. We taught them how to live. We educated their children. We became a light to the world. And in our prosperity, we grew lax.

"Alliances were made with the Christian kings in the north. Their soldiers were employed to fight our wars. Their religious darkness was even permitted to flourish. And since truth was permitted to exist alongside error, Allah's sight darkened, and this land was taken from us. However, this time we will not lose it again."

The crowd was becoming agitated. The people were beginning to whisper to each other, and some were becoming animated with excitement. The rising murmur of voices threatened to drown out the speaker. Farax paused and held up his hand. The sound died away, and was replaced by the silence of expectant tenseness.

"This is the message that Ibrahim brings from the Sultan: that Allah will not bless us if we leave even one Christian on these shores.

"The errors of those who came before us will not be repeated!" Farax shouted. "This land will be thoroughly cleansed. And when we are done, there will be only Islam. For we will burn their churches, burn their cities!"

They roared in excitement. Young Morisco men began shaking their fists, their faces contorted. Their shrieks echoed off the buildings. Farax let the people shout, and eventually the voices organized themselves into the repeated chant, "Great is Allah, Great is Allah!"

Eventually Farax raised both hands. The chanting faded. "And what might the king do if we rise? He will not be able to stop us! He has only a few hundred soldiers in this region, and what are a few hundred against an army of Janissaries? No, he will not stop us. We will bring Allah's sword to complete victory.

"Allah will bless us with the houses and goods of the slain Christians. Their children will be our slaves, and their maidens will become our wives. This land, with its delightful climate and its beautiful women, will become for us a foretaste of that heaven which is promised for those who fight against the enemies of Allah, the only holy. Great is Allah!" Farax's voice ended with piercing shriek of hate. His last words were picked up by the crowd and repeated again and again.

Maria was shaking. Her anxiety over her father's trust in Farax had been prophetic. She slid down the doorpost, her legs no longer able to support her. That was the worst thing she could have done.

The church door was pushed open as she collapsed against it, and the shouting of those nearest to the church turned to cries of excitement as they saw her huddled in the open doorway. "There is one!" one of them shouted. "That is one of the Christian girls!" The young men nearest the church cheered and surged toward Maria.

Maria leapt up and ran into the church. Gone was the paralyzing terror, and in its place was blind panic. Gathering her skirts about her, she sprinted toward the altar as the young men came through the door.

Without slowing down as she crossed in front of the altar, Maria threw her shoulder against the sacristy door. It flew open and Maria lost her balance, stumbled and ran toward the door that led outside.

She flung aside the door and lost her footing. She had missed the steps outside the door and tumbled. She landed on her hands and slid, her knees banging into the paving stones. Scrambling to stand, her feet catching in her dress, she was dimly aware that her hands hurt. She got her feet under her, and standing, sprinted down the alleyway, her pursuers close behind her.

Maria could hear them just behind her and tried to run faster. She had only run a few yards from the church when she felt a hand close on her dress. She spun and jerked as hard as she could. Her assailant staggered, and she heard the hiss of tearing cloth. Leaping forward, she flew toward the alley.

To her left a door opened. "In here, Señorita!" Maria looked and saw Father Menendez, the priest who had said mass. "In here. Hurry!" he called again.

Maria turned and sprinted through the open door. Father Menendez slammed it shut, and threw his weight against it. The door shook as the Moriscos banged into it. "Come, you are safe now." Maria felt an arm about her shoulders, and turning, saw Father Ramos, the elderly priest in charge of the church.

"Oh, Father," she gasped and collapsed against him. Her panic faded, and her body shook with gasping sobs. The elderly priest gathered her in his arms. "Peace, child," said Father Ramos soothingly, "they won't bother you now."

Father Menendez braced his shoulders against the door. He was a giant of a priest, and the Maria's pursuers found his bulk hard to move. There was silence outside for a few seconds, and then a hoarse shout. The door moved, pushing Father Mendez back as a pair of men threw their weight against it. Father Menendez forced the door closed, his broad shoulders straining against the confines of his cassock. He reached for Father Ramos' heavy cane that leaned against a table next to the entry.

"Give way," he shouted, "or by all that is holy, I will brain any who crosses this threshold."

Jeering laughter came from outside, and the door shook again as the Moriscos threw themselves against it. The door was slowly being forced open, and Father Menendez was struggling to get it closed again. Slowly he shoved the door until it closed on an arm that had reached around it. There was a hoarse cry of pain. "Be off!" shouted Father Menendez. He threw the door open, and jumped to the side.

The six men outside shouted and ran for the open door. Father Menendez raised the cane as the first man came through the doorway and brought the brass knob down against his head. The man collapsed. Father Menendez raised the cane again and swung it sideways. The knob caught the second man in the mouth, snapping his head back. He fell backward, causing the one behind him to stumble. Stepping over the fallen men, the priest grabbed the front of the shirt of the Morisco closest to him, lifted him

off his feet, and threw him backwards. He landed on his back in the alley.

"How dare you attempt to molest this young
lady," he roared. "Get out of here. By God, I will
smash your heads in if you don't."

The three remaining men hesitated. They
had almost had the girl, and then this priest
had appeared in the doorway like a black robed
archangel. He radiated fury, which grew as he
stood there. They backed away. Father Menendez took one step forward, and they broke into
a run. As they rounded the corner at the end of
the alley, Father Menendez moved the two he
had struck outside and closed the door.

Father Ramos eased Maria, still sobbing violently, into a chair. He knelt down in front of
her, holding her arms. "Maria, they are gone,"
he said. He looked at Father Menendez. "Get
me a glass of wine," he ordered.

Father Menendez ran out of the room and
came back a minute later with a cup half full
with wine. He gave the cup to Father Ramos
and set the bottle next to Maria. "I had better
get someone to help me drag those two someplace else," he said nodding toward the door.
"They're not going to move on their own. I hit
them pretty hard."

"And send a message to her father. Tell Señor Montoya to come here at once," instructed
Father Ramos. "Here drink this," he said to Maria after the violence of her sobbing had sub-

sided. Maria took the cup and swallowed its contents. There was blood on the cup when she handed it back to the priest.

"My child, your hands!" exclaimed the priest. He turned her palms up. Her palms were raw and covered with blood and dirt. Maria stared at them. "I will be right back," said the priest. He stood and hurried out of the room.

Maria wiped her eyes with her sleeve and struggled to compose herself. The growing pain in her hands helped. When Father Ramos returned with a basin of water and a towel, her breathing had slowed, and other than the occasional gasping sob, she had herself under control.

Her father came into the room as Father Ramos was washing the last bit of dirt out of her scraped hands. He stopped short. "Maria, your hands!" he exclaimed. "Your dress. What happened?" He knelt next to his daughter and put an arm around her.

"Papa," said Maria turning her face into his chest. "We have to leave. I can't stay here another day."

"What happened?" asked Montoya again. He held her head and pushed back her hair out of her face.

"There was a gathering of Moriscos," said Father Ramos. He tore strips of cloth and bound Maria's hands as he spoke. "Someone by the name of Farax was preaching revolution.

He claimed that the Ottomans would be sending an army. He threatened death for all who refuse Islam. It seems that a few of the younger Moriscos caught sight of her and chased her through the church. Father Menendez brought her in here and dealt with her pursuers."

Montoya stared at the priest in shock. "Farax? It can't be."

"It was him," said the priest. "I was at the edge of the courtyard when he started. He named himself."

"I don't believe it." Montoya shook his head. "It had to have been someone else."

"It was Farax," said Maria. She lifted her head. "I saw him."

Montoya stood and walked over to the window, his hands clasped behind his back. Now that the initial disbelief had vanished, he felt rage building inside of him. He had been lied to. Farax had assured him no one wanted violence, yet all along he had been scheming to rebel!

"Papa, do you believe now?" asked Maria. "We have to leave."

Montoya took a deep breath. He went back to his daughter. "I am sorry. I should have listened to you. You were right. We will leave. Do you feel like you can make it back to the house?"

Maria stood stiffly. Her legs were trembling slightly and her knees hurt. She felt her torn dress start to slide off her shoulder. Reaching up, she tried to hold it in place.

"Here," said Father Ramos. He draped his cloak around Maria's shoulders. "You can have Carlos bring it back." He turned to Montoya. "God be praised, your daughter escaped. She almost did not."

"Thank you for helping her, and thank Father Menendez for me." Montoya put his arm around Maria. He led her through the house and out the front door.

Night had come when Montoya knocked on Maria's door and entered. She had spent the remainder of the day in her room while her father was discussing the situation with Carlos and some of the other tradesmen.

"Maria," said Montoya. He crossed the room and sat slowly on the bed. He took one of her hands. "How are they? Do they hurt much?"

"As long as I don't touch anything," said Maria. "My fingers are fine, though. It is just the palms."

"Again, I apologize for not listening. I had Carlos finding out what happened in the square. And I was talking to Father Menendez. I shouldn't have let you go alone this morning. I should have gone to mass with you. I am sorry."

Maria moved over to her father, took his arm and leaned her head against his shoulder.

"There is nothing to be sorry for, Papa. You were lied to. And Father Menendez was there to stop those who chased me." She paused and lifted her head. "By the way, did you find out if those two men survived?"

"You are a strange one," Montoya chuckled. "They came close to abusing you and you are concerned about their health?"

"No, Papa. I am more concerned about Father Menendez. I don't want him to have the death of anyone on his conscience. Even if he was defending me."

"They are still alive, though one of them will have a hard time eating meat from now on." Maria sighed with relief and laid her head back on Montoya's shoulder. "Carlos and I have learned more about that meeting in the square. Farax was recruiting followers. He wasn't planning to start anything today. He was trying to get men to join him in the mountains."

"Did any go?" asked Maria.

"According to Carlos, Farax was seen leaving the city with about twenty men."

"So he is building an army."

"He is trying to. Twenty men are not enough for an army. He may get more men as time goes on. The general feeling in the city is that he will not start anything until the spring when the weather is better for campaigning. The Sultan's army will not be here before spring, anyway."

"And we will be gone?" asked Maria.

"Yes, we will be gone. But not for a few months. It will take a little time to complete the process of relocating my business to Valencia. Everything should be ready in December. We will leave shortly after Christmas."

Maria sighed. They would still be here for almost four months. She was counting on departing within a couple of weeks. "Don't worry," said Montoya, "if our estimation of when Farax will start his uprising is wrong, we will leave at once. I would like to not have to start my business all over again, if it can be avoided."

"But Carlos will still be around when you are away making those arrangements?"

"No, Carlos will make the arrangements for me. I will stay here with you. In a few weeks, Carlos will head to Valencia. I will employ someone to help me here when he is gone. You will not have to go out alone again."

Montoya closed the door after saying goodnight. Maria stood and went to her window. She opened the shutters and looked out over the darkened street. A few lights showed the windows of the houses that lined the far side of the street. The night was clear, but the moon had not yet risen, and the people in the street remained dark shadows that moved almost soundlessly past. Occasionally she heard quiet voices and the sound of laughter. The city seemed peaceful in spite of the events of the morning.

She would have to write to Marlo and let him know of their plans. He would be relieved of her father's decision. Their move would save him the winter trip across the mountains to Granada.

A man's voice followed by a woman's delighted peal of laughter came from down the street. Maria breathed in the night air and smiled. She closed the shutters and prepared for bed. She felt at peace for the first time in a year. Gone was the lingering anxiety that she had never been without for the last year. Her father finally saw the danger. They would be leaving in a few months before the troubles could tear the region apart. Long before spring, the Montoyas would be gone.

Maria climbed into bed. The house was quiet. She pulled the covers around her and smiled again. Her father was going to take her to Valencia where she would have no more fear. In the spring, when the armies of Farax and Selim came, they would find the house and shop empty. Maria lifted herself up and blew out the candle. Darkness closed around her, and she fell asleep. No nightmares would disturb her that night.

Epilogue

High in the mountains of Italy, the Tiber River began its run to the sea. Down hills and cliffs it plunged, at times flowing tranquilly through trees, and at times crashing over rocks until it reached the plains where it flowed peacefully past farm and village, and on into a great city.

The river had long carried the blessings of God to this city. Rome, Eternal Rome, who had been Mistress of the World for almost two thousand years. On her seven hills, the river had bestowed its blessing, and from those same seven hills, the course of history had been shaped. On the Plains of Latium, this city had arisen, and the world had learned to bow before her.

Over the centuries, the same river witnessed man's greed and arrogance bring destruction to this city, and with each destruction, the river gave, as if from an eternal well-spring of life, new vigor. And the city rose again to new greatness. From the Carthaginians to the Great Fire, from political upheaval to its destruction by the Visigoths, from the loss of the Emperor to the birth of a new civilization, Rome never failed. And the world was still filled with her glory.

For her glory was no longer that of an emperor, nor that of a great army, rather it was the glory of a church – a church unlike any that had existed in the past. For this church changed the world, and the world became God's kingdom.

In a small chapel on the Vatican Hill, the old pope knelt in prayer. His shoulders were stooped, his beard white with care, and from his hands dangled a rosary. In his hands also was a letter, and it was because of this letter that he was praying.

The letter brought news, and like all news of that troubled time, it was both good and bad. The heir to the Spanish throne was dead, and Philip now had no successor. While King Philip had disinherited his son, there had always been hope of reconciliation. Now that Prince Carlos had passed away, who would care for the people of Spain when the king himself died?

The letter brought news, also, of a gathering of a great army in the east, and of the building of siege engines. Selim was massing his forces on the Bosporus, ships were being readied, and the preparations for a great siege were nearing completion.

The letter further spoke of a certain wool dyer in the Aljuperas who had returned to Granada from his self-imposed exile, accompanied by a mysterious bearded man who whispered in his ear. The renegade and his companion showed no fear of consequence. They spoke openly in that city of what they would do to the Christian inhabitants in the months to come, and they promised their followers that, in a year's time, there would no longer be a Christian left to darken Granada's streets.

And yet, the letter told of a young Captain who had completed his first action against the darkness threatening the world. The Algerians had fled to their harbors in terror, understanding that, at last, the retribution of Spain was coming. The captain, filled with the noble spirit of El Cid and the daring of Caesar, had patrolled the western waters of the Mediterranean with such courage that Turk and Algerian alike had fled, lest they encounter him.

The letter told too, how in a land far away, in jungle and desert, the native peoples had joyfully celebrated the coming of an Aztec princess, who was born aloft by an angel and stood upon the crescent. Her glory was that of the sun. And she was with child. The Virgin of

Guadalupe. In this foreign land, the reign of evil had been overthrown, and the enslavement and the sacrificing of whole peoples had come to an end. And the reign of this princess was victorious.

The old pope closed his eyes on his tears. His heart ached for his people. And he prayed lest the crescent crush the people of the world. His heart ached also for those who were already pressed under the weight of that black moon, and yet, in the midst of his pain, he smiled. The Virgin had, as a Roman general from days long past would have done, marched triumphant, crushing the standard of her enemies under her feet. In a land far away, she had conquered. And now she trod upon the standard of the crescent.

The river continued its slow way to the sea, imperturbable, and unchanging. Though storms troubled its waters, and rains flooded its banks, the river still remained through the passing of years, bringing the blessings of Rome to a turbulent world.

~~~
~~~